Beyond
the
Olive
Grove

BOOKS BY KATE HEWITT

A Mother's Goodbye
Secrets We Keep
Not My Daughter
No Time to Say Goodbye
A Hope for Emily
Into the Darkest Day
When You Were Mine
The Girl from Berlin
The Edelweiss Sisters

THE FAR HORIZONS TRILOGY
The Heart Goes On
Her Rebel Heart
This Fragile Heart

THE AMHERST ISLAND TRILOGY
The Orphan's Island
Dreams of the Island
Return to the Island

KATE HEWITT

Beyond
the
Olive
Grove

bookouture

Published by Bookouture in 2021

An imprint of Storyfire Ltd.
Carmelite House
50 Victoria Embankment
London EC4Y 0DZ

www.bookouture.com

ISBN: 978-1-80019-909-5
eBook ISBN: 978-1-80019-908-8

Dedicated to my brother Geordie, who first gave me a love of Greece on our travels many years ago. Love you!

CHAPTER ONE

Now

Ava Lancet peered through the unrelenting night as she fought down a growing sense of panic. Darkness had fallen twenty minutes ago and she had no idea where she was—or where she was meant to go.

She glanced at the map crumpled on the passenger seat of her rental car, wishing that the agent had provided a GPS instead of the seemingly obsolete, old-fashioned fold-out map that he'd assured her would help her drive from Athens to the tiny village of Iousidous. And perhaps it would have if she could have made any sense of the wiggly lines and incomprehensible Greek names. Not that reading Greek even mattered now because darkness had fallen and she could barely make out the road signs on Greece's National Highway.

She'd been in this country for just a few hours and already she was completely lost, both literally and figuratively. Spiritually, emotionally, hopelessly lost. A fortnight ago, escaping a cold, wet spring in England had seemed like a wonderful idea, a desperate lifeline, since her own life—and marriage—had been put on hold. That's how Ava liked to think of it anyway, because to consider anything else was too final. Too much of a failure.

She drew a deep breath, her fingers clenched around the steering wheel, her knuckles whitening, and she craned her head forward in an attempt to read one of the road signs that loomed out of the darkness. At first the Greek letters looked like so much nonsense, squiggly hieroglyphics, despite her crash course in Greek—ten hours' worth of online lessons, and countless more hours poring over textbooks. Yet as she continued to squint hopefully through the darkness, she saw the Roman alphabet printed underneath and felt a wave of relief. *Iousidous*. It would be her home for the foreseeable future.

Muttering a prayer of heartfelt thanks, Ava flipped on her signal and turned off the highway. The narrow road that now led through the scrubby hills of central Greece was even darker and more alarmingly strange than the far wider highway she'd just left. According to the map, Iousidous was only three kilometers from the National Highway, but already it felt longer.

The road wound its way through the hills, the steeply rising mountains nothing but jagged black shapes in the darkness. The only turnings were dirt or pebbly tracks that looked as if they led straight into the densely forested heights, and so Ava kept on the little road, hoping that it would lead, if not to Iousidous, then at least to somewhere.

Three kilometers, she decided, was an unbearably long distance when you were driving through the dark. It was certainly long enough to question whether you were on the right road at all, or even in the right country. It gave her ample time to wonder why she'd decided to leave her life in England and come to Greece—*move* to Greece—where she didn't know a single soul and all she had was a set of keys to a farmhouse no one had lived in for over sixty years.

"Right," Ava said aloud, the sound of her own voice seeming lonely and yet oddly reassuring in the confines of the car. "If I don't see something in the next thirty seconds, I'm turning round and going back to Athens." The thought of driving several hours back to the city was a most unappealing prospect, but at this moment, so was continuing on. She glanced at the clock, knowing a full minute had passed, and yet still reluctant to turn around. Besides, there was no easy place to turn the car round on this narrow, twisting road.

Then she came round a rather sharp bend and suddenly, stretched out before her on several terraced hills, she saw a village, or at least the lights of a village. A small white sign with black letters standing crookedly by the side of the road told her she was indeed approaching Iousidous. She could make out that much Greek, at least.

Ava breathed a sigh of relief that came halfway to a shudder. She was here. She'd made it. Sort of. Now she just had to find her grandmother's house.

The high street of Iousidous, if it could even be called a high street, was lined with low stone houses with tiled roofs, their painted shutters closed tightly for the night. The place looked nearly abandoned, Ava observed as she parked the car along the side of the street. The village seemed much smaller than she'd anticipated, just a few narrow streets of houses huddled on a hillside. She couldn't even see any shops, never mind the reassuring, boxy solidity of a large supermarket or store. And she was supposed to live here indefinitely? What on earth had she been thinking?

She hadn't been thinking, not really. She'd been reacting to the dissolution of both her hopes and her marriage. Too much loss. Escaping had felt like the only option, the only way to stay remotely sane.

And it wasn't as if there had been anything to stay in England for any more.

Forcing such thoughts away, and the accompanying savage twist of pain inside, Ava got out of the car. The air was colder and clearer than in Athens, and it smelled sharp with pine resin. She stretched, glancing around, imagining that her arrival in such a sleepy place would cause something of a stir. But the only movement came from a rail-thin cat perched on a stone wall; the animal glared at her before stalking away, tail bristling high in the air.

Ava blinked, trying to get used to the darkness, which was only relieved by the light of the moon and the occasional lamp winking from inside one of the houses on the street, its glow filtering between the cracks in the shutters. It was eight o'clock at night, yet the place seemed utterly still, strangely devoid of life, the only sound was the wind rustling high in the pines standing sentry above the sleepy little village. Standing there, realizing she didn't even know which house had belonged to her grandmother, Ava wondered just how crazy and desperate she'd been to come all this way with no hope and little plan.

The solicitor in Leeds who had handled her grandmother's estate had possessed only one photograph of the house, taken decades ago. Ava hadn't even known that her grandmother had had a house in Greece until the will had been read; Sophia had lived in Leeds since right after the Second World War. Yet gazing at that grainy photo, Ava had been intrigued, almost transfixed, even though she recognized that the solicitor's words, "charming and rustic," really meant antiquated and falling down. Still, she'd admired the house's tiled roof and painted door, the small over-grown garden, the darkness of the mountains in the background, looking like a large smudge of ink.

"Has anyone been living there?" she'd asked, and the solicitor had shrugged.

"Not for many years. The house came into your grandmother's possession after the war. She had an estate agent from a nearby town handle sublets for about ten years. Apparently the area experienced a great deal of emigration, and there was no interest in letting the house after that period, although your grandmother continued to have the minimum amount of maintenance done to keep the place in repair, and pay the property taxes, of course."

Ava shook her head slowly, trying to take it all in. A house…
a house in a village in Greece, sitting there empty and even cared
for—sort of—all that time, and no one had ever even known.
"And she never went back?"

"Apparently not."

Clearly he had not been her grandmother's confidant. Ava
wondered whether anyone had. Her memories of her grandmother were of a stern woman, softened occasionally by smiles,
briskly determined not to dwell in the past. *Why would I want
to talk about all that?* she would say dismissively if asked, and
so hardly anyone ever did. For the last five years she'd been in a
nursing home; Ava was ashamed now she hadn't visited her more,
what with her own troubles to bear.

But why, in all those years, had her grandmother never
mentioned a house? Why hadn't she sold it or gone back? And
why, Ava couldn't help but wonder, had her grandmother given
it to her?

Her mother, Susan, had been pragmatic. "I'm not surprised
she didn't sell it. Who would buy a place like that? It's in the
middle of nowhere, isn't it? Hardly worth anything, I'd imagine."

"Still, a farmhouse—in a village—"

"It's not Provence or even Italy," her mother had reminded
her. "You're bound to romanticize it, I know, but it's Greece,
rural Greece, not some holiday hotspot, and that's very different.
Very old world."

"And you know this how?" Ava had returned with a little smile.

"I backpacked through Europe in the early seventies, before
you were born."

She'd vaguely remembered her mother mentioning such a
trip, irrelevant to her teenage self. "You went to rural Greece?"

"Not Iousidous, because your grandmother would never even
say the name of the place, although I knew she came from near
the mountains. But I'm half Greek, Ava, and I wanted to see my

own country. I traveled through a few places and, trust me, it was like stepping back in time. In the mountains whole villages didn't have electricity, even in the 1970s."

"But that was fifty years ago, and this isn't really in the mountains, is it?"

"Close enough, I should think, and not on any 'Places to Travel' lists. I doubt much has changed. And the house certainly hasn't, if it hasn't been lived in for that long. It might be close to falling down by now. Are you sure you want to go?"

"I don't know if I want to," Ava had said, her throat turning tight, "but I need to."

Her mother had nodded, her gaze turning tender and all too knowing. "It's been a hard year, Ava, for both you and Simon. It might be good for you to get away, find a little distance."

Ava had looked away, a lump forming in her throat. Nearly a year on and she still hadn't been coping. That much had been obvious to her mother, to Simon, to everyone. Even her supervisor at the primary school where she'd worked part-time as an art teacher had mentioned it. *Maybe the budget cuts are a good thing for you, Ava. You could get some rest.*

As if resting would help. As if she was merely tired. It would just give her more time to think. And as for finding distance… how could you find distance from something that still felt so enmeshed in your very soul, tangled up in every part of you, if you even wanted to? Ava wasn't sure she did. If she let go of the grief, she might lose herself as well. There might be nothing left at all.

"I still don't know why she left it to me," she'd said to her mother, determined to keep the conversation about the house. Her grandmother had five grandchildren besides Ava: her cousins were spread all over the globe, two in England, two in Australia, and one in the States. "She could have left it to anyone."

"She always favored you, I think," her mother said. "She used to say you were like her."

Ava thought of the austere-looking woman from her childhood holding court from the plastic-swathed three-piece suite in the front room of her semidetached house in Leeds. She'd visited her grandmother a few times a year as a child and had accepted boiled sweets and a rather firm pat on the cheek, and not much else. When her grandmother had died six months ago, she'd felt sad but not devastated. She'd been dealing with a deeper, more raw grief, and Sophia Matthews had been in her nineties, and had been suffering from dementia for several years. In some ways it had been a relief, the gentle slip into death rather than the brutal tearing away.

"How am I like her?" Ava had asked, and Susan smiled sadly.

"She told me once you reminded her of herself, back when she lived in Greece. Strong, she said. Stronger than you think."

"Stronger than I think? Or stronger than she thought?"

"Does it matter?" Susan had asked with a smile. "Strong, in any case."

But Ava didn't feel strong. She felt weak, horribly, pathetically weak, like some spineless, slithery creature, shell-less and exposed, which could not even care for itself. A stronger woman would move on after the loss of her child. A stronger woman would want to. *And a stronger woman would be able to save her marriage.*

"In any case," Susan said, "she didn't speak any more of it. You know she never talked about her time in Greece. She hated if we so much as mentioned it." She sighed, shaking her head, and Ava thought of her mother traveling through Greece back in the 1970s, young and hopeful and yet still somehow lost, trying to rediscover part of her forgotten heritage. Had her mother found any answers on that trip? Would she?

Ava had never even really considered herself Greek at all; her grandmother had been so determinedly English. As far as Sophia Matthews had been concerned, her life had begun in England, in 1946, when she was twenty-six and married to an Englishman, Ava's grandfather Edward, who had worked in a bank and died before she was born. Sophia had worked hard at making her children appear completely English, learning the language herself and refusing to speak Greek to them or anyone. As Sophia came from a country with a fierce national pride, this decision made so many years ago now added to the sense of loss. Had Sophia missed the land of her birth, or her family? Had she thought in Greek, or dreamed in it? Perhaps she'd been conflicted in herself, even if she never gave anything away. Ava had felt a prickling of shame that such thoughts had never crossed her mind before.

"I doubt there's anyone alive in the village who remembers the war," she'd told her mother. "They'd have to be over ninety, at the least."

"Probably not. But if you're really interested, you could do some digging at a local library or historical society."

"I don't read Greek, or speak it beyond a few key phrases. I doubt I'd find much."

"True." Her mother had smiled and patted her hand. "Perhaps it's best to let it lie, then. Your grandmother must have had a reason not to talk about it, and regardless of who lived in the house before, at least it's a place for you to stay. Rest." Her eyebrows had drawn together. "Regain yourself."

"I'm not lost," Ava had said, half joking, half warning. She couldn't take any more pity, not from her mother anyway. Simon certainly hadn't shown her any; one of their last fights had started because he'd told her to stop moping.

Moping, as if she were a sulky child. The implication had so obviously been that he'd moved on from the death of their daughter—why couldn't she? As if it were a choice she was too stubborn to make. Resentment had burned in Ava's chest and churned in her gut even then, when she was talking to her mother a month later.

Now, standing in the village, the night air crisp and quiet and so very dark, Ava swallowed down the anger, knowing there was no point to thinking about any of it now. She and Simon had surely said all they could say to each other, which in the end hadn't been very much, and it was that knowledge, perhaps, that hurt the most. Taking a deep breath, she started down the street.

In the darkness every house looked the same: whitewashed stone, tiled roof, painted door. Small gardens shrouded in darkness released the dry, dusty scents of rosemary and lavender, sage and thyme. The narrow street hugged the hillside, then curved sharply upwards, presumably to a street much like it farther up the hill, and perhaps another one after that, zigzagging towards the peak. Her grandmother really had lived in the mountains, or at least closer to them than Ava had realized.

How on earth was she going to be able to find her house? Ava possessed an old-fashioned iron key but no address beyond the name of the village. Somehow, in her vague imaginings, she'd pictured herself arriving in daylight, strolling down a sunny street, chatting to friendly villagers and soon-to-be neighbors in her clumsy Greek; someone would smile and clap their hands as they pointed out the house and everyone would make her feel welcome. It was something more from a romcom than reality, she acknowledged now as she continued making her way down the street, alone in the darkness.

Presumably her grandmother's house was the one most in disrepair, but she couldn't make the houses out well enough to know, and in any case there were several that looked less than neat and tidy. She stopped in the middle of the street and listened to a cat—perhaps the thin one on the fence—yowl in the distance. A light switched off, casting the little street into deeper darkness. Ava fought the urge to cry, more from fatigue than sorrow, but the tears felt the same.

It was typical of her that she'd rushed into this whole adventure without properly thinking it through. Simon had always accused her of rushing into things, of being too hasty and emotional.

Once she'd brought home a stray dog without consulting him; she'd thrown away her birth control pills with blithe thoughtlessness. The dog had died years ago, and the pills hadn't mattered in the end, but still. Once upon a time, she'd happily traipsed through life. That felt like a long time ago, but it still seemed she was adept at making poor decisions.

They were a sorry pair, Ava thought sadly, with her own volatile emotions and Simon's refusal to be even remotely ruffled. It had been his unending, stony silence in the face of their shared loss that had led her to ask for a separation, and then make this move to Greece. Simon might have considered it foolhardy, but Ava had known instinctively that she needed a change, a new start, at least for a little while. Life had simply become too bleak to face.

Gazing around at the darkened, empty street, she decided this was certainly a new start, yet the trouble was she wasn't sure how to begin.

The squeaky sound of a shutter opening had her turning around. A face poked out of a window in the house opposite, hair swathed in a head scarf, eyes narrowed in suspicion and lost in wrinkles.

"*Pos se lene? Stamata!*" the older woman demanded. She issued a series of barked commands that had every Greek phrase flying out of Ava's head.

"*Den katalaveno,*" she finally managed. I don't understand. Perhaps the most important words to speak in a foreign language.

The woman's frown grew even more ferocious. She started to say something Ava knew she wouldn't understand, then stopped. "*Anglitha?*" she asked, and Ava nodded in relief.

"Yes… I mean *ne… Anglitha*. I'm English. Do you speak English? *Anglitha?*"

The woman shrugged. "Some."

Better than nothing, Ava thought with both gratitude and desperation. She stepped towards the woman, who was now leaning out of the window, her elbows braced on the stone sill. She looked to be in her mid-seventies, about forty years older than Ava. "I've come to stay in a house here," Ava explained hesitantly. "It belonged to Sophia..." She realized that in her panic and dismay she'd forgotten her grandmother's maiden name. Helplessly she fished the key, heavy and antiquated, from her pocket and showed it to the woman who gave it no more than a cursory glance.

"*Ne, ne.* You must be the one who bought the Paranoussis place."

Paranoussis! Yes. Ava remembered her grandmother's name, and she nodded almost frantically. "Yes. That's right. Sophia Paranoussis is—was—my grandmother. Do you know where her house is?'

The woman nodded, alert now. "Your grandmother, *ne*? One moment." She closed the shutters and emerged a few seconds later in the doorway of her house, a sweater now draped over her rounded shoulders. She called back into the house to someone in Greek and then turned to Ava. "I am Eleni."

"I'm Ava." She reached out to shake Eleni's hand. "Ava Lancet."

"And your grandmother, she lived in Iousidous?"

Ava nodded. "A long time ago. She left right after the war."

"As did most the village's young," Eleni said with a sigh, although if she'd been alive then, she would have only just been born. "Come."

Ava followed the older woman down the darkened street past half a dozen shuttered houses. It was hard to tell whether they were lived in or not, although Ava saw a few cars parked on the street. She strained to hear something other than the rustle of the wind in the trees and the crunch of pebbles under their feet, but there was nothing. All around them the village was dark, silent and still.

They walked quietly for just a few minutes before Eleni stopped in front of a house perched in the sharp curve of the street that twisted up farther into the hills and the darkness. Even without the benefit of street lamps, Ava could tell that this house was clearly a bit more dilapidated than the rest. One peeling shutter hung askew and the lightless windows and weedy garden gave every indication that no one lived there, or had lived there for a very long time.

"Here it is," Eleni said, and Ava stepped forward.

"Wonderful, thank you," she murmured. She fit the old key into the lock as Eleni watched, clearly curious about the *Anglitha* who appeared to have come to live in a falling-down farmhouse sight unseen. The key stuck, and Ava jiggled it for a few alarmed seconds before it finally turned. With a creaky sigh of surrender the door opened, and she stepped into her grandmother's house.

CHAPTER TWO

Now

The house smelled old and unused, the air damp and musty. It smelled, Ava thought, forgotten. In the darkness all she could make out were a few bulky shapes, and she fumbled for a light switch that she assumed—or at least hoped—was by the door.

"Here." Eleni reached for it, and the click was audible and dispiriting in the darkness, for nothing happened. Eleni made a grunt of disgust, and Ava felt the panic that had skirted around the edges of her mind now swamp it completely.

"I arranged to have the electricity turned on—" Her voice, she heard, sounded alarmingly shrill. She'd spent over an hour on the telephone last week, racking up an enormous bill, attempting to communicate her needs to the local electric company. She'd thought they'd reached an understanding; apparently they had not.

Eleni shrugged. "It is not the Greek way."

"What isn't? Light?" Ava fought down the urge to start laughing hysterically, for that would surely only give way to tears. She was exhausted and emotionally drained and she just wanted something to *work*. She desperately needed sleep. And yet here she was in a lightless house that clearly—from the smell alone—was not fit for human habitation.

Once again she'd been absurdly impulsive and chased a dream, just as Simon had always accused her of doing. She'd thought something difficult and improbable would be if not exactly fun then at least doable, and here she was in a place like a pigsty, realizing, just as Simon had always said, that life didn't follow her heedless fantasies.

No, it most certainly did not.

"It is not the Greek way to do things quickly," Eleni explained, her voice calm and surprisingly soothing. "Especially as you—the owner—were not here. We Greeks, we like to talk and look and maybe have a drink before we do anything." She smiled. "We get things done in our own time."

Ava drew in a steadying breath. "I see."

Eleni withdrew a torch from the pocket of her trousers and flicked it on; the narrow beam revealed a room appalling in its unfinished state. A few rickety wooden chairs and a warped low table were the only furniture. Ava had been planning to buy some new things anyway, but the stark barrenness of the place still shocked her, even though she realized it shouldn't have. From England she had been determined to turn it all into an adventure. *A house in Greece! In a tiny village, so picturesque!* Her best friend, Julie, had said she was envious. Her boss had told her it sounded perfect. Ava had pictured herself here as if on holiday, sipping thick Greek coffee from a tiny porcelain cup at a small sidewalk café, or in her lovely little garden, planting pots of trailing bougainvillea and clematis, maybe an orange tree. Healing herself with these small kindnesses, tender acts of mercy for her own soul. In light of this absolute hovel, it all seemed ridiculous. Her adventure was a joke, or worse, a catastrophe.

Her gaze moved slowly around the room now illuminated by the thin light of the torch, taking in the sticks of old furniture, and then the floor, thick with dust, the stone walls begrimed with smoke and dirt. It was awful. Really, really awful. And unlivable, at least as far as tonight was concerned.

Eleni clucked her tongue. "It needs a good clean."

"You could say that," Ava managed to reply. Silently she wondered whether it needed to be torn down and a new house needed to be built in its place. She forced herself to smile. "I suppose I should have considered something like this happening," she said, trying to keep her voice bright, as if this were nothing more than a mild and even amusing inconvenience. "The solicitor mentioned that it hadn't been lived in for sixty years—"

Eleni clucked her tongue again. "Half the houses in this village haven't been lived in for that long," she said dismissively, and Ava wondered if any of the others might be in a better state than this one. Perhaps she could trade. "At least this one has been modernized," Eleni added, although Ava begged to disagree. Nothing about this place looked modern. Eleni tapped her foot against the floor and flicked the useless switch again. "Tile floor, electricity. And a kitchen and bathroom. All that would have been added after the war."

"Really?" Ava knew she had no real idea what life had been like here seventy years ago. She'd assumed, naïvely, she saw now, that life in rural Greece wouldn't have been that different from that in, say, Dorset. Her mother had warned her, but Ava had ignored the warning, just as she'd ignored anything that didn't fit into her plans, because she'd been so desperate to go. She swallowed. "What would the house have been like then, before the additions?"

"Dirt floor and no kitchen. That was the kitchen." Eleni gestured to the fireplace, which took up most of one wall. "And the toilet—outside. What do you call it?"

"A privy?"

Eleni nodded. "Yes. And no electric, of course. No running water. So, yes, it is modern. Lucky for you."

"Indeed," Ava murmured. "The solicitor mentioned that some minimal repairs were done over the years."

"Yes, everyone thought it strange. People always wondered who kept this place. If they would ever come back." She slapped one wall, the way you might slap the flank of a cow or horse. "Well, with the electric and water, a bit of whitewash, it should not be so bad for you. You will stay?"

"I'm hoping to," Ava answered, although she felt that Eleni was a touch more optimistic than she was. She glanced at the empty room cast into looming shadows by the torch's thin beam and wondered whether she should sleep on the dirty floor, or if the upstairs might be more promising. Perhaps she could sleep in the car. Or could she face the prospect of finding a hotel at nine o'clock at night, in the middle of nowhere? She'd seen that a fair-sized town, Lamia, was about ten kilometers away, but she didn't know if that black dot on the map meant a big enough town to have a decent hotel, or even a shop. Perhaps it was more or less the same as Iousidous—dilapidated and forgotten. It was just one more thing she hadn't bothered to check, yet now she felt she'd sell her soul for a soft bed, a hot bath, and a glass of wine.

None, she knew, would be forthcoming. Despair, all too close an emotion for the last year, flooded through her again. Tears rose and she blinked them back fiercely. She'd agreed to this adventure. She just had no idea it would be like… this.

Then, to her surprise, Eleni patted her arm. "Do not worry. You cannot stay the night here with it like this. It is not fit for pigs right now. Come back with me. You eat at my house. You sleep there."

Eleni spoke firmly, and Ava knew her offer was genuine. *Yet to sleep in a stranger's house?* She felt both humbled and uncomfortable. This was not how things were done in England. "I couldn't—"

"And what else will you do?" Eleni asked practically. She swept an arm towards the grimy room, as depressing on second glance as it had been on the first, or even more so. Ava saw there was some kind of animal's nest in the wide hearth and she swallowed audibly. "You cannot stay here," Eleni insisted again.

"I know, but—"

"Come." Smiling and shaking her head, refusing to listen to any more protests, Eleni ushered her outside again.

Eleni waited while Ava locked up, and then led her to her own house, the same kind of low stone building with a terracotta tiled roof and a painted door, yet in every other way completely different. The small garden was neatly tended, pots of rosemary and thyme sat on the wide window sill, and inside warm lamplight illuminated a comfortable sitting room with a worn sofa and a couple of chairs by the fireplace, each piece draped in hand-embroidered covers. The warmth enveloped her as she stepped inside.

"You must eat," Eleni said, and went to the small kitchen at the back of the house.

"You're really too kind," Ava called out. She felt both grateful for Eleni's spontaneous generosity and annoyed at herself for getting into such a predicament as this in the first place. She should have checked that the house was ready. She should have booked into a hotel while she fixed it up. It seemed so obvious now, and yet in England all she'd been able to think about was getting away. She hadn't wanted to consider delays or dangers; she'd just wanted to *go*. To escape. For a little while, at least. So she'd closed her mind to anything that could possibly go wrong and ended up—here.

"So what is an *Anglitha* doing in such a place as this?" Eleni asked. Ava had moved to the doorway of the kitchen and was watching as Eleni placed several little bowls on the small table—olives swimming in brine and oil, a lump of feta cheese, some chunks of stewed meat mixed with spices.

"I wanted to try something new," Ava explained rather hesitantly. "May I help?"

Eleni reached for a loaf of crusty bread and began to slice it with brisk movements. "No, no. You must be tired. Did you drive all the way from Athens today?"

"Yes, I have a rental car for a few weeks. I'm not sure what I'll do after that."

Eleni turned to her, one eyebrow raised. "You stay for more than weeks, then?"

Ava flushed. It sounded so strange, to just turn up here with nothing to do, nowhere else to go. "Well, I'm not sure how long I'll stay," she said. "But at least a few months, I think." It suddenly seemed a very long time. What would she even do? She had a little money saved, and surely it wouldn't cost too much to live frugally in a place like this, but even so, Ava thought Eleni looked skeptical. As skeptical as she herself now felt.

Eleni gestured to the set table. "Come. Eat."

Murmuring her thanks, Ava went to sit down. "This looks delicious. I can't thank you enough for helping me out like this. I don't know what I would have done—"

Eleni waved a hand in dismissal. "This is nothing. And if your grandmother lived in the village, and now you are going to, for however long, then of course I must help you. We help each other here. That is our way."

"You are so kind," Ava said, meaning it utterly, and then from the other room she heard the slap of slippered feet against the tile floor. She looked up to see an elderly woman—in her eighties at least—standing in the doorway. Her face was a mass of wrinkles, her hair a silvery-white wispy cloud, but even so her eyes were bright and sharp and dark.

"*Pya ine afti?*" she asked, and Eleni spoke rapidly in Greek before turning to Ava and speaking in English.

"This is my mother, Parthenope. She has lived here a long time."

"*Anglitha…*" Parthenope murmured, and Ava rose from the table and held out her hand.

"It's nice to meet you," she said, haltingly, for she had no idea whether the older woman could understand English.

To Ava's surprise, as Parthenope turned to look at her, she squinted, seeming to do a double take, and then her face paled, her mouth slackening in shock. Her hands trembled and she clutched at the cardigan draped over her humped shoulders. "Sophia…" she whispered, and Ava felt a thrill of shocked recognition at the name.

Eleni, clearly dismayed, waved her hands and spoke again in Greek. "*Ochi, ochi…*" No, no. She turned apologetically to Ava. "I'm sorry. I have not known her to be confused—"

"I don't think she's confused," Ava said quietly. "My grandmother's first name was Sophia. My mother said I looked like her when she was younger." And acted like her too. Strong, apparently, stronger than Ava thought, even though she certainly didn't feel it now.

Now Eleni's face slackened in surprise, and Parthenope crossed the room to clasp Ava's hands tightly in her own. "Sophia, Sophia," she crooned, the name a lullaby. To her shock Ava saw tears trickling down Parthenope's deeply wrinkled cheeks. "*Signomi,*" she whispered. "*Signomi.*"

Ava recognized the phrase from her online lessons, yet she still didn't understand why Parthenope was saying it. *I'm sorry.* "Did you know my grandmother?" she asked uncertainly, and Parthenope spoke rapidly in Greek once more.

"My mother said, 'Yes, I did,'" Eleni translated. She still looked surprised and even troubled as she continued to translate her mother's words. "'Sophia worked in the coffeehouse here in the village, before the Germans closed it down. She was my friend, and a good woman.'"

"I had no idea," Ava said, strangely moved by this admission. She felt as if she'd been given a gift, a thread that connected her to this place, to these people. Amazing how it suddenly made her feel less alone. She had assumed that no one from her grandmother's time would be left in the village. She hadn't expected a connection to the past, no matter how tenuous. She hadn't even considered it.

"Nor had I," Eleni said slowly. "My mother never talks about that time."

"My grandmother didn't either. I'm afraid I hardly ever really thought about my grandmother even being Greek. She left Greece right after the war, and my grandfather was English. She never talked about anything to do with Greece."

"It was a very hard time," Eleni replied. She glanced at her mother, who had released Ava's hand and now stood quietly shaking her head, her eyes still filled with tears. "No one talks about it now. No one ever has."

Ava nodded and they continued eating in a thoughtful silence. She wanted to ask Parthenope about her grandmother, yet she knew the language barrier would prove too difficult, and whatever memories Parthenope held were obviously painful and perhaps even traumatic. *I'm sorry.* Why? For what? Ava knew she couldn't ask, at least not yet. Eleni had said no one talked about it, and her grandmother certainly hadn't.

Life is for living, Ava remembered Sophia saying whenever she'd been asked questions about her time in Greece. *There is no need to remember.*

Remember what? Ava thought of what Parthenope had said and she felt as if she'd been given a small piece of a puzzle she'd never expected to fit together. A puzzle that she hadn't even known existed, and yet she now felt a surprising, deep-seated desire to complete it, and see its whole troubling picture.

CHAPTER THREE

July 1942

"You're a good woman, Sophia—"

Sophia Paranoussis dodged the arm of the sentimental farmer who might have had a glass too many of the local retsina and went to the back room of the coffeehouse for another tray of glasses. She disliked her evenings here, when the farmers stomped in with the mud still on their boots and drank away their sorrows and what little money they had. She hated the thick fog of hand-rolled cigarettes and the oily smoke of the paraffin lamps that filled the room and whose reeking smell never truly left her hair or her clothes. The men would drink their retsina or coffee and talk of politics and farming over games of backgammon made from bottle caps until they finally went home to their wives and children, and to the prospect of another day eking out a meager existence from this hard and unforgiving earth.

Yet even though she disliked it, working several evenings in the coffeehouse brought in a little more money, and in these uncertain times those few drachmas were needed. Not that she was always paid in drachmas. With the Italians and Germans demanding half a harvest and inflation turning notes nearly worthless, sometimes she was paid in oil or wheat, or even tobacco, which she gave to her father.

Sighing, Sophia swiped a sweaty strand of hair away from her forehead and placed the tray of dirty glasses onto the low wooden table. It was July, and the heat of high summer made the back room nearly unbearable. Sophia spent most of her time in here, washing glasses and refilling jugs, keeping out of sight of the men. Today she'd gone into the front room only because Spiro had been called away.

Kristina, the owner of the coffeehouse, bustled in wearing her widow's black, her hair piled on top of her head and covered with a scarf. A year ago, when she was forty, she'd been widowed even before the fighting between the Resistance and the Germans had become too dangerous, with bullets spewing across the streets in Athens. Her husband, Georgios, had gone there to sell the pine resin he'd harvested, and in a sudden fit of patriotic rage he'd pulled down a banner emblazoned with a swastika and thrown it to the ground. A German soldier had seen him and shot him on the spot.

When the news had traveled back to the village, everyone had been shocked into a respectful silence for Kristina and her son, Spiro, then just sixteen years old. Georgios's act of defiance had been considered bravery rather than foolish bravado. Sophia would have rather had a husband at home, bringing in the harvest, but she'd said nothing. Villagers possessed both a fierce pride and courage, even if sometimes she felt she had neither, at least not in the same measure.

Yet in the year and a half since the Germans had marched on Athens, no Nazi had been seen in Iousidous or even near it. They'd heard rumors and stories, of course, ever since Greece had been carved up like a loaf of *psomi* by the Axis: the Bulgarians in Macedonia, the Germans taking Athens and the islands, and the Italians occupying the rest. Lax, even lazy, the Italian army had not caused life to change much in the village, unless you counted the soldiers who occasionally sauntered in and groped the girls; better to keep your daughters in the kitchens or lock them in the barns. If any Italian soldiers were seen in Iousidous, Sophia didn't come to the coffeehouse, not even to stay in the back room. Yet even so, despite some of the soldiers' lechery, no Italian took out his gun and shot a man in the head.

After Georgios's death Kristina gained an unexpected liberty; most widows were forced to live quietly in their houses, talking to no one and barely lifting their eyes from the ground, yet thanks to her husband's noble act the village accepted Kristina's running both the coffeehouse and her husband's smallholding, alongside her son.

Men tipped their peaked caps to her in the square, and with murmured blessings women gave her eggs packed in straw and rounds of goats' cheese swimming in brine. In a small village rife with gossip and possessing strict rules about the roles of men and women, such concessions were a testament to the villagers' respect for Georgios.

Now Kristina pressed her hands to the small of her back and closed her eyes. Sophia suspected she did not like working among all the men either, even though they respected her and few became actually drunk, which would be considered a disgrace. A glass of retsina and a story or song was the way to end the day, not stumbling home in the dark, out of your senses.

"One more hour, Sophia, and then we are done." Kristina had asked Sophia to help at the coffeehouse after Georgios died, and it was accepted because a man could hardly work alone with, or under, a woman. Things were changing even in a small place like Iousidous.

"Where is Spiro?" Sophia asked. She did not wish to go out in the front room again.

A funny little smile played around Kristina's mouth even as she tensed. "Out." She took a handful of tarnished coins from the pocket of her apron and placed them in the old cigar box where she kept her money, up on a high shelf. Sophia didn't ask any more questions, even though she was curious. It was dark, late, and no one went out at night in a village like this, especially not in these uncertain times.

Kristina glanced at her, that funny little smile widening. "You are not going to ask questions?"

Sophia turned back to her tray of dirty glasses. "It is not my business."

"No, it is not. Not yet, perhaps." Kristina gave a little laugh, although the sound held no humor. Who was really laughing these days?

Sophia held her tongue, her head bent over the washing basin.

"At least Dimitrios has left, thank God," Kristina said. She gave Sophia a knowing look.

Sophia kept her head lowered and pretended not to notice. She did not want to think about Dimitrios—or her sister, Angelika, who was pretty and playful and destined for trouble.

"You will have to worry about that one, eh?" Kristina persisted.

"He is nothing to do with me."

"Not with you, no. But your sister?" Kristina laughed again, and this time the sound chilled Sophia. Dimitrios Atrikes had been in the coffeehouse earlier, swaggering about and laughing too loudly, as usual. He was only twenty, a farmer's son like nearly every other boy in Iousidous, but he had fiery ideas and a loose tongue, and he liked to tap the side of his nose and wink as if he knew more than he was letting on. Sophia was afraid, for her sister's sake, that he might.

"You don't gossip like the other girls, do you, Sophia?" Kristina said as she reached for one of the dusty bottles of retsina. "But you know what I'm talking about all the same."

Sophia glanced at her, discomfited by the knowing gleam in the older woman's eyes. She watched in surprise as Kristina poured herself a glass of retsina; she'd never seen the woman drink before.

"You're a quiet one," Kristina said, almost thoughtfully, and from somewhere Sophia found her voice.

"I prefer listening to speaking." It was safer that way.

Kristina smiled. "That's good," she said, and drained her glass. "In these times, that's good."

These times. These uncertain and terrible times. Sophia turned away from Kristina, closing her eyes as she offered a brief and fervent prayer to Theotokos, the mother of God and bearer of sorrows, to keep her sister safe, her family safe, even all of Greece safe, for since the Nazis had marched into Athens in April 1941, safety was no longer a guarantee. Sometimes it felt like a miracle.

Although their little village had escaped any real attention, there was a garrison of Italian soldiers only ten kilometers away in Lamia. The Nazis stayed to the cities, but Sophia had heard whispers of the atrocities committed in their name, battles fought right in the street between the soldiers and the *andartes,* the Greek Resistance. Thank God such things did not happen here... yet.

Even so, almost as frightening to Sophia as the thought of soldiers—Italian or German—was that of the *andartes* themselves. Sophia had heard whispers of the People's Liberation Army, or ELAS, the communist-led Resistance movement that was growing in strength and, if some whispers were to be believed, could be as vicious and violent as the Nazis themselves. They marched into villages and demanded bread and blankets and sometimes even a sheep or a goat, although it could cost a man his livelihood, or even his very life if the Nazis discovered he'd been aiding, willingly or not, the Liberation Army.

One of the bands of guerrillas, Sophia had heard, was led by the ruthless Aris Velouchiotis. She had heard stories of how he had shot a man in the head for stealing a bit of bread... just like the Nazi had shot Georgios in Athens.

And Dimitrios Atrikes, her sister's foolish admirer, was whispered to belong to that bloodthirsty band. Sophia had heard him in the coffeehouse, boasting about his rusty old rifle, given to him, he insisted, by Velouchiotis himself. Many of the men in the village, and women too, approved of Velouchiotis and his growing army, and Sophia suspected some secretly gave him and his men food and supplies even though whole villages had been burned for less. Still, that was the Greek way. Fight. Resist always, as a matter of pride and courage, no matter the consequence.

Yet Sophia felt only fear. She'd seen her sister, Angelika, listen to Dimitrios's boasting, clearly taken by his broad shoulders and self-confident swagger, but Sophia knew better than to be charmed by such folly. Now, more than ever, was a time to keep your head down and go quietly about your business, attracting no attention, causing no alarm. Staying safe, until this endless war was finally over.

Angelika, however, didn't think like Sophia. She never had. From a young age, she'd always had an eye for pretty things, easy pleasures. And in truth Sophia had been happy to spoil her; Angelika could be like a kitten she wanted to stroke, reveling in any attention or praise. But when it came to Dimitrios Atrikes… Sophia had seen how Angelika listened to him, *liked* him. Whenever she could, she was by Dimitrios, or as close as she could get, considering that in a village like theirs men and women were not left alone until words had been spoken and an agreement between parents made. Still, at the last feast day she'd smiled up at him and tossed her shiny dark curls. Who knew where it would lead? Girls had been ruined by less.

Sighing, Sophia gave Kristina a weary smile and then loaded her tray with clean glasses before heading back out to the smoky front room. She would talk to her sister tonight, and God willing, make her see some sense. That, she thought wryly, was what a good woman would do.

Yet when she slipped through the darkened streets back to her father's farmhouse, which was nestled in the first curve of the street, its tidy front garden filled with pots of tomatoes and fat bulbs of garlic, the clothes mangle and the mud oven used for baking in the heat of the summer, she found it all quiet and dark. Her father, tired because it was the busy time of year, the threshing of wheat, had already gone to bed, having settled their cow, four sheep, and three goats in the shed on the side of the house.

Many of the villagers of Iousidous still slept with their animals in their front room with them, the hens roosting on the rafters, the sheep curled up by the hearth. Sophia's mother, who had been a shopkeeper's daughter from Lamia, had said she wouldn't live like a beast, and so her father, Evangelos, had built a shed. Now, as Sophia put her pay in the dented tin on the mantel above the hearth, she was grateful for the clean space with its woven rug and a framed print her mother had bought on a trip to Athens as a girl. Her mother might have died just over five years ago from a weak chest, but the animals still stayed in their shed.

The money put away, Sophia went back outside to the stairs on the side of the house that led to the second floor, another luxury demanded by her mother. Most farmhouses were long and low, only one story. But Katerina Paranoussis had wanted bedrooms, and so her adoring husband had built two on top of the front room, with an outside staircase. Her mother had died in the front bedroom, the sheets speckled with her coughed-up blood. Sophia shared the second one with her sister, and even though it was after ten o'clock at night, the room was dark and empty, the cover on her sister's bed still pulled tight across the thin mattress.

Sophia stopped short at the sight of that empty bed, knowing there was no decent or honorable reason why her sister should not be stretched out on it, asleep. What self-respecting woman was out and about at this hour, never mind during the war? Her sister needed to be more careful if she wished one day to see herself established as a married woman in this village. The gossip, Sophia knew, could be quick and brutal, tongues being as deadly, in their own way, as those terrible guns.

Just then she heard the clatter of her sister's boots on the steps outside, and then along the hallway. Even when her sister was trying to be quiet, she was loud, overwhelming and impossible to ignore. She peeked into the bedroom, checking to see if Sophia had returned, and Sophia clucked her tongue loudly.

"And where have you been?"

"Oh, Sophia!" One hand flew to her chest and Angelika slipped into the room. Her eyes were bright, her cheeks flushed. "I thought you might be asleep."

"You knew I was working at the coffeehouse. I've only just returned."

"Oh, the coffeehouse," Angelika said with a laugh, and Sophia tried to suppress the small stab of resentment her sister's attitude sometimes caused her. She did not like working at the coffeehouse, but she was glad Kristina had asked her to help. What with the taxes levied by the occupying soldiers and the war's inflated prices, the money they gained from selling wheat, wool, and pine resin did not go far. Often they went to bed with their bellies still half empty, although out in the country it was not nearly as bad as in Athens, where Sophia had heard they were eating rubbish and rats.

Sophia had been surprised when Evangelos had given his grudging acceptance for her to work; it was not fitting, of course, for a woman to work outside the home, but since Kristina was doing it, and they needed the money, he had said yes. He hardly spoke now, except to grunt a grace before their evening meal. The life had been leached out of him by her mother's death, so sometimes Sophia thought he held as much spirit as the painted icons adorning Saint Stephen's, perched high above the village, their unblinking eyes watching over them all.

Angelika had said nothing when Sophia had asked her father's permission and made only a paltry effort to help either at the coffeehouse or at home. As well-intentioned as her sister could be, Sophia knew that Angelika had neither the diligence nor the interest to complete the many household tasks that needed to be done. She would start a chore, whether it was fetching water or kneading bread, and then she would wander off, the thing half finished, only to return with floods of apologies and even tears and yet do the same thing all over again. Most days Sophia could not even resent her sister for it. Angelika was too young, too pretty, and too naturally loving to stay angry with for long. It was like being angry with a kitten; Sophia only felt guilty when she scolded her.

"Yes, the coffeehouse," she said now as her sister uncovered her head—she'd kept her head scarf on, at least—and began to take the pins out of her hair. "And where were you?"

"Just getting water from the fountain." Angelika glanced up at her, her brown eyes guileless and full of appeal. "I wanted to save you the chore in the morning."

"Fetching water on a dark night! I've never heard of such nonsense." Sophia tried not to be softened by her sister's obvious ploy. "You were out hoping to catch sight of Dimitrios stumbling back from the coffeehouse, weren't you?"

"He wasn't stumbling," Angelika said with a giggle, and Sophia clucked her tongue.

"Angelika, *louloudi mou*, you could be ruined, completely ruined, for such a thing. Surely you know that? No decent man would marry you if he heard you'd been out by yourself, being stupid with a boy like Dimitrios."

Angelika only laughed, looking delighted rather than alarmed. "Oh, Sophia, you fuss so. There was no harm in it. After five years of mourning, I think I deserve a little fun, and it really was only a little, I promise. I wouldn't bring shame to our family."

Sophia pressed her lips together. In other circumstances, she might have agreed. Five years, the expected length of mourning for the death of a mother, was a long time for a young girl to wear black and stay mostly inside, singing no songs except in church and making sure not to laugh or talk too loudly. Angelika, naturally so cheerful and sometimes even boisterous, had understandably chafed against the restrictions, but now that the time of mourning was finally over, she enjoyed her relative freedom a little too much. People would talk, and she would be called shameless or stupid, the worst insults for an unmarried girl. Besides, Sophia thought with a weary resignation, there was a war going on, little that her sister seemed to realize it. They lived in an enemy-occupied country fraught with danger, overwhelmed by deprivation. It was hardly the time for *fun*.

Sophia took a breath and forced herself to speak kindly. "I know you want your fun, and I understand it. You are young and pretty, and life has been quiet and hard. But Angelika, you know you cannot be seen alone with a man when you are unmarried."

Angelika pouted. "We didn't even talk—"

"Even so."

"Don't, Sophia, please." Angelika's face crumpled. She couldn't bear being scolded, not even gently. She had been that way since she was a child, indulged perhaps because her mother knew that no more children would come; something had happened to her insides during Angelika's birth. Even before her mother's death Angelika had done little work, often playing with her rag doll or a bit of dough in a corner of the yard while Sophia and Katerina baked bread, salted tomatoes, or rubbed corn from the cobs. Sophia had never begrudged her for it; she'd wanted to protect her, just as she did now.

"Angelika, I worry for you. I want to see you settled, with a husband of your own, children too—"

"And maybe I will be, even before you are," Angelika returned with a little laugh. "Who knows?"

Sophia felt as if a chill hand had reached inside her and taken hold of her heart. Please God, not that fool Dimitrios. She did not want the communist *andartes* brought into her life, into her very home, with their rifles and curses, and that was not even considering Dimitrios's foolishness. "Maybe," she allowed, "but not if—"

"Oh, stop, Sophia, please!" Angelika raised her voice, and in the next bedroom they both heard their father let out a shuddering snore. They stared silently at each other in the moonlit room, the tension snapping between them.

"Things are different now," Angelika stated more quietly. "The war makes them so; you see it yourself. Could you have worked in a coffeehouse before the soldiers came? In the old days such a thing would not have been allowed. You would have brought as much shame to our father as I might simply by talking in the square!"

"So you did talk!"

Angelika just spun away and Sophia tried to suppress the needling hurt she felt at her sister's accusation. "Are you saying I bring shame to our father?" she asked quietly, and Angelika turned back to her.

"No, no, forgive me," she exclaimed, and with her childlike impulsiveness she hurried to Sophia, dropping to her knees to lay her head in her sister's lap. Gently Sophia touched the dark curls, which were still as soft and lustrous as a baby's. "I don't mean any harm," Angelika said, gazing up at her with dark eyes now luminous with tears. "You know I don't. I just want to have a bit of fun, that's all—"

Fun. It was a concept that felt completely alien to Sophia. There was work and need and duty, hunger and money and fear. There was no *fun.* But Angelika was only eighteen, and she'd lived in a dour household mourning her mother for too many years already. She was made for singing, for pleasure, for *life.* Sighing, Sophia touched her sister's curls again, threading her fingers through their softness.

Angelika preened under her caress like a cat, her cheek pressed against Sophia's skirt. Sophia felt herself soften as she stroked her hair, enjoying the moment of tenderness. "Don't you ever want more?" Angelika asked, a soft note of longing in her voice. "More than this?"

Sophia's fingers stilled. *More?* What more could there be than a house with a shed and two bedrooms, healthy animals, a good harvest? The only more Sophia wanted was safety, but she did not think her sister meant that.

"We need to find you a husband, *moraki mou,*" Sophia said with a sigh. "Then you will have this more. A home of your own, a child. That is what you need."

Angelika closed her eyes and didn't answer, which Sophia knew was her way of avoiding the conversation. Making no promises. But then Sophia could hardly make any, either. There were few husbands to be found in their village now, and Angelika would be considered young to marry. She dropped her hand. "Please be careful," she said quietly. "That is all I'm asking."

Angelika lifted her head and opened her eyes, gazing at her with liquid innocence. "I will," she promised, and rose to take off her boots.

Sophia sat on her bed, fatigue overwhelming her. The air in the bedroom was still and stifling, and if she'd had more energy, she would have dragged her mattress downstairs and slept in the great room, where it was cooler. As it was, she barely felt able to undress and lie on top of the covers.

Tomorrow she would wake before the dawn, make coffee and bread and cheese for her father to take to the fields, and then set about her tasks for the day: weeding the garden, milking their cow, tending their sheep and goats, darning and sewing, cleaning and cooking, an endless round of duties that Angelika would help with, for a while at least. Then some errand would call her away for far longer than it should take—fetching water, feeding the goats... and Sophia would not see her until the afternoon.

A husband, Sophia thought again. Her sister needed a husband—no matter that she was several years younger than most girls were when they were married. If their father had been more attentive, he would have begun to arrange Sophia's own marriage, but she knew he had not thought of it, much less talked to his sister, Andra, who would act as the negotiator. In any case, marriage-age men were scarce. A dozen boys from the village had already joined the Greek army two years ago, to fight off the invasion by the Italians from Albania; when the Germans had swept in, they'd fled, apparently all the way to Egypt, to be equipped and trained by the British forces stationed there. Sophia could not even imagine such a place, so far away from all she'd known, the round humps of the hills, the sharp smell of pine trees.

Others, like Dimitrios, had joined the *andartes* and melted into the hills, appearing occasionally to swagger around the square or demand food. Their names were whispered with quiet reverence; you never knew who was listening. And as for those young men who remained... Sophia ran through the motley bunch in her head. The baker's son, who was a bit simple; a farming boy who was too young, another who had a squint, and one who was cruel to his mule. Maybe a few others who worked the farms between Iousidous and Lamia. None of them, Sophia knew, would make the kind of husband she'd normally want for her sister, yet who could be choosy in times like these?

Sighing, she closed her eyes, but despite her exhaustion sleep would not come. Things are different now, Angelika had said. Sophia knew her sister was right, but Angelika had spoken with the confidence of the naïve, the blind faith of the innocent. She spoke as if change would be good, as if it were welcome, as if nothing could touch her. Yet how could any of it be welcome, with men being shot in their heads and whole villages disappearing in the space of a single night? Jews in Salonika, it was whispered, were being sent on trains God only knew where, packed in like cattle in a shed, and thousands of people died every day in Athens, from starvation.

Again Sophia felt that chill inside, like winter entering her bones, turning her old. She would not be surprised if her hair turned white before her twenty-first birthday. She wanted only to stay safe, to keep Angelika and her father safe. Was it too much to ask in this dangerous age? "*Things are different now.*"

Yes, Angelika, she answered silently, closing her eyes and willing herself to sleep, *but I do not wish them to be.*

CHAPTER FOUR

Now

Ava woke to brilliant sunlight slanting through the slats of the window's shutters. For a moment before she opened her eyes and faced the day, she pretended she was back in the terraced house in York she'd bought with Simon years ago, their first and only home. She did this every morning, no matter where she woke. It was her painful little ritual, with several precious steps, and she could not keep herself from doing it even though it hurt, sometimes almost unbearably.

Lying there, her eyes still shut, she imagined the sunlight was streaming in from the large window by their bed, filtered through the leaves of the horse chestnut tree in the back garden that they both loved. She slid one hand under her T-shirt, onto the soft flatness of her belly, and imagined it was firm and round. She could almost feel a tiny foot kicking into her palm, even though all was, of course, still. Then she pictured Simon next to her, sleeping on his back with his hands folded over his chest, as he always did. Ava used to tease him that he didn't just sleep like the dead, he *looked* like he was dead. That joke had stopped being funny a year ago, when she'd held the tiny, still form of her daughter in her arms. Her little fingers had been pleated together under her chin, her eyes closed, and her mouth furled up like a rosebud.

Ava opened her eyes, blinking slowly in the bright, hard sunlight, so different from the gentle, more diffused light of England,

and felt the pain open inside her again, as fresh and raw as ever. She knew she needed to stop imagining, every morning, how things could have been. How they used to be. Yet even though it hurt, she craved just the memory of the hope and joy she'd felt then; the remnants of those feelings sometimes felt like all that sustained her now. And, she feared, to stop doing it would be to allow herself to forget, and she could not ever let herself do that.

She stretched, swinging her legs over the side of the bed as the events of the evening before trickled through her consciousness. The drive from Athens. The dilapidated farmhouse. The kindness of Eleni. And perhaps most surprising of all, Parthenope's confused apology.

I'm sorry. Such a strange—and sad—thing to say after seventy years. What on earth could Parthenope be sorry for now? What had happened all those years ago? Or had seeing Ava simply triggered a memory that held no meaning after all this time? Lying there, Ava remembered how the tears had slipped down Parthenope's papery cheeks. Hardly a meaningless memory. Perhaps grief never lessened, not after one year, not after seventy. The thought offered both hope and sorrow. She wasn't ready to let go of her own grief, but she wanted to believe she could one day. At least she thought she did. She could not imagine living this way forever.

And as for Parthenope... Ava knew she couldn't ask the elderly woman what had troubled her so, at least not yet. Last night she had seemed genuinely distressed, and that in turn had distressed Eleni. As their guest, Ava had no intention of upsetting either of them, and yet she was intensely curious. As she dressed, she wondered whether there was anyone else in the village she could ask about it, and then she wondered if she even wanted to know. Whatever it was, it couldn't be good. There was a reason no one talked about that time, just as her mother had warned her. Besides, Parthenope's tears and apology did not suggest a happy memory; surely she'd experienced enough sadness and loss already.

Sighing, she ran a brush through her unruly hair and went to find Eleni in the kitchen. The older woman stood by the sink, spooning yogurt into a bowl. In the sunlight her gray hair looked almost blond, the light touching the crow's feet at the corners of her eyes and the deep laugh lines that Ava saw as Eleni turned to her and smiled.

"So, you are awake. And hungry too, I think."

"Starving," Ava admitted a bit sheepishly. She still felt a little uncomfortable and even guilty taking this stranger's hospitality. She could hardly imagine such a thing happening back in England, but life seemed different here in the rural heartland of Greece, as if she'd fallen back in time, to a simpler age.

"Let me help," she said, starting forward, but Eleni shook her head firmly.

"No, no, it is all finished. You drink coffee?"

"Yes, please."

Eleni arched an eyebrow, a smile curving her lips. "Greek coffee?"

Ava had heard about Greek coffee; it was a strong, syrupy espresso that you could stand a spoon in. "Yes, please," she said again, smiling, and Eleni nodded in approval.

"*Poli kala*," she said, and from a small copper pot she poured Ava a little ceramic cup of what looked like brown sludge. She pushed the sugar bowl towards her. "This will help."

Ava murmured her thanks, then spooned the sugar into the coffee and stirred. Eleni began to slice a melon. "So will you go back to your grandmother's house?" she asked as she fanned the succulent slices out on a plate. "Perhaps it will not be so bad in the light of day."

"Or perhaps it will be worse," Ava couldn't keep herself from saying with a little laugh. "Either way, I need to have another look. You've been kind enough to let me stay one night—"

Eleni waved a hand. "It is no bother. We do not have visitors in this village too often, I can assure you."

"You are very kind." Ava took a tiny sip of coffee. It was so strong, it was hard not to wince or even shudder at the taste. "I suppose I'll need to ring the electric company again—"

Eleni waved a hand again. "My cousin Vasileios works for Public Power. He can sort out the electric."

Another seemingly insurmountable obstacle so easily pushed aside. If only all of her life could be so simple, so easy. "I don't know what I'd have done if I hadn't met you last night." Gone back to Athens, probably, in tears, and then maybe even all the way back to England, defeated.

Eleni shrugged, the movement both philosophical and dismissive. "You don't need to worry about such things. After all, you are one of us." She placed a bowl of thick Greek yogurt in front of Ava, a dollop of golden honey spreading in its center. "So your grandmother's house…" she continued, turning back to the sink, "it has been empty a long time."

"Over sixty years, I think. My grandmother, Sophia, moved to England sometime after the war. I really don't know anything about her life in Greece." She'd never even been curious. The thought shamed her now, at least a little. Why were the young never curious about what came before them?

She took a breath and let it out slowly before she added hesitantly, "It's wonderful that your mother knew her. If she could tell me some things—memories—or tell you, rather, that would be—" She stopped as she saw Eleni shaking her head with the same kind of firm dismissal with which she'd discussed the electricity.

"My mother never talks about the war. No one does. It is as if it did not happen. In truth I am amazed she spoke to you at all." She glanced away, her lips pressed in a firm line. "Even I do not know all of what happened here during that time, although of course there are stories."

Ava was not really that surprised, but she still felt a flicker of disappointment. She stirred her creamy yogurt, watching as the golden honey melted into it. "Stories?" she repeated quietly.

"Terrible stories, about terrible things." Eleni shook her head. "Violence of all kinds. Of course, at that time, such things happened everywhere, all over Europe. But in Greece… there was more. Starvation because of the Allied blockades, and the Germans, they took all the food. The economy—the whole country—was ruined for at least two generations, perhaps more if you consider the sorry state of affairs today." She gave a small, sad smile and Ava nodded her understanding. She knew Greece's economy had been something of a national disaster— it had been in the news enough back in England—even if it didn't seem to touch daily life in this remote little spot. "And," Eleni continued, "during the war 300,000 people died of starvation in Athens alone. Here, in the country, it was a little better. At least we could grow our own food, although that was taken too, first by the Italians and Nazis, and then by the *andartes*."

"*Andartes*?" Ava had never heard the word.

"Soldiers of the Resistance. Communists on one side and monarchy-hating republicans on the other. Both violent." She shook her head with a grimace. "When the Germans finally left, they fought each other and tore the country apart even further in a civil war that lasted years. Everyone suffered."

"I didn't even know there was a Greek Resistance," Ava admitted. "Or a civil war." Her lack of knowledge embarrassed her, but Eleni, like with so much else, shrugged it off philosophically.

"Oh, yes, the Resistance was very strong, especially the communists. They hid up in the mountains, attacked outposts and gendarmeries. Some of the villagers helped feed and shelter them, and of course the Nazis did not like that at all. They burned whole villages to the ground for giving a bit of bread. By the end of the war, Iousidous was nearly ruined. It was a mercy there was anything left at all."

"When did the civil war end?"

"In 1949. I was a year old."

Nearly ten years of brutal, unrelenting violence and bloodshed. And her grandmother, presumably, had lived through most of that—although she'd left Greece, as far as Ava knew, in 1946. How had Sophia got out of the country? It surely couldn't have been easy, with the end of the Second World War and the continuing Greek Civil War, and yet Ava had never given it a second's thought. Again she felt that flicker of shame. She'd seen her grandmother at least once a month all through her childhood, had sat on her stiff, plastic-swathed sofa and never even thought to ask. All she remembered about those endless Sunday afternoons was being almost painfully bored, wearing a dress that usually itched, and wishing she could drink something other than the orange squash her grandmother made, which was always far too strong, a bit like the coffee she was now taking in tiny medicinal sips.

"And what happened to the village after the civil war?" she asked, taking another sip of coffee. The taste, it seemed, was growing on her. A little bit, anyway. She didn't feel the need to wince.

"The economy was terrible, and young people wanted new lives in the city or even in another country. They left. It is understandable—even I left, for a time. Just about anyone who could, did."

"So you haven't lived here all your life?"

"I spent a year in England, working as an au pair," Eleni said with a shrug. "Over fifty years ago now. It is how I learned my English." She smiled, pouring herself a cup of coffee and settling in a chair opposite Ava. "But I came back to Greece after, and worked in Lamia. My husband, he was from the next town over.

We both wanted to settle here. The young people want to leave, but I think, at some time in life, you need to go home and see what is there."

Ava nodded, wondering when that time would be for her, if ever. Her only desire had been to leave home. Leave all the sorrow and regrets and memories. She wasn't even sure what home was now. Was it the house in York? Simon? Or the hopes for their little family that she had long since lost? Perhaps home wasn't something that could be found any more.

"So," Eleni asked briskly, "what brings you to Greece?" She glanced rather pointedly at Ava's wedding ring. "For as long a time as you say?"

Ava laughed shakily. Eleni sounded both disapproving and curious. She supposed she was traditional about things like a marriage, a woman her age in a small, remote village like this. "I'm separated from my husband," she admitted, the words sounding strange coming from her own mouth. Even though she barely knew Eleni, after everything that the woman had done for her already, she surely deserved her honesty. "We decided we—we needed to take some time away from each other and see what happened."

A rather innocuous way to put it, but Ava couldn't manage anything more. When they'd separated a month ago, it had seemed so painfully final and yet so horribly ordinary. She had despised the stilted conversation as they navigated the prosaic details of a life apart, deciding in an awkward, diffident way which credit cards to cancel and whether to divide the furniture. It had been awful, worse somehow than the first conversation about whether or not to separate at all, the way they'd dismantled their joined existence like an old washing machine. Could you put such a thing back together again, even if you wanted to, or would it just stay a collection of jumbled, rusty parts?

"I don't know about these modern marriages," Eleni said, taking a sip of her own coffee. "My husband and I never spent a night apart until he died two years ago now. How can any problems be fixed if you don't solve them together?"

"Sometimes you need a break from solving problems," Ava said quietly. She stared down at her coffee, her throat turning thick with tears, her vision clouding. "Sometimes you need a break from how hard it is," she added, then pressed her lips together before she said any more or broke down completely. Nearly a year later it was all still so fresh, so raw, so painful. When would it get better? When would she be able to talk about her daughter and her husband and the family she'd expected to have without feeling as if her soul was being ripped into ragged pieces? *Soon*, she hoped, even as she continued to cling to her grief.

Eleni reached over and covered her hand with her own work-worn one. "I am sorry. It is not my business to ask."

Ava looked up and tried to smile. "No, it's all right. You've been so good to me—"

"It is nothing," Eleni said, releasing Ava's hand and standing up. "But now, I think, you must go see what this house of yours looks like in daylight. I will have supper ready this evening. You will not be able to cook in that place until tomorrow."

Fifteen minutes later Ava left Eleni's house and strolled down the street towards her grandmother's. Her own house. The sun was lemony bright, the sky hard and blue. She tilted her face up towards the warmth, enjoyed the feel of the sun on her face as well as the crisp, cool mountain air.

Iousidous did not look much livelier in the morning than it had in the lonely darkness of last night. A few shutters had been opened to the sunshine, and as Ava walked she saw one or two older women, wearing head scarves and aprons, stooped over in their small front gardens. She smiled tentatively at them but they only stared balefully back. Clearly this was not a place for outsiders. Ava recalled how Eleni had spoken sharply to her last night, until she had stammered something out about her grandmother. She wondered whether other villagers might warm up to her if they knew about Sophia. The women in their gardens, although elderly, did not look old enough to have been alive during the war. Would anyone, besides Parthenope, remember that time?

Ava pushed such thoughts aside as she came to the front of the house. It looked even more dilapidated in the bright sunshine. She was half amazed it was standing at all. The roof tiles were broken, the shutters falling from their hinges. At least the door opened with a little less resistance this time, and once more she stepped inside.

It felt different to last night, when it had been nothing more than a depressing-looking hovel. Now, in light of Parthenope's confused memory of Sophia Paranoussis, Ava was acutely aware that this had been her grandmother's home. She had been born here, had grown up here, lived and perhaps loved here. Yet the musty, near-empty room gave nothing away.

Ava wandered through the downstairs; besides the large living room, there was only a small kitchen and a bathroom, both seeming grudgingly tacked on at a later date, as well as a small side room that looked to have been some kind of storage area. The walls were rough and unfinished in that room, and the floor was just stones over packed earth, weeds poking through the cracks. The kitchen held only a stone sink and an ancient-looking gas stove. She'd seen a second floor from the outside, but it took her at least ten minutes to find the stairs on the outside of the house. Obscured by a tangle of overgrown vines, they were barely visible from the front of the house. Ava hesitated, debating their safety before she took a cautious step upwards. The rusted iron creaked underfoot but held, and slowly, grasping the railing, she made it to the second floor. The door at the top was locked, but it opened with some jiggling of the same rusty key she'd used downstairs.

Ava took a step inside a dark, narrow corridor; two doors led off it. She peeked inside one bedroom, saw sunshine filtering in through the cracks in the closed shutters, touching an old iron bedstead with light. Ava took a step inside the room and her foot went through the rotted wooden floorboards; she gasped aloud, imagining herself falling to the floor below, thudding on the stone as lifeless as a rag doll, but then her foot hit what looked like roof tile. She realized the bedrooms must have been added on later—built directly onto the roof.

Shaky with relief, her heart racing, she stepped back out into the hallway. The second bedroom was much like the first, but with two bed frames instead of one. Empty and silent, dust motes dancing through the air, the room revealed nothing. Ava felt a spasm of helpless frustration, for she could not even begin to envision her grandmother in this room. She could not remotely imagine what her grandmother might have said or worn, much less thought or dreamed. Her own ignorance made the room's silence feel strangely like a reproach. *Who was the woman who had lived here? What had her life been like?*

Ava heard a car drive slowly down the village road, its engine sputtering a little, and the bleat of a goat or sheep in the distance. The entire landscape felt foreign, impenetrable, a world apart. Shaking her head, she stepped back into the dark corridor and then downstairs.

A door led off the kitchen into the back garden, now no more than a patch of weeds and a few twisted, stunted-looking trees. Ava sat on a wide, sun-warmed stone that served as a stoop, and rested her elbows on her knees. About twenty meters away the garden disappeared into scrub, which in turn led into dense pine forest. The hills in the distance were dark green with trees, and, with the only sound the wind, she felt very much alone.

She closed her eyes, tried to imagine the house not as it once had been, when her grandmother had lived here, but as it could be, with some scrubbing and repairs. She could find out whether the stove worked and buy a refrigerator. Perhaps Eleni would know someone who could repair the floorboards and whitewash the walls. With a few bits of furniture, it could at least be livable.

And to her surprise, despite last night's difficult start, she realized she *wanted* to live here. For a little while at least. She still wasn't sure what she would do, or just how she might manage, but she knew she wanted to try. The possibility made her feel peaceful—almost. As close to peace as she'd been in a long while, perhaps.

She heard a whisper in the grass and opened her eyes to see the scrawny cat from last night staring at her with lamp-like eyes. At least she thought it was the same one; in the darkness she hadn't noticed the animal's color, but she thought she recognized that unblinking stare.

"Sorry," she said. "I don't have any food. But I will later, if you come back."

The cat let out a reproachful meow and then turned and stalked away through the weeds.

After a moment Ava rose again, locked up the house, and went back out into the sleepy street. She would explore the rest of the village, and then perhaps in the afternoon she would drive to Lamia for furniture and food.

Hardly anyone was about as Ava made her way up the hillside. In daylight she saw that Iousidous was really no more than one winding street that snaked up the hillside, turning in on itself several times, houses lining either side. For every house with a garden or car or some sign of life, there were two that were clearly uninhabited, as dilapidated as her grandmother's or worse. Some were complete ruins, the roofs or windows missing, weeds growing in the great rooms, an air of forlorn emptiness shrouding them like a mist.

Halfway up the hill the ground leveled out to form a surprisingly pleasant square with a fountain in the middle. To Ava's happy surprise she saw a café on one side of the square, no more than a small storefront with an awning and a few tables outside, but at this point she'd hardly expected Iousidous to have any businesses at all. She made her way over to the café and smiled at the stout woman sweeping the floor who gazed back in obvious suspicion.

"Do you speak English?"

"Enough."

Ava wasn't sure what that meant, but she widened her smile anyway. "Could I have a cup of coffee?" Perhaps the only way to get used to Greek coffee was to keep drinking it.

The woman nodded tersely and pointed to one of the tables. Ava was the only customer. She sat down as the woman disappeared inside, and then gazed round the square.

Besides the café, there was a little post office and a small shop that looked to sell basic groceries. The rest of the whitewashed buildings were either shut up or appeared to be homes, although Ava imagined that once—perhaps in her grandmother's lifetime—the square had been bustling with activity and enterprise.

If she couldn't imagine her grandmother in the house, perhaps she could imagine her here, young and vibrant, a wicker shopping basket on her arm, her hair dark, eyes bright.

Still it was impossible; she was imagining a made-up person, someone who might never have existed. The only grandmother Ava could imagine was the elderly woman from her childhood and adolescence, her dark eyes faded yet her chin still tilted proudly as she beckoned with one claw-like finger for Ava to fetch the tin of boiled sweets she kept on the top shelf of the pantry.

The woman came back with her coffee, and Ava thanked her. "*Efharisto.*"

The woman glanced at her, eyes narrowed. "You do not speak Greek."

So much for her attempt at the language, Ava thought wryly. "No, not really."

"On holiday?"

"Sort of." The woman frowned, not understanding, and Ava explained, "I'm staying here for a while. In the Paranoussis house, at the first curve in the street. Do you know it?"

The woman still looked uncomprehending, and Ava gave her an apologetic little smile and a shrug. "My grandmother lived here."

This gained no response either, finally Ava pointed at the coffee. "*Efharisto*," she said again. "*Nostimos.*" Delicious.

The woman merely grunted and returned to her sweeping.

Ava sipped the coffee slowly as she gazed around the empty square. She wondered how the woman at the café made a living if she sold only one coffee a morning. Did any young people live here at all? The whole village seemed so silent and empty, as if it had been forgotten by time itself.

Fighting a sudden pang of loneliness, she slipped her mobile phone out of her pocket and glanced at the blank screen. No received or missed calls, but then the reception was patchy here. Someone might not get through. Who, Ava wondered as she put her phone away, was she hoping would ring? Her mother? Her best friend, Julie? Or Simon?

Simon always used to ring her to make sure she'd arrived safely somewhere. His diligence had annoyed her sometimes, made her feel as if he thought she was a scatterbrained child, yet now, sitting alone in the empty silence of this square, she found she missed it. For a moment she craved the comfort and security of knowing someone wanted to hear from her, knowing she was missed and maybe even loved. The phone was as silent as the house had been, revealing nothing. Simon probably wasn't thinking of her at all.

After she'd drunk and paid for her coffee—deciding that two cups a day of Greek coffee was at least one more than she needed—Ava continued her walk through the village and up the hillside. She walked along another snaking street of houses, and then past a small modern building that looked to be a school.

Then the road turned sharply once more and she was suddenly at the top of the hill, with a tiny blue-domed, whitewashed church perched on its rocky summit, a scrubby patch of grass and a few plane trees out in front. The pine-covered hills stretched all around her, a vast, undulating blanket of dark green, and in the distance she spied the crystalline sparkle of water, like light reflecting off a mirror.

She turned towards the church and saw that one of the wooden doors had been left slightly ajar. After a second's hesitation Ava slipped inside, her eyes adjusting to the dim light. The air smelled of beeswax and incense and she saw that the church was just one small, empty room, devoid of any chairs, with some peeling but brightly painted icons on the walls, and two ornately decorated wooden screens in front, hiding the altar from view. She stood there a moment, breathing in the unfamiliar yet weirdly comforting scents, amazed to find herself in such a strange place: a little church on top of a hill in the middle of Greece. How had she got here?

Perhaps she could picture her grandmother here, standing with the other villagers, head bowed, listening to the priest chant the Mass. She wasn't quite sure what a Greek Orthodox service looked like, although she had a vague recollection of semi-Catholic practices, yet with a more culturally ethnic feel. She realized she didn't even know what—if anything—her grandmother had believed.

And what did she believe? The last time she'd been in a church had been for her daughter's funeral. The casket had been tiny, the size of a bread box, white with silver handles. Stony-faced, Simon had carried it in his arms and placed it on the altar, like some kind of awful sacrifice, before the service had begun. At that point, only three days after her labor, still bleeding, her empty stomach sagging, her breasts full and aching with milk that hadn't dried up yet despite the pills she'd been given, Ava had felt too numb to cry, too shocked even to process what was happening.

Yet when the minister, some round-cheeked balding man whose parish they happened to live in, took the casket in his arms and headed out of the church, Ava had cried out. It had been an ugly animal sound, more of a growl than a scream, and utterly instinctive. Simon had drawn her quickly to him, and Ava thought he would have put his hand over her mouth if she hadn't jerked away again. He was embarrassed, and she was in agony. She felt as if she had drunk poison, as if her insides were writhing in a desperate and tortured denial. *This can't be happening.* She had wondered if this was what dying felt like, but knew it wasn't, for she kept relentlessly living, on and on, and surely that was the greater tragedy.

The smell of the incense was making her dizzy, or maybe it was just the memories, but either way Ava knew she had to get out of the church. Letting out a breath she hadn't realized she'd been holding, she headed back into sunlight, and down the hill.

She walked slowly, feeling tired now, the sun surprisingly hot overhead for the middle of March. As she passed the low concrete building she'd assumed was a school, schoolchildren spilled out of its doors, dark-haired children shouting excitedly in Greek, the girls in red-and-white checked pinafores, the boys in red jumpers and flannel trousers. She slowed to a stop by the fence, watching them play; the youngest ones couldn't be more than five or six. In their red uniforms they reminded her of apples, glossy and brimming with health and vitality. The children barely took notice of her, yet Ava ached as she looked at them.

It shouldn't hurt. She knew that. She'd been an art teacher at a primary school, for heaven's sake, before her job had been axed because of austerity measures and the relentless budget cuts. She'd taught several classes of thirty children every day, except for the six weeks' compassionate leave, not maternity, she'd been granted. She'd somehow got herself through all that without falling apart, so why did she feel so close to it now? Was it being in such a strange, new place, or having just remembered the funeral while in the little church at the top of the village? Or was it simply that the grief was always inside her, and sometimes it raised its head and sniffed the air, a crouching beast ready to spring and devour?

A teacher, a woman about the same age as Ava, came to the door of the school. She was dressed casually in jeans and a jumper, and her long, dark hair was pulled back into a ponytail. She was striking rather than pretty, with dark eyes and heavy, straight eyebrows, and as she stared at Ava, Ava realized it might look a bit suspicious to have a stranger lurking about this little village school. With a little grimacing smile of apology, she started down the hill, and as she turned, she saw the woman smile back and wave, and her heart lightened just a little.

CHAPTER FIVE

Now

After she'd returned from her walk, Ava decided to drive to Lamia. Eleni had promised her that the power would be on by the time she finished her shopping; the older woman had also offered to help with the scrubbing and sweeping. Ava, in usual fashion, was both humbled and cheered, and Eleni brushed her stammering thanks aside.

"It is nothing," she said, and in so firm a voice that Ava believed her.

It made her wonder what kind of community her grandmother had lived in. Had the villagers been close, helped each other with the demands of a harsh life farming this mountainous country, not to mention the challenges of the war? Had Sophia had friends, or even a boyfriend? She must have been in her early twenties when she'd left. Had it been hard to leave, or even heart wrenching? Had she missed anyone?

It was impossible to envisage. Ava could not fathom what life was like in rural Greece seventy years ago. Eleni had mentioned that the houses wouldn't have had running water or electricity at that time; that was hard enough to imagine, never mind the customs, traditions, societal rules… It was a different world, an alien universe, and in her mind Ava peopled it with cardboard figures, girls in wide skirts and embroidered blouses, men in vaguely medieval-looking poet shirts and leather boots. *Ridicu-lous*. She had no idea what any of it would have really been like.

Sighing, she wished again she could ask Parthenope what she'd meant by that tearful apology, but she knew Eleni had practically forbidden it. After accepting so much hospitality, Ava could hardly go against her host's wishes. Yet she had no idea how else to find out more about her grandmother's life. The house held no answers, and there could surely be only a handful of people left who remembered the war, who had lived through it.

She let her mind drift as she drove to Lamia, the road winding through the steep hills, the pine forests giving way to a sudden, fertile plain and the whitewashed huddle of buildings; the town was clearly much larger than Iousidous yet still seemed quaint.

In the central square Ava strolled alongside stalls with a basket she'd bought on her arm, the sun warm on her face as she inspected ropes of onions and fat bulbs of garlic, baskets of shiny, plump tomatoes and lumps of feta cheese swimming in brine. She found a little stall on a side street that sold towels and bed sheets for a couple of euros apiece, and she bought a set of basic dishes in pleasingly thick white china. She visited a shop that sold furniture along with just about everything, it seemed, that you needed to do up a house. Pots and pans lay haphazardly stacked next to duvet covers, and a dozen plastic-framed prints of da Vinci's *Madonna of the Rocks* leaned against one wall.

The shopkeeper didn't speak much English, but somehow, with a combination of Ava's hesitant Greek, his bits of English, and a lot of pointing and miming, she managed to buy a table, chairs, a sofa, a mattress, and even a fridge. She flinched a little at the price, doing a mental conversion to pounds, but she'd received a severance package from the school and she needed only a few things. The man promised to deliver the items later that afternoon, putting his hand over his heart and nodding vigorously, which Ava hoped was a sign of serious intent.

Satisfied with her purchases, she had lunch at a little café in the central square, eating crispy *souvlaki* and burning her fingers. By the time she made it back to her rental car it was mid-afternoon, and she was both tired and relaxed, humming under her breath as she drove out of Lamia and up the steep, twisting road that led to Iousidous. It felt good to be productive, to have actually accomplished something. Perhaps she could even sleep in the house tonight. The thought gave her a little leap of excitement, along with a pulse of alarm.

She was a few kilometers outside of the village, or so she assumed, when she heard a strange popping sound and then the car bumped and rumbled to a stop. She just had time to pull onto the shoulder, not that there was much of one, before turning off the engine and going to discover what had happened.

A flat tire. *Of course.* Her good mood burst, as fragile as a soap bubble. If she had been one of those calm, competent, capable women, she would have known how to change a tire. This wouldn't have fazed her at all.

The sun beat down and the air was still and silent, the only sound the faint rustling of the wind in the pines high above. She felt like the last person left on earth. Taking a deep breath, Ava brushed a tendril of hair away from her face and strove not to panic. Even so she could feel the sharp little claws of anxiety digging into her skull, clutching at her soul. Two months after the stillbirth she'd been prescribed antidepressants, but the pills just made her feel woozy and sick and so she had stopped taking them, had insisted she could conquer her anxiety with a combination of homeopathy, yoga, and simple mind over matter.

She hadn't conquered it, hadn't even really tried.

Simon had been patient with her, she acknowledged now, even if it had been in a long-suffering aren't-I-so-patient kind of way. But then he'd always accused her of panicking, of rushing into worst-case scenarios on very little evidence. She'd been the one to suggest they buy gold bars when the stock market plunged; she'd even, ridiculously she saw now, hoarded flour and salt after reading a book on the necessity of self-sufficiency.

"What," Simon had asked her, smiling just a little, "are you going to do with fifty kilograms of salt?"

The book she'd read had insisted on stockpiling salt, and belatedly Ava realized that it was useful only if you intended to kill, skin, and preserve your own meat, hardly a possibility in urban England even if she'd been interested in such a thing, which she most certainly had not.

Yet even though she'd overreacted over those absurd things, she hadn't when it had come to her child. After years of trying, fertility drugs, endless rounds of IVF, she'd been strangely, smugly complacent about her pregnancy. Why hadn't she panicked then, when it had mattered? When so much had been at stake?

With effort Ava pushed the thoughts away. The point was she shouldn't panic now, when she had a flat tire and no means of changing it, and she was on a deserted road several kilometers from her destination with no mobile reception.

It didn't look good, yet what was the worst that could happen? She'd walk back to Iousidous, ask for Eleni's help, and drive back with someone who could change her tire. Eleni probably could. She certainly seemed capable, and Ava doubted it would even surprise the older woman that she had never changed a tire in her life.

"It is nothing," Eleni would say with a dismissive wave, and Ava would feel both grateful and pathetic. She wanted, she realized now, to do something for herself for once, and yet she acknowledged she didn't even know how.

She heard the sound of a motor in the distance, and with a wary relief she saw a battered pickup truck approach. She stood back, unsure whether she should smile, wave, or make some internationally known signal of distress. *SOS?* Hadn't she read something about putting a pillowcase in the window to indicate you were in trouble? It must have been some true-story drama in a magazine, yet who kept pillowcases in the car? Although, she realized ruefully, she actually had some in the trunk.

In the end she just stood there, looking, she was sure, abject and quite helpless.

The truck slowed to a stop, sending up plumes of dust. A man rolled down the window and poked his head out; Ava saw he was a bit older than she was, in his forties probably, with curly, dark hair going gray at the temples and serious, liquid eyes. He spoke rapidly in Greek, and Ava, feeling even more pathetic, gave a little shrug and spread her hands.

"*Me sighorite*—"

"You are English?"

Relief pulsed through her. "Yes—"

"And you have a flat tire, it seems."

"Yes." Another wave of relief. "You speak English—"

He waved his hand in a so-so gesture. "Some." He sounded practically fluent to her, especially considering her own lamentable attempts at his language. "I could change it for you. You have a spare?"

Ava hadn't even checked. Why bother, when she couldn't change a tire herself? She tried to smile back. "I think so—"

"It is a hire car, yes? Let me look." He pulled in front of her car on the shoulder; Ava saw there was a sulky-looking teenaged girl in the passenger seat of the truck. The girl crossed her arms and stared straight in front of her as the man got out.

"You are here on holiday?" he asked as he opened the trunk of her car. He raised his eyebrows at all the packages there, and Ava hurried to move them.

"Sort of," she said, pushing aside a pile of sheets and a couple of saucepans. "An extended one." She was not about to explain the complexities of her impulsive move to Greece to this stranger, friendly as he was.

"So it seems." He opened the well of the trunk, and they both stared in silent dismay at the cavernous space where a spare tire should have been. "It appears you were not the first to have a flat in this car," the man said.

Ava said nothing. She suddenly felt too tired and overwhelmed to speak, much less act. Fatigue from the plane journey, emotional exhaustion, panic—it all came crashing down and she nearly swayed where she stood.

"Don't worry," the man said and Ava refocused on his face. He was frowning, studying her in obvious concern. "I can give you a lift."

"Oh—"

"That is, if you are not going too far?"

"Iousidous."

"Just a few kilometers. I live right outside the village." He held out one weathered hand. "Andreas Lethikos."

"Ava Lancet."

She took his hand, feeling a faint flash of something almost like comfort at the way his hand enveloped hers. It made her feel, bizarrely and momentarily, safe. "I'm sorry. I only arrived in Greece yesterday and I think the tiredness from traveling just hit me." Among other things.

"Let me put your things in my truck." Ava tried to help him shift all of her new belongings, but Andreas would have none of it. So she stood on the side of the dusty road and watched, feeling helpless yet again.

Finally he opened the cab of the truck and gestured inside. The teenage girl glared at her as Ava scrambled into the truck. She didn't usually get in cars—or trucks—with strange men, but the presence of the sulky girl who eyed her with blatant suspicion actually made her feel safer, as did the wedding ring she saw on Andreas's finger.

The girl spoke in Greek, and Andreas answered a bit sharply. Looking extremely put out, the girl moved over a few inches so Ava could sit rather awkwardly between them.

"This is my daughter, Kalista," Andreas said as he started the truck.

The girl spoke again, and Ava wished she'd taken the time to learn more Greek; she couldn't catch a single word. She tuned out of their rather tense conversation and rested her head back against the seat. She felt as if she could fall asleep right there, bouncing between Andreas and his angry daughter.

While driving back to Iousidous, she'd been buoyed by a fragile new optimism that had now, in the light of reality, blown away like so much dust. She didn't just feel tired, she knew; she felt homesick. She wanted, suddenly and painfully, to ring Simon. To hear his voice, so steady and reassuring.

Not that she was going to act on that impulse. When she'd told Simon she was moving to Greece, just as when she'd told him she wanted to separate, he'd hardly said anything at all. His face had remained expressionless as he simply nodded and said, "If that's what you want to do."

Ava had wanted to cry out that of course it wasn't, but all the things she had wanted were impossible now. A baby. A family. Simon smiling at her, his hand cradling her bump of a belly, his other arm around her shoulders. Instead, he stared at her with that awful blank look—indifference, really, was what it was—and shrugged twelve years of marriage away in the space of a second.

And so she had gone.

She realized that Andreas and Kalista had stopped speaking, and the silence in the cab of the truck was taut with suppressed tension. Tight-lipped, Andreas glanced at Ava. "I'm so very sorry, but my daughter needs to return home before I take you to Iousidous. She has homework for school, and I would like to help you move your things and change your tire."

"Oh—" Ava said, struggling to sit up a bit. She had not considered the practicalities of leaving her car on the side of the road. If Simon had been here, he would have thought of it. He would have had a plan, and he would have executed it with the brisk efficiency that mostly gratified but occasionally annoyed her. "That's very kind of you," she finally said, inadequately. "Of course I don't mind."

Andreas nodded. "Thank you for your understanding. I do apologize."

They drove in silence along the steep mountain road until Andreas turned down a narrow gravel lane that led into a prosperous-looking property; a five-bar gate opened up to a well-tended track that wound through the pine forest.

"What do you farm?" Ava asked as the truck pulled in front of a low, rambling whitewashed villa. It looked about five times bigger than her house in its downstairs alone, and its modern conveniences most certainly extended past a tottering gas stove and running water.

"Olives," Andreas replied. "We make olive oil, although, long ago, before the civil war we had wheat fields as well. The Lethikos family has owned this farm for over a hundred years." He spoke proudly, yet there was a slight edge to his voice and he glanced rather pointedly at his daughter, who shrugged and looked away. Ava's curiosity was piqued, but she said nothing. "Would you like to come inside?" Andreas asked. "For a glass of water or fruit juice? It must have been very hot and dusty to sit by the side of the road. How long were you there?"

"Not too long," Ava replied, although with the panic creeping up on her it had felt endless. "A glass of fruit juice sounds lovely, thank you."

She followed Andreas into the villa and watched as Kalista disappeared into one of the bedrooms without a backward glance. The living room was airy and comfortable, with a huge stone fireplace taking up most of one wall. The windows were open to the veranda, pots of flowers and herbs lining the steps. Ava glanced in appreciation at the view of the mountainside dotted with the twisted trunks of olive trees. Far below she could see the white churning foam of a river.

"*Visinada*," Andreas told her as he joined her by the window. He handed her the glass of juice and Ava murmured her thanks. "Made with cherry juice, a Greek specialty. I hope you like it."

She took a sip; it was both tart and sweet. "Delicious, thank you."

He nodded towards the view of the mountainside, the river foaming far below. "That is the Gorgopotamos. There is a railroad bridge across it, but the area around the river is a protected site."

"Really? Why?"

"There was a viaduct across it before the Second World War, very important for bringing supplies to Athens. The Resistance bombed it in 1942. Very…" He snapped his fingers, searching for the word. "Successful."

"Goodness," Ava murmured, and Andreas smiled.

"These things don't seem so long ago to us. Nothing really changes here, as my daughter complains." He paused. "I'm sorry for her—difficulty. We have been alone these last two years since my wife died, and it has not been easy."

"I'm sorry," Ava said, and meant it. She knew about loss; she could only imagine how trying it must be for a man to raise a willful teenage daughter on his own.

"And what brings you to Greece?"

"I inherited a little house in Iousidous from my grandmother. She was from this region, although she left after the war. When I learned about the farmhouse, it seemed like a good opportunity to come and try something new." It was a tidy little speech, if a bit bizarre. Ava thought she could probably guess what Andreas was thinking. Why would a woman move to rural Greece on her own, with no obvious plan or job? "My life in England was at a bit of a—stopping point," she explained, and then, since Andreas had told her about his wife, she added stiltedly, "I lost my job due to budget cuts, and my husband and I are separated."

"I'm sorry. I don't mean to ask so many questions. Your business is your own, of course."

Ava nodded, although it didn't feel as if her business was her own. She'd only been in Greece for twenty-four hours and already she was telling people things she hadn't shared with many friends back in England, at least not easily. Even her best friend Julie had only been given scant details. And yet here she felt as if she'd fallen down a rabbit hole into a world where people didn't guard their secrets or avoid looking you in the eye; they opened their homes and maybe even their hearts, and she could not help but respond—impulsively perhaps—in kind. Simon, Ava thought, would have shaken his head at the way she'd accepted Eleni's offer to stay the night, and Andreas's offer of a lift. He would have told her she was too trusting, too dependent, and perhaps he would have been right. Or maybe she'd been living with Simon's stoic silence for too long.

"I'm sorry, but I should get back to Iousidous," she finally said. "I don't want the shopping to spoil."

"Of course," Andreas said. "I'm sorry to have delayed you."

They were just climbing back into his truck when Ava's mobile phone trilled tinnily. Surprised, she dug it out of her handbag and flipped it open.

"I didn't think there was reception here—" she said, only to stop, her heart seeming to freeze in her chest, as she looked at the number on the luminous little screen. It was Simon.

Andreas glanced across at Ava as he started the engine of his truck. "Ava? Are you all right? You look as if—what is the expression?—you've seen a ghost."

"It's nothing." The screen of her mobile had darkened as the call went to her voicemail. Ava slipped her phone back into her handbag. Her fingers were shaking. *Simon.*

Undoubtedly he'd rung to check whether she'd arrived safely. Typical Simon. He would have expected her to run into trouble—and even if she had, it still annoyed and touched her all at once. Ava knew she was being contrary to feel even the slightest bit irritated by his solicitude. Some part of her would have rather he was too hurt or angry to call; his concern bordered, absurdly perhaps, on indifference, just a man doing his tedious duty. It made her wonder if he'd ever loved her at all. The breakdown of their marriage had left him so unruffled, so utterly unaffected. Ringing her—speaking to her—was not a torment, the way it would be for her. It was just something to tick off on his to-do list.

"It should only take a few minutes to drive to Iousidous," Andreas said, pulling Ava back into the present. "I don't think your shopping will spoil."

"Oh… good." With effort she made herself think about every-day things, about her shopping in the back of Andreas's truck and the bright blue sky stretching out ahead of them. "Thank you," she added belatedly. "This is really very kind of you."

Andreas lifted one shoulder in a little shrug. "It is nothing," he said, a phrase Ava was beginning to recognize—and slightly resent.

It is something, she wanted to say. *It means something to me.* She didn't want it to be nothing. She really needed to get a handle on her emotions. She knew Andreas was being nothing but kind.

"I am happy to welcome you to our small corner of the world," he added. "Perhaps we will see more of each other."

He gave her a tentative, sideways smile that, after a second's hesitation, Ava returned. She supposed, in such a small place, they would see more of each other, although she did not know whether Andreas meant that they might see each other intentionally.

Back in Iousidous, Andreas helped Ava unload her shopping into the house. Under a stranger's scrutiny Ava was acutely conscious of just how dilapidated the place really was. She thought of Andreas's villa, with its sweeping views and airy spaciousness, and gave a self-conscious laugh. "It's not much, I know. And it needs a good clean."

"It was your grandmother's house?"

"Yes, but she left right after the war."

"As did many people. At least she survived it."

"Your family was here then?" Ava asked, remembering he'd said something about his olive grove being in his family's possession for a hundred years. Andreas nodded.

"My father was just a boy at the time."

"I wonder if he knew my grandmother."

"I would ask him, but he died five years ago," Andreas replied with a small, sad smile. "And he never spoke of the war. No one does."

Just as Eleni had said. Clearly finding anything out about her grandmother was going to be very difficult indeed. People were friendly and open here, but not about the past.

"It was an awful time," Ava offered hesitantly, for she was keenly aware that she had absolutely no idea of what she was talking about.

"Yes, and we Greeks prefer to act as if it didn't happen. If we don't like it, it does not exist." He smiled faintly, and Ava smiled back, her heart twisting inside her. If only that could be true. "If you need any furniture," he continued, "we might have some pieces—"

"I'm having a few things delivered," Ava said quickly. She felt reluctant to accept any more of Andreas's generosity. "Any moment now, actually. And in any case, I don't know how long I'll be here." It sounded like a warning.

Andreas raised his eyebrows. "You did not buy a return ticket?"

"No, but I'll have to go back at some point." Ava tried to keep her voice light. "You always do, don't you?"

"I hope so." Andreas glanced away. "I hope you can always go back."

Curiosity flared inside her. He sounded so wistful, and even sad. Still she did not press. She wasn't about to ask for more personal details. She knew how excruciating it could be to have them prised from you.

"Well, thank you," she said, awkwardly, for it sounded like a dismissal, which she supposed it was.

"I am happy to help," Andreas said. "I will change your tire, yes? And perhaps drive you back out to collect it."

"Oh, right…" In a welter of embarrassment Ava realized she'd forgotten about the car. "That would be fantastic."

"I'll be back in a little while?" he said, eyebrows raised expectantly, and Ava nodded.

"Brilliant. Thank you."

What, she wondered as Andreas left the house, would she have done without these people? By this time she'd probably have been on a plane back to Manchester Airport.

She sank on top of a cardboard box that held her new dishes, and let out a long, slow sigh. She was utterly grateful for the help Andreas and Eleni had given her, but it still somehow made her feel miserable. Pathetic. She slipped her mobile out of her bag and stared at the screen. No messages. Before she could even consider whether to ring Simon back now or not, a quick knock sounded at the door and Eleni poked her head in.

"Was that Andreas Lethikos here?" she asked, eyes bright with shrewd curiosity.

"Yes—"

"How do you know him already?"

Quickly Ava explained about her car. Eleni looked both interested and impressed. "He is a good man, Andreas. Sad about his wife." Ava didn't ask about that; surely Andreas's widowed status was none of her business. Eleni must have sensed her reluctance, for she put her hands on her hips and glanced around at the piles of boxes and bags. "You buy everything you need?"

"And then some. Lamia was lovely. I'm having a bunch of things delivered—"

"Spiro turned the power on while you were gone." Smiling triumphantly, Eleni flicked the switch and the living room was bathed in electric light.

Ava blinked, heartened by this small sign of modern life. "Oh, Eleni, thank you. That's wonderful." She smiled, awkward again with the sense of beholden gratitude. "You've done so much for me already."

Eleni shrugged. "It is good to have more young people here. For however long." She gave Ava an openly speculative look that Ava chose to ignore. She knew Eleni was curious about her marriage, and why she was in Greece alone, but she also knew she wasn't ready to talk about it.

"There is a picnic up at the church, after services on Sunday. It is an important day—Greek Independence Day. You know it?"

Ava shook her head, realizing that she knew very little about Greek history.

"We celebrate our freedom from the Turks. The Ottoman. And it is also the feast day of the…" Eleni paused, clearly searching for a word. "The Annunciation of the Theotokos." Ava stared at her blankly, and for a second Eleni looked both amused and just a tiny bit annoyed. "The Virgin? The Mother of God?"

"Oh, right." She did not know about any special days in the church calendar except Christmas and Easter. But maybe the Church of England didn't celebrate the Annunciation.

"You come?" Eleni prompted. "To the picnic? Everyone from the village will be there."

"Oh…" Ava hesitated. Of course, she could hardly say no, not after all Eleni had done for her. And she did want to meet people in the village and become a part of things. She really did—it was just the prospect of all those introductions, and explaining who she was and how she'd got here, and enduring all the speculative looks and silences, perhaps even some pointed questions from the more blunt villagers... Ava smiled tiredly. "Yes, of course, I'd love to come."

"Good," Eleni said approvingly. "And now—we clean." She rolled up the sleeves of her old cardigan and headed to the kitchen for soap and water.

Two hours later Ava was even more exhausted than before, and the downstairs of the house was, if not sparkling, then certainly habitable.

"The walls need more whitewash," Eleni said. "I'll bring some next time. And you leave the upstairs for now—too dangerous. I'll get someone to repair the stairs."

By the time Eleni had left, the sun was sinking towards the ragged fringe of pines on the horizon. She'd invited Ava to dinner, but Ava had refused.

"Thank you so much for the offer, but I'm shattered and I think I'll just eat here."

Eleni wrinkled her forehead. "Shattered? You mean, broken?"

Laughing a little, Ava had explained. "No—just tired. Really, really tired."

"Ah. Yes. You rest." She patted Ava's arm with maternal concern. "That is good. I will bring you some *souvlaki*, yes? And perhaps some soup?"

Ava wanted to refuse, because at this point she just wanted to be alone. Yet looking at Eleni's kindly but determined expression, she had a feeling refusing would cause offense, so she smiled instead.

"Thank you. You're so kind."

With Eleni gone the house felt very quiet. Very empty. Outside, darkness fell quickly, like a cloak, and with it came a chill in the mountain air, reminding Ava that her grandmother's house might possess a few modern conveniences, but central heating was not one of them. She gazed around the main room with its fireplace and two rickety chairs and wondered just what she had taken on. This didn't feel remotely like a home. All the things she'd bought in Lamia, including the delivered furniture, were piled in various boxes and bags in the center of the room. She felt too tired to unpack them now. An hour ago all she'd wanted was space and solitude, and now she had both, she felt as if she could scream.

"Hello?" Andreas poked his head round the door, thankfully startling Ava out of her melancholy thoughts. "I've changed the tire on your car. Shall I drive you there now?"

"Oh, wonderful. Yes, please. I'll just leave a note for Eleni." Fifteen minutes alone in her new house and she couldn't wait to leave.

Outside Ava slid into the passenger's side of Andreas's truck, conscious of the strange intimacy of the two of them alone in the truck, in the darkness. As they drove out of Iousidous, the endless night seemed to swallow them up.

"It looks better," Andreas said, clearing his throat. "The house."

"Oh, yes. I had help. Eleni—do you know her?" Ava realized she didn't even know Eleni's last name.

"Eleni Kefalas? Yes. I know her."

"I suppose everyone knows everyone else in a place like this."

"It is a small place, yes. A community, you know?"

"Yes."

He gave her a sympathetic sideways glance. "You might become a part of it, yes? Like your grandmother."

"If I stay long enough."

"You are thinking of leaving already?" He gave a little laugh, but Ava heard a certain sharpness in it that she didn't expect or understand.

"No, not really, but I didn't expect the house to be in such a state. I should have, I know that. I knew it had been abandoned. But..." She let out a long, low breath and shook her head.

"It needs much work."

"Yes."

"But you'll do it? And then?" Andreas lifted his shoulders in a smiling shrug. "It will be good. It will all be good."

Ava let out a rather shaky laugh. "I hope so," she said quietly, and wondered whether Andreas heard the waver of doubt and sadness she felt in her voice.

CHAPTER SIX

July 1942

Two days after Sophia had come home to see Angelika's bed unmade and unslept in, she decided to pay a visit to her father's sister, her aunt Andra.

Such a visit required a certain level of formality; although they were kin, the ties had never been close because of Evangelos's marriage to a town girl, and in any case Sophia knew this visit would be both unexpected and important. She waited until her daily tasks were finished, the bread made, the house swept, the water fetched, the corn ground, and the tomatoes picked. She put on her clothes for church, a navy-blue-and-white striped skirt of scratchy wool and a white blouse embroidered with blue thread. She wrapped a clean kerchief around her hair, put a basket containing freshly made *psomi* and six fresh eggs on her arm, and set off.

Although Sophia walked alone to the coffeehouse three nights a week, and often enough to the fountain in the village square that supplied everyone's water, she still felt conspicuous. She was wearing her best clothes, and that could only mean she was on an errand of some importance. Women stopped their scrubbing and baking in their front yards and stared at her in open speculation as she marched past, her head held high. Some called out a greeting, and Sophia replied with dignity, although she felt her face flush. By mid-afternoon everyone would know what she was doing, or at least be able to guess.

She was after a husband.

Taking a deep breath, she came to her aunt's house, similar to her own although without the second story. Her two cousins, plain-faced girls in their mid-teens, stared at her in open curiosity, taking in her formal dress, the basket on her arm.

"I'll get Mama," one of them said, and the other, Talia, ushered Sophia into the yard with all the requisite expressions of delighted hospitality.

A few minutes later Andra, tall and spare with red cheeks and a hooked nose, bustled forward, kissing both of Sophia's cheeks before drawing her into the house. Sophia laid her gifts on the table, and her aunt and cousins dutifully exclaimed in delight over each offering: fresh *psomi*! You make it so light! And eggs! Look at the size of them! So nice and brown! A few minutes later the gifts were whisked away and Sophia was bid to sit down in the most comfortable chair and plied with bread, cheese, and coffee from her aunt's kitchen. Sophia knew she must eat a little of each, even though, like her own, her aunt's kitchen was sparsely supplied. After the tax levied by the Italians, there was little food left to go around, although at least no one in Iousidous was starving yet.

They ate for a while and chatted rather awkwardly about village matters: the wheat, the weather, the death of a neighbor's mule. Andra touched darkly on the war, the famine, and the cruel soldiers who had raped a girl in the next village.

"Animals," she said, spitting on the ground, and Sophia held her tongue. She did not want to talk about soldiers or rape. Eventually an anticipatory silence fell, and Andra shooed her daughters away. Sophia took a breath.

"It is time," she began, "to find a husband."

"Hah!" Andra sucked her teeth. "If only it were so easy."

"I know there are not many men—"

Andra shook her head firmly. "This is your father's duty, Sophia. Not yours. For a young girl to beg for her own husband!"

Her face tightened in familiar lines of disapproval; Andra had always suspected her and Angelika of being too like their mother, with aspirations for more, even though Sophia had never harbored any. "It's a sad world we live in now, for it to come to this."

"I'm not asking for myself," Sophia said, both startled and stung. She realized she should have expected her aunt to assume such a thing. She was four years older than her sister, after all, but she would never go begging for her own husband.

"Not you?" Andra's heavy eyebrows rose towards her widow's peak of coarse black hair. "Then Angelika?"

"Yes. Yes, of course, Angelika. I thought perhaps you could ask—"

"She is only eighteen. She has years yet. This wretched war might be over before you have to think of seeing her safely married."

Sophia had expected such an objection. Most girls in the village did not marry until they were in their mid-twenties; they needed to help their mothers until then. "She is not needed at home," she said carefully. "I can manage."

"Hah!" Andra sat back in her chair and folded her arms across her thin bosom. "Just as you have managed all these years," she observed rather slyly, and Sophia said nothing. She would not admit to her sister's failings in her duties, even if they were evident to every woman in the village. "Your sister is your mother's daughter, for certain," Andra added, and Sophia determinedly did not rise to the bait. Andra had never liked Katerina, with her elegant ways and second floor, the animals kept in a shed instead of the great room. She'd been too good for village life, Sophia knew, and in the end it had killed her.

She took a deep, calming breath. "I thought, perhaps, you could think on it. Consider who might be suitable—"

Andra sighed and shook her head, cutting short Sophia's hesitant suggestion, phrased with such painful care. "I cannot."

"There are still a few men in the village," Sophia protested. She could not be so bold as to name one in particular, but surely certain names would come to mind? Agisilaos, whose father had a farm similar in size to her own. Admittedly, Agisilaos was not the most handsome man: he was stout and squat and missing a front tooth. But still, in these times, he was a man, he had the prospect of a farm and a good living, and he was healthy.

"Sophia, I cannot marry off a girl of eighteen," Andra told her sharply. "It would cause talk—"

"Only about how clever she is," Sophia protested. If a girl managed to snag a husband, no matter what the reason, she was lauded. Only a stupid girl ended up alone, or worse, shamed.

"And what of the other girls in this village, girls who are twenty or nearing thirty, and have no husbands? What about my own daughters? Should Angelika step in front of them all and demand a man for herself? She's little more than a child."

"She's eighteen, not—"

"A child," Andra stated flatly. "And she acts as one, too. Carousing about, making eyes at the boys, avoiding her work. Shameless, although I would never say such a thing."

You just did, Sophia thought, but stayed silent. She could not argue with her aunt.

"And," Andra continued, sounding almost angry, "you are as foolish as your mother was, for coming here and thinking I would help you with such a thing."

Sophia bit her lip. Her aunt was right; it had been foolish to come here; she saw that now. Even if Andra had agreed to consider opening negotiations with another family, Angelika wouldn't. Angelika would never agree to marry a man like Agisilaos. As for Dimitrios, he would not consider marriage for another five or ten years at least. His father would not allow him, and if not marriage, then what? She shuddered to think.

"I'm sorry," she said, rising from the table. "You're right, this was foolishness. I only want to see Angelika well settled. I am concerned for her."

Andra waved a hand dismissively. "Settle her at your own hearth, then. Let her become a woman who works her own garden, her own home. What man wants a woman who flutters about doing nothing? When she's learned some responsibility, then you can marry her off, as long as there is still a man left with a pair of eyes, two legs and what goes between!" She let out a loud guffaw at her own coarse humor. Sophia blushed and said nothing. "And you should think of your own marriage," Andra continued in a slightly softer tone. "Surely there is someone you have looked at, at least? You are almost of an age."

Quickly she shook her head. "I am too busy, *Thia* Andra. And I am happy at home."

Andra shrugged her acceptance. She'd never bothered herself overmuch with either Sophia or Angelika, not even after Katerina had died. She certainly wouldn't now.

That night Sophia washed trays of dirty glasses in the back room of the coffeehouse, the heat causing her blouse to stick to her back and large patches of sweat to dampen the thin cotton under her arms. She wiped her forehead, longing only for the safety and stillness of home. Surely Angelika would not get up to more mischief, with these absurd claims of fetching water under the cover of darkness. Once Sophia had glanced into the crowded, smoky front room and she had not seen Dimitrios. She had not heard his loud, braying laugh, either, and if he was not here, then where was he? He was not, Sophia knew, the type of man to stay safely at home when he could be out boasting at the taverna. Please God he was not dallying with Angelika and bringing shame to their family.

She had been stupid, she saw that now, to go to her aunt. Stupid and blind, to do something so publicly. Now everyone would talk, whisper about little Sophia thinking of catching herself a man. The men at the coffeehouse would make remarks. Perhaps people would guess she was worried about Angelika, and that would make things worse. And in any case it had all been completely pointless, because just as her sister had proudly told her, things were changing. The old ways were crumbling under the pressures of war, giving way to this new and different life Sophia didn't want. And when the war was over—whenever that distant day might be—who knew what life would be like then? What would still remain?

A guffaw of hard laughter came from the front room, louder than usual. All evening Sophia had sensed a tense male energy she didn't like. News had come from Athens that afternoon, of a village on the outskirts of the city that had been burned to the ground for hiding *andartes*. Men had been led from their homes, trussed like chickens, and shot in front of their wives and children. Some women, too, had died, and even little ones. It was horrifying, unbelievable, and yet Sophia knew it to be true. She could imagine it: the misery, the blood, the children's lifeless limbs splayed out like spent matchsticks. And it could happen here, to her, to Angelika, especially if her sister persisted in this innocent yet dangerous fascination with Dimitrios.

What if he enlisted her foolish aid for the communists, the ELAS men led by Velouchiotis that he bragged about being a part of? Sophia had kept a sharp eye at home on the little larder, counting tomatoes and dried corn, making sure a loaf of *psomi* didn't go missing. She knew there were other women in the village who brought food to the *andartes*. They wrapped a loaf in cloth and left it in the base of a stone wall, in the cleft of a rock. Silently, secretly, under the cover of night someone came and took it. No one spoke of it; no one watched, and yet somehow everyone knew.

Sophia knew her own unwillingness to do the same could be a source of unspoken shame if it were known. Perhaps it already was, and she was being silently judged, yet she would not even consider it, not for a moment. Her life for a loaf of bread? Her sister's or her father's? And she did not believe these *andartes*, for all their courageous ways, were men to be admired. They swaggered and shot their rifles and talked of killing. They were not so different from the Italians or even the Nazis; they just didn't wear a proper uniform. Some of them had ridden into villages already, demanded food and supplies and beaten or even shot those who did not give it readily. No, she thought grimly, not different at all.

And if Dimitrios really was one of them…

The soapy glass she was holding suddenly slid from her hands, shattering as it hit the edge of the basin, the jagged pieces scattering over the floor of packed earth.

"Sophia! It is not like you to be clumsy."

Sophia turned to see Kristina standing in the doorway, her hands on her hips. She didn't sound particularly angry, but Sophia felt a fierce stab of regret all the same. A glass was a glass, and not easily replaced. "I'm sorry. It is the news from that village that has upset me—you heard?"

"Of course I heard." Kristina pursed her lips. "Pigs," she said under her breath. "*Poutanas gioi.*" Sophia stiffened at the surprising curse word. *Sons of bitches.*

"It is terrible," she said inadequately, wanting to fill the awkward silence Kristina's cursing had caused. "If only something could be done."

Kristina gave her a hard stare, that strange little smile on her lips once more. A ripple of unease, cold despite the stifling heat of the kitchen, snaked down Sophia's spine. She didn't like that smile of Kristina's. "If only," Kristina said, and turned to leave the kitchen. She stopped in the doorway, one hand on the wall. Sophia watched her uneasily, sensing the same coiled tension in the widow that she'd felt from the men in the front room. "Go fetch more water," Kristina called over her shoulder. "From the barrel. There could be broken glass in that basin, and I do not wish you to cut your fingers."

Obediently Sophia heaved the basin to the back patch of garden and dumped the dirty water into the weeds. She was just reaching for the pail to fetch some fresh water from the barrel when a strong hand suddenly clasped her wrist.

Sophia could not think to scream. She stared at that hand, so unfamiliar and yet holding her so surely—when had a man touched her bare skin?—and her mind completely emptied out, like water onto the parched earth. In an instant it was gone.

"*Parakalo*," a voice whispered in her ear. *Please*. "Do not be afraid, and do not make any noise. It will be bad for us both."

Sophia said nothing, but when the man still didn't release her, she gave a short nod to indicate she'd understood. Slowly he took his hand from her arm; she could see a red mark all around her wrist. She clutched her arm to her chest as if it were broken, as if he had crushed it with that firm grasp, and spun around to face her assailant.

He smiled, a neat, narrow-faced man, not much taller than she was. "I am not here to hurt you," he said.

She glanced down at her arm. "No?"

He gave a little huff of laughter. "No."

Sophia stared at the stranger, fear licking at her belly and fraying her nerves. He gazed back at her with dark, fathomless eyes, and Sophia could not think what he wanted. Had he been waiting for her here, in this dark patch of weeds? How had he known she would be out here? Had Kristina sent her for this very reason—but why?

"Sophia. I have heard good things of you."

She licked her lips and found her voice. "How could you have heard of me?"

He smiled faintly. "There are ways. You are not like your sister."

Dread pooled coldly inside her. *This was about Angelika. Of course.* She should have said something earlier, warned her. "My sister is silly," she told the man quickly, tripping over her words. "Harmless, though, truly. She never means anything by what she does. She can't keep her tongue in her head, that is all, but I will speak to her." And please God, Angelika would finally see sense.

"No, indeed, she cannot." The man folded his arms, his eyes narrowing. "But you can."

Sophia swallowed. "What do you want?" she whispered. She was amazed that no one had called for her, that Kristina or Spiro hadn't seen her out here with a strange man and called out—unless Kristina really did know. But why…? And, she acknowledged numbly, she had thought Angelika might be ruined. Her very life, never mind her reputation, was in this man's power.

"Someone wants to talk to you," the man said quietly. "Midnight, tomorrow, in the Lethikos olive grove, twenty minutes' walk from the village. You know it?"

"Yes, but—" Sophia licked her lips again. Her throat was so very dry and her heart beat with hard, painful thuds. Was she in trouble? What could she have done? Or was it still about Angelika? Questions fluttered through her mind like birds scattering at the sound of an animal, the sight of a beast. Trying to flee, wings beating in rapid fear. "I don't know anything," she said, choking on the words. "I just work and keep my head down. That's all I ever want to do."

"Which makes you suitable for our purpose," the man replied calmly. He leaned forward so his voice was no more than a hiss, a breath. "But this war will not be won by keeping your head down. We must act. Quickly, quietly. There are those already at work, doing things you cannot even imagine."

And then, of course, she knew who this man was, or at least whom he worked for. She had, in some part of her, known who he was from the moment his hand had circled her wrist. He worked for the Resistance. She shook her head, the movement one of violent instinct.

"No—"

"You must do your duty, Sophia."

"You are a communist," she choked and he shook his head.

"No. I do not work for those animals."

So he was a republican. His calm, precise manner spoke of military organization, not the wild, uncontrolled tactics of the guerrillas. He must work under General Zervas for EDES, the republican Resistance group that clashed with men like Velouchiotis and his troop of bloodthirsty men, creating yet more violence. Yet did it even matter that much? Both groups demanded action, violence. Both groups promised danger, or even death.

"I can't—"

"Twelve o'clock, in Lethikos's grove," the man cut across her swiftly. Sophia just shook her head, helpless now. Could she not refuse?

"There are others," she began, "who want—"

"We need you."

"Why?"

He smiled, no more than a glint of teeth in the darkness. "The reasons do not matter. Do you want this war to be won, Sophia? Do you want it to be over?"

"Yes, of course I do," she whispered, because there was no other answer. She just didn't want to be involved in such danger. To risk not just her own life, but her father's and Angelika's, the safety she'd tried so hard to hoard, like the drachmas in the tin above the hearth. Yet you could not cling to such things; you could not count them like coins. In a moment they were snatched away, as if they'd never been at all.

"Please—" she tried again, but she might as well have been speaking to a stone.

"You will answer to a man named Perseus. He will be waiting for you." And with that he was gone, his presence marked only by a dusty boot print in the dirt.

Sophia sagged against the wall, her whole body trembling with the aftershocks of the encounter. Why—and how—had a man in the Resistance found her? Recruited her? Surely she was unsuitable. She was afraid. Didn't that make her a risk? And yet already she might know too much. Already her fear made her a liability, and if they saw it, it could mean her death. The Resistance groups did not scruple to kill someone who was a threat to them, whether they were German, Italian—or Greek.

"All I wanted was to stay safe," she whispered, although whether she was talking to herself or to God, she could not say. How could she fault God for bringing her to this when so many more terrible things were happening to others? And yet it had seemed such a small, simple request. Safety. She would surrender other dreams—frail hopes of marriage, children, even this elusive fun Angelika went on about. Just safety. Life itself. A beating heart, a breath, a bit of food to eat. That was all she'd asked for, all she wanted. Yet such things, Sophia recognized with a shudder, were now as much a foolish hope as the others. In this new and terrible world, safety was no more than a helpless yearning, a troubadour's song.

CHAPTER SEVEN

Now

Greek Independence Day dawned cool and clear, with a hard, bright blue sky. Ava sat outside on the warm slab of stone that was her back stoop and listened to the sounds of the village coming to life; she could almost feel the energy pulsating in the usually sleepy streets. According to Eleni, everyone came out for the celebrations, the church service and picnic afterwards, dancing and even a parade. Ava realized that despite her earlier trepidation she was looking forward to being a part of it, no matter how small.

She'd been living in her grandmother's house for nearly a week, and most of that time had been spent sorting out her furniture and making a dusty, unused farmhouse a home, at least of sorts. She'd gone to Lamia again and bought some rugs and colorful throws and pillows, and with her few pieces of furniture it looked fairly decent, if a little sparse. Wandering through the few rooms, she often wondered what it had looked like in her grandmother's day, yet she could imagine very little. The details of her grandmother's life remained frustratingly elusive.

In the last week she'd shared several meals with Eleni, and although she'd wanted to ask Parthenope more questions, she'd held her tongue. Whenever Eleni's mother joined them, Eleni gave Ava a sharp warning glance that couldn't be misunderstood. Conversation about the past was still strictly off limits. In any case, Parthenope seemed to have forgotten her emotional outburst from when she'd first met Ava. She never apologized again, and Ava's presence seemed a matter of indifferent acceptance. Ava wondered whether the precious memories of her grandmother were locked away forever.

In the last week Simon hadn't rung again. Ava kept checking her phone, staring at its blank screen as if it held the answers to the universe. Or at least her world, which was ridiculous because she wasn't even sure she wanted to speak to Simon. She did know that she wanted him to ring, and she was afraid to ask herself why. Her marriage might not be definitively over, but it was on its last breath. A year of taut silences and sudden angry outbursts was surely a testament to that.

She had talked to her mother, keeping the conversation safely on practicalities and descriptions of the village and house. Her mother had followed her lead and not asked any questions about Simon.

Her best friend, Julie, had been another matter. Ava, Julie, and Simon had all been friends since their university days. In fact, Julie had been Simon's friend first, both of them in the sailing club, and Ava had become friends with her when she'd started dating Simon. The dynamics had never bothered her, not once, in the nearly twenty years they'd known each other, yet when she talked to Julie now, they suddenly did.

"Do you want to hear about Simon?" her friend had asked bluntly, and Ava had felt suddenly breathless with shock and pain. Of course Julie was still in touch with Simon. Ava and Simon's separation didn't mean Julie had stopped being friends with him. It was obvious, and yet unpalatable. Was Simon moaning to Julie about how over the top and absurd Ava was being, haring off to Greece? Was he crying on her shoulder?

But no, Simon never moaned or cried. He had the emotional sensitivity of a rock, even if he denied it. In one of their last arguments Ava, enraged by his unflappable calm after their baby's stillbirth, had screamed, "Did you even care about our daughter, Simon? Do you miss her at all?"

Simon had stared at her with that impossibly expressionless look. How could you be married to someone for over ten years and still not know what he was thinking? "I can't miss her, because I never knew her," he said, and Ava let out a choked sob.

"I can't believe you said that."

"You asked."

"Do you feel anything," she had demanded in a raw voice, "at all?"

Still expressionless, mouth compressed and eyes narrowed, he'd simply said, "I'm not a stone."

He'd felt like one to her. On the phone she'd told Julie, quite firmly, that she did not want to hear about Simon. She didn't want to think about Simon, and yet he invaded her thoughts, and in too many moments she caught herself imagining what he would think of things, the house, the grim-faced café owner Ava visited every morning for her cup of syrupy sludge, the skinny cat she'd started feeding from her back stoop.

Don't feed strays, Ava; they'll never leave you alone. The cat's feral; it can probably fell a goat.

Sometimes she even found herself smiling, or saying something in response, as if they were actually having a conversation.

But it's cute, and I've always wanted a cat.

His response: *I'm sorry I'm allergic.*

Sorry not sorry, she would have teased, and he would have given her a rueful grin of acknowledgement.

A week of near solitude and she was going mad.

At least her isolation had caused her to look forward to meeting other villagers and being out in the pine-scented sunshine. They might ask uncomfortable questions or stare at the wedding ring that she couldn't yet bear to take off, but at least there would be someone to talk to.

Ava walked up towards the church alone, since Eleni needed to drive with Parthenope. The village felt livelier than it had since her arrival, with children racing along the street, and the central square decked with bright garlands of flowers. A few people smiled and nodded at her, and some children ran up to her and said something unintelligible in Greek, and Ava did her best to answer, calling "*Kalimera*" and waving. Still, she felt conspicuous, a stranger in a place where strangers were rarely seen.

By the time she reached the church, the happy bustle of the celebration overtook her self-consciousness. She found Eleni, with Parthenope clutching her arm and leaning on her as she shuffled towards the church doors.

"Come, let me introduce you before the service starts," Eleni said, and led her to a group of women chatting next to the church.

Ava didn't catch many of the names, but she heard the hellos and saw the smiles, and felt cheered even though it was clear not everyone had nearly as good a mastery of English as Eleni did. She really should have learned more Greek.

She was just heading into the little church when she saw a familiar figure coming up the hill from the village. It was the school-teacher, with her straight eyebrows and plait of dark hair, her stride long and sure. Ava smiled hesitantly, and she was cheered when the woman smiled back and even lifted her hand in recognition.

Her fragile cheer faltered when she entered the incense-scented interior of the church, and felt dizzying panic clutch at her, taking her by surprise yet again. *A tiny casket, the priest's sonorous and lamenting voice. Her own harsh cry...*

It had been almost a year, and for the first time she was tired of her own instinctive reaction, tired of herself and her endless grief. Sweat trickled between her shoulder blades and she took a gulp of the dusty air. She might not be willing to let go of her grief, but she should be able to function at least. Put it to one side, at least for a little while.

Eleni placed a hand on her shoulder. "Ava," she murmured, "*Ise kala?*"

Are you all right. Ava swallowed. Nodded. Yes, she was. She would be. She did not want to fall apart here, in front of all these strangers. She did not want to fall apart, full stop. She was tired, so very tired, of feeling useless and fragile.

"I'm fine," she whispered, and thankfully there was no more time to talk as the priest, sporting a bushy black beard and wearing a long black cassock, moved to the front of the church.

Ava let the Greek prayers and chants wash over her, unfamiliar enough to be bizarrely soothing. Some of her tension eased even as her legs started to ache from standing; Orthodox churches had no seating, except for the very old, like Parthenope. And then it was over, and Eleni was ushering her outside, the sun glinting off the near-blinding whiteness of the church.

"Now we eat," Eleni said, "and dance. You must learn some of the Greek dances." Ava smiled noncommittally, and Eleni glanced at her with a frown. "What happened in there? You looked so pale. Ill, almost."

"Just tired." Ava did not meet Eleni's searching gaze. The older woman might have befriended her—saved her, even—but she'd known her only a week. She wasn't about to pour out all the grief and misery in her heart, and especially not at a joyous occasion like this.

"Then you dance. There is a book, a book that all Greeks know and love. *Zorba the Greek.* Do you know it?"

Mystified by the sudden change in conversation, Ava just shook her head.

"Zorba is a man with much wisdom. When his little boy died, you know what he did?" Eleni waited for her to guess, but Ava only shook her head again. She felt a hot clutch of emotion grab at her chest. What did Eleni know, or at least guess, about her own life, her own pain? "He danced," Eleni said simply. "And everyone, they said Zorba is mad, to dance when he should be grieving. But Zorba, he said he *must* dance. Because it is only dancing that stops the pain."

Ava just shook her head yet again and looked away. She felt the hot press of tears at the back of her lids, the aching lump in her throat. She didn't want to cry, didn't want anyone to see her cry, and with a muttered excuse she pushed past Eleni and went to stand alone under a plane tree, the sun already hot even though the air was mountain-crisp as she struggled to control her emotions.

"I saw you at the school. You are English, yes?"

Ava drew in a quick breath and turned to see the school-teacher smiling tentatively at her. She nodded, forced that rush of emotion back. There was no way Eleni could know about the loss of her daughter. She'd just been relating a story, something to make Ava join in the dancing. "Yes," she said, managing a smile, "I am English. *Anglitha.* How did you know?"

"I've heard talk of the Englishwoman who has moved here, and since you are the only stranger, I knew it must be you." The woman smiled and stuck out her hand, which Ava took. "My name is Helena."

"Ava."

"What brings you to such a tiny place as Iousidous?" Helena's English was nearly flawless.

"You might have also heard that my grandmother lived here many years ago—"

"Yes, I did. Sophia Paranoussis."

Helena's knowledgeable assurance took her a bit aback. "I'm living in her house, for a little while at least—"

"Yes, the old Paranoussis place. I know it. But why come here?" she smiled, lifting her shoulders. "Most people leave a place like this, as your grandmother did. Why did you come back?"

Did no one shy away from blunt questions here? Ava wondered. Was nosiness a Greek trait? Maybe just a village trait, although Helena's questions felt too pointed to be run-of-the-mill curiosity. She sounded almost as if she were testing her, trying to figure her out.

"I was at a bit of a stopping point," Ava said, trying to sound both friendly and repressive. "My grandmother died, leaving me her house. It seemed like a good time to come here, discover a bit about my roots."

Helena looked pleased. "So you are interested in Greek history?"

She could get in trouble here. She was clueless about Greek history. "I'm interested in my grandmother's history," Ava said, and then decided full disclosure was needed. "Although, to be honest, I wasn't all that interested until I arrived and realized I didn't actually know anything about my grandmother's life. And no one seems to speak of that time—the war and everything." She sounded rather inane, but Helena nodded in agreement.

"No one does. It is very difficult. I moved back here to teach, but also to record a history of life here during the war. My own grandparents were killed here, you see, during the civil war that erupted after the Nazis left. My mother was just a small child, raised by relatives in Athens. But I always wondered about my own history, and I have hopes of learning more."

"How?" Ava asked, genuinely curious now. "I admit I haven't tried very hard, but I have no idea how to learn about my grandmother. No one wants to tell me anything." Eleni didn't even want her to ask.

"There are five survivors of the war left in Iousidous," Helena said matter-of-factly, "and three have agreed to talk to me. This is after I have lived in the village for four years and won the trust of some of the older people." She gave a wry smile. "When I first moved back, there were eleven survivors. But time is running out. Their stories might be lost forever, and I would hate for that to happen."

Like her grandmother's story, only known, it seemed, to Parthenope. "Have you talked to the survivors?" Ava asked. Iousidous was such a small place. One of them would surely remember her grandmother.

"Not yet. My first meeting is next week. But I heard you had come here to stay in your grandmother's house, and I thought perhaps you would be interested."

"Interested?"

"In accompanying me. I do not know if all three will agree, but I could ask. You might learn something about your grandmother, and it would be good to have someone else listening."

"Oh…" Surprise temporarily robbed Ava of words. "That would be wonderful," she said at last. "I never imagined such a thing, but yes. Thank you for suggesting it. Please do ask."

Helena smiled and nodded, and Ava saw that people were moving over towards a small, scrubby patch of grass where a couple of trestle tables had been set up and were already near to buckling with plates of food. Together they walked over to the group, and Ava joined Eleni and Parthenope. She was soon filling her plate with *souvlaki*, cucumber and yogurt salad, and *baklava* sticky with honey and studded with nuts.

They all sat under the shade of a plane tree, and ate and watched the various entertainments: children performing a folk dance, a little play that Ava got only the gist of, and then the men in traditional village garb from about two hundred years ago—blousy white shirts and what were basically skirts—made a circle with their arms around each other's shoulders and began to dance. It was a vigorous, joyful celebration, surprisingly masculine. Ava saw Andreas in the group, his head thrown back as he sang along with the others. The sunlight caught the gray threads in his curly hair, the browned column of his throat, and Ava felt a funny tightening in her middle.

No, she couldn't be thinking about Andreas Lethikos that way. She barely knew him, and in any case she was still, technically, married to Simon.

And more than that, Ava didn't want her marriage to be over, even if she had a sinking certainty that it was. She was not remotely ready to think about anyone else that way.

"Ava. Come dance." Eleni stood in front of her, smiling and flushed, and she saw that everyone was joining in the dancing now, half a dozen circles of people spread out on the grass. Eleni held out her hand, and Ava shook her head.

"I'm sorry. I'm not... I'm not ready to dance." Even if it stopped the pain. She might have felt frustrated with her inability to function in the church, but she wasn't sure she was ready to do as Eleni said and stop the pain. She wasn't ready to let go of her grief or her marriage.

Eleni stared at her for a long moment, and then dropped her hand. "I understand," she said quietly, and turned to join the other dancers. Ava watched them all dance with a sense of longing; the dancers' easy joy was infectious, and yet she felt so distant from it. She almost wished she had accepted Eleni's invitation to dance, and yet she knew she wouldn't have been capable of it. Watching, for now, had to be enough.

By late afternoon, the celebrations were winding down, and everyone began to head back down the hill, sleepy children hoisted on parents' shoulders, the echo of laughter still lingering in the crisp air.

"I will let you know," Helena promised, touching Ava's arm, "about the interviews."

"Thank you." Ava waved goodbye and then slid her phone out of her bag; she hadn't checked it all afternoon and she felt as if a fist had squeezed around her heart when she saw the missed call. Simon had rung again and this time he had left a voicemail.

She waited until she was back at the house, having said her goodbyes to Eleni and Parthenope, to listen to the message. The sun was starting to sink towards the ragged fringe of pines on the hilly horizon, and the air felt cold with the onset of evening. Ava pulled a throw around her shoulders and curled up on the sofa before dialing her voicemail.

"Ava, it's Simon." His voice sounded the same, wonderfully the same, brisk and no-nonsense with that tiny hint of wryness she'd always loved. "Just checking to see how you are and that the house hasn't fallen down around your ears. Not that it would." That last bit sounded like a concession, almost an apology. Then, back to brusqueness. "No need to ring back. Bye."

And that was it. The whole message was eight seconds long. Ava almost pressed delete, and then stupidly didn't. She remained on the sofa, her knees tucked into her chest, the phone cradled against her heart.

No need to call him back? Had he talked to Julie and heard she was fine, or at least alive, and so that was that? She swallowed past the tightness in her throat. Why did that pithy little message hurt so much? Because it did. It hurt almost unbearably, and she was too tired and emotionally wrung out—still—to figure out why.

Ava let out a sigh and tossed the phone onto the sofa. It stared at her, as silent and unblinking as the cat that had taken to visiting her garden. She fed it scraps, but it never came close enough for her to stroke it. Taking with nothing to give.

Fine. No need to call Simon back, so she wouldn't. She'd get on with her life, she'd think about accompanying Helena on those interviews, maybe she'd even plant something. An orange tree, as she'd envisioned. And she'd build something here, something good and true, even if it was totally different from the way she'd wanted her life to be.

CHAPTER EIGHT

Now

The next day, with an almost grim determination, Ava began the rebuilding process. She drove to Lamia and bought a bunch of seeds and plants, unsure exactly what she'd bought since all the labels were in Greek and the shopkeeper spoke no English. Never mind. She'd plant something, and she hoped it would be pretty.

It felt good to work in the little garden, out in the sun, using her muscles and breaking out in a sweat. The earth was dry and crumbly, easy to dig through at first, until she got through the thin layer of topsoil and realized how rocky and barren it really was. How did anyone grow anything here at all?

An hour later she'd planted two little shrubs, made something close to a flower bed and scattered it with seeds. The cat emerged from the scrub and watched her unblinkingly.

"Don't eat these seeds," Ava warned it severely, although she didn't really know if cats ate seeds. "I'll get you something else." Humming a bit under her breath, she went to the kitchen and found some scraps from the *souvlaki* that Eleni had brought a few days ago. She left them in a dish and stood about a foot away, watching and waiting just as the cat was.

It didn't want to come and get the food when she was so close, even if it was starving. Still, Ava wouldn't budge. She wasn't expecting to turn a feral cat into a house pet, but she wanted something back.

"You've got to want it," she told the cat, and it stared at her for a long moment before retreating back into the trees.

Damn. Ava stared at the empty place where it had been and wondered just why she had pushed. Couldn't she give a cat food without expecting something? Was she really that needy, that demanding?

Sighing, she turned back to the garden, only to hear her phone trill against her hip. She slipped it out of her jeans pocket and saw that it was Julie.

"Hey, Jules."

"Please tell me you're sitting at a café, drinking espresso, and ogling the gorgeous Greek men."

Ava let out a rusty laugh, glad Julie was going for light. They'd had too many heavy, painful conversations lately. "No. But I just chased a feral cat back into the woods."

"That's a relief. Was it dangerous?"

"It was a cat. No, it's not dangerous. It's starving." She gazed at the dish of meat scraps and decided to leave it out in case the cat returned.

"Still, it's a wild animal, right? I don't fancy those so much."

"Well, it's gone now." She went inside and kicked the door closed behind her. "How are you?"

"Oh, fine. Weather's miserable; job's OK. Same, same."

"Right. Well it's a balmy twenty-three degrees here with cloudless blue skies, so I do feel sorry for you."

"*Nyah, nyah* to you too," Julie said, laughing, and then there was a pause. "I saw Simon last night."

Ava felt her fingers curl tighter around the phone, hurting. Her breath slammed through her chest. "And?" she asked as levelly as she could, even though she, absurdly, hated the thought of Julie's seeing Simon. *I saw Simon last night.* It almost sounded like a date.

"He seems pretty down, actually. He was really quiet, like he had a lot on his mind."

"Julie, that's how Simon always seems." She'd thought she'd liked the strong, silent types, and she had, oh, she had, until she'd finally needed something back. Some emotion, some sympathy, something more than solid reliability, stony silences and good sex, although they hadn't even had sex in nearly a year. That, Ava knew, was mostly her fault.

"Well, more quiet than usual," Julie said and Ava let out a short laugh.

"I'm not sure that's possible."

"Be fair, Ava—"

"Don't take his side," she cut across her friend sharply. "I can't stand it if you do. You're my best friend, Julie—"

"I don't even want there to be sides," Julie told her, sighing. "But if we're talking about whose friend I am, Ava, I was Simon's friend first."

Ava blinked. She felt as if Julie had just punched her in the stomach. "I can't believe you just said that."

"I'm sorry," Julie said quietly. "You're right. I shouldn't have. But... he *is* my friend, and I don't like seeing him so miserable. Have you rung him?"

"No." Jealousy picked at her, little pinpricks of doubt. Why did Julie care so much about what Simon felt? Did she have more loyalty to Simon than to her, especially now she was three thousand kilometers away? "The whole point of coming here was to get some distance, remember?"

"I remember." Julie sighed again. "I think he misses you, Ava."

If only. Just the thought that Simon might miss her caused her heart to give a stupid little lurch, even as that jealousy kept picking at her. Julie seemed very interested in Simon's feelings—what few he had.

"I'll believe it when I hear it from him."

"You know Simon. You won't. He doesn't do that kind of thing." Emoting. It had been a joke between them all, back at university. Stoic Simon. They used to laugh about it, tease him when they watched a sappy film. *Is that a tear, Si? Are your eyes suspiciously bright? Surely not.*

She would have loved him to shed even one tear a year ago. To show he cared just a little, that he felt a tenth or even a hundredth of what she was feeling as they'd buried their tiny daughter.

"I know how Simon is, Julie. Trust me. We've been married for twelve years." Too late she realized she should have used the past tense, although she supposed they were still technically married now. A separation wasn't a divorce, even if it had felt just as final.

"I'm sorry," Julie said. "I'm obviously handling this all wrong. I just hate seeing Simon so down."

Ava felt those little pinpricks of doubt sharpen into claws. So Julie hated seeing Simon down? What about her? She'd been overwhelmed with grief and sorrow for nearly a year. Julie had been supportive—of course she had. As supportive, Ava supposed, as she had let Julie be. Some grief was too deep and intimate to share with just anyone, even your best friend. The person she'd wanted to share it with had been Simon, and he hadn't been interested.

"If he's really missing me, he can call," Ava said shortly. And not just leave a bloody eight-second message.

"Why don't you call him?"

Ava said nothing. She didn't think Julie would understand how ringing first would feel like giving in. Showing her weakness. She'd showed enough weakness to Simon over the last year, with her tears and migraines and antidepressants. With her begging and pleading, desperate for him to give her *something* back. All of it had seemed only to annoy him; she wasn't about to show him any more.

"OK, I get the message," Julie said with a sigh. "I'll leave it alone."

"Thank you."

"Have you seen any gorgeous Greek men? Maybe I should come over for a holiday."

"Not really, but one lives in hope," Ava joked weakly. She thought, bizarrely, of Andreas. She wouldn't classify him as gorgeous, exactly, but there was certainly something attractive about his curly hair and dark, molten eyes. She remembered how he'd danced with the other men at the Independence Day celebration, his head thrown back, the column of his throat visible under the bright noonday sun. He'd looked so happy then, happy and free, and Ava didn't know whether that sense of easy joy was what had attracted her in that moment or the man himself.

In any case, it was way too early to be thinking about attraction in any form.

"I'd love for you to come over," she said to Julie, "if you can find the time off work." And despite her earlier absurd jealousy, she knew she'd be glad to see her friend. "It's not Corfu, though. We're talking rural Greece. No beaches, no piña coladas. No mobile phone reception, even."

"No problem," Julie said breezily, and Ava laughed. She couldn't quite imagine Julie in Iousidous, but she still wasn't quite sure if she could imagine herself here, and yet here she was.

The phone call finished, she sat in the sitting room, her gaze on the huge fireplace that dominated one wall. She'd swept it out, but she hadn't had a fire in the hearth yet. She had no idea what the state of the chimney was. Seventy years ago, when her grandmother had lived here, she would have used the fireplace for cooking as well as heating the house. Ava imagined her bent in front of it, baking bread or stirring soup or—what? She still only had the haziest images of what life would have been like here. What her grandmother's life would have been like.

She hadn't heard from Helena about the interviews, but she hoped the people Helena was talking to would agree. Finally she might begin to understand what her grandmother's life might have been like, even if she still didn't have any sense of the details.

Her phone, still clasped loosely in her hand, trilled suddenly, startling her out of her mini-reverie. *Simon.* The name—the hope—was like a lightning bolt streaking through her mind. It wasn't Simon, though; it was a local number, and as Ava answered it, she hoped it was Helena.

"Ava? It's Andreas."

Shock temporarily robbed her of speech. She'd completely forgotten that she'd given him her number when he'd changed her tire. It had been a matter of expediency rather than an invitation, and yet she didn't think he was ringing about her car now.

"Ava?"

"Sorry, sorry, um, bad connection. It's better now." A flush fought its way up her face. "Hi, Andreas."

"I was wondering, if you are free, if you would like to come lunch on Saturday." He sounded hesitant, although whether that was his careful English or the nature of his invitation Ava couldn't tell. She was speechless with surprise yet again, although she found her voice a bit more quickly this time.

"Oh—thank you for the invitation—"

"Kalista would like to practice her English," Andreas said quickly, and Ava knew this was code for *this is not a date.* Still, Andreas's English was really very good. She couldn't see why his daughter would need to practice with her. "She prefers to speak with someone other than her boring old father," Andreas said with a laugh, and Ava wondered whether he could read her mind.

"That sounds lovely," she said, rather firmly. This too would be part of her moving on. Finding her own life here in Greece. "Thank you so much."

"Would you like to come round about noon? Do you remember the way?"

She had a hopeless sense of direction, so Ava took instructions on how to get there before ringing off. She put her phone back in her pocket and headed outside, stopping short when she saw that every scrap of meat was gone from the dish.

"Coward," she called to the silent scrub. "You're going to have to face me sometime." The only answer was the sighing of the wind in the pines high above her.

That evening Ava went round to Eleni's for supper. She'd brought a dish of marinated olives she'd bought in Lamia, hoping Eleni wouldn't be offended. She seemed determined to do everything for her, Ava knew, but she was ready to do some—admittedly small—things for herself.

Eleni kissed her on both cheeks as she arrived. "You look well," she said approvingly, stepping back to survey Ava from top to toe. "There is color in your cheeks, a sparkle in your eye."

"Is there?" Ava gave a little uncertain laugh. She hadn't quite realized it until that moment, but even after Julie's unsettling call she'd been kind of happy today. She'd kept busy in the garden and hadn't thought of other things too much. "Here. I brought you some olives."

Eleni clucked and insisted she shouldn't have, but she took them all the same. Ava came into the little kitchen, looking around for Parthenope, but she didn't see her anywhere.

"She is sleeping," Eleni said quietly. "The celebrations on Sunday tired her greatly."

"Oh. Right." Ava drew a deep breath. "Do you know Helena, the schoolteacher?"

Eleni slid her an amused look as she transferred the olives to a ceramic dish and put them on the table. "Iousidous has only about six hundred people, and I have lived here for much of my life. I know everyone."

"Of course you do," Ava acknowledged with a little laugh. "Do you know that Helena is trying to get together a sort of oral history of those who survived the war?" Eleni frowned, and Ava wondered if she'd understood what she'd meant. She also wondered, belatedly, whether she should have told Eleni about Helena's plans. Maybe Helena wanted to keep them quiet, for some reason.

"I know," Eleni said shortly, and Ava was relieved on both counts, even though it seemed to be a topic of conversation the older woman did not wish to pursue.

"Has she asked your mother to participate?"

Eleni turned away, busying herself at the oven. A mouthwatering aroma of garlic, rosemary, and roasting meat wafted from the oven's open door. "I told her no."

"You did?" Ava said in surprise, before she could think better of it.

Eleni turned back to her, looking annoyed for the first time since Ava had seen her at the window the night she'd arrived. "Yes, I did. My mother is ninety-eight years old. She does not need someone coming here asking questions about things she'd rather forget."

Eleni's accent had thickened throughout this abrupt speech, making it hard for Ava to understand her. She understood the gist perfectly well, though. Eleni did not want anyone, not Ava, not Helena, stirring up her mother's past.

"I'm sorry," she said quietly. "I know you didn't want to upset your mother when she thought I was my grandmother, but…" She took a deep breath and recklessly plunged on. "Don't you think it might help? To talk about it—whatever it is? Whatever is bothering her, for her to say sorry after so many years?"

Eleni stared at her for a long moment. "No, I don't think it can help," she finally said, sounding more resigned now than angry. "Whatever happened, happened. It was terrible—I know that. More terrible than anything either you or I have lived through. Why bring it up? Why…" Eleni snapped her fingers, scrunching her face up impatiently before she remembered the word. "Why pry?"

Pry. It made Ava feel like a snoop. But this was her grandmother they were talking about, and Parthenope obviously had some memory or association with Sophia Paranoussis. "I don't think of it as prying," she replied carefully, "when it's my own relative. And if there was anything I could learn about my grandmother—"

"What if it is something sad? Something tragic? Something you wished you had never known?" Eleni gazed at her steadily. "Haven't you had enough sorrow, Ava? In your own life?"

Ava stared at her, all thoughts of her grandmother evaporating in the knowing light in Eleni's eyes. "What," she asked, her mouth dry, "do you mean?"

"I'm not certain what happened," Eleni said, "but sadness covers you like—like a cloak." Ava said nothing, her throat suddenly tight. "It was a child, wasn't it?" Eleni sighed. "Now I am the one who is—what did I say?—prying."

"How did you know?" Ava asked when she finally felt able to speak.

"You touch your belly, like this." Eleni pressed one hand against her stomach. "Like you are missing something, a part of you." Ava swallowed. She hadn't realized she did that. Had anyone else noticed, or even guessed the reason why? "And," Eleni continued, "I know, at least a little, of that sorrow."

"You had a—"

"I was never so blessed. But my husband and I longed for children." Her smile curved wryly. "He was Greek: of course he wanted a large family. Sons and daughters. But none came." She spread her hands wide. "No babies."

"I'm so sorry, Eleni."

The older woman just shrugged, but Ava saw a lingering sadness in her eyes. A different kind of grief, but one she still carried. *Did it ever end?*

"Do you want to talk about it?" Eleni asked after a moment. "What happened?"

Ava opened her mouth to say no, she did not, she wasn't ready. Instead she heard herself say, to her own surprise, "Her name was Charlotte."

Eleni's face softened into a sad smile. "A pretty name."

Ava nodded, glanced down at the floor, and then continued. "We'd been trying for years to have a baby. I wanted a family almost as soon as we got married. Simon didn't want to rush, and in the end that wasn't an issue, because nothing ever happened. The doctors didn't even have a reason—unexplained infertility, they said. Apparently it's quite common."

"Yes."

"We did the tests, the fertility drugs, the IVF. Rounds and rounds." She spoke faster, hearing the pain in her voice, like something broken. "It was stressful for both of us, I know that, and there's some horrible percentage rate of couples who split up after too many rounds of IVF. But I couldn't let go of it. The dream. I wanted a baby so very much."

"Of course you did," Eleni murmured.

Ava was still staring at the floor, blinking hard, talking faster and faster. "In the end we decided to take a break. From the IVF, not each other. Not then. Just a couple of months to focus on each other again, to reconnect. And amazingly, three weeks later, I found out I was pregnant. Naturally." She let out a shuddering breath. "It felt like such a damned miracle." Her gaze flew up to meet Eleni's as she realized that to the older, more traditional woman, the word might cause offense. "Sorry, sorry. I shouldn't have—"

Eleni waved a hand, smiling faintly. "I don't think I know that English word."

Ava smiled back even though she could feel the tears, heavy and hot, crowding her eyes and thickening in her throat. "No, I don't suppose you would."

"So." Eleni sat down at the table, her chin propped in her hands. "You were pregnant."

"Yes, and the strange thing, the stupid thing, really, was I thought that was it. Nothing could go wrong now. It had been so bloody hard—sorry—so hard to actually get pregnant, and then when it happened naturally..." She shook her head, helpless in the face of her memories, and the almost smug complacency she'd lapsed into once she knew she was pregnant. "I thought it was meant to be. I was sure everything was going to be fine. It *had* to be."

"Perhaps," Eleni said, "you needed a rest from worry. From fear."

"But in the end I should have been afraid. I should have been afraid, and worried, and maybe—" Ava stopped, not wanting to give voice to the thought. Not wanting to believe that she could have changed the outcome. One more ultrasound. Another doctor's visit. Not going for that jog. *Something.*

"What happens, happens," Eleni said quietly. "There is a reason, lost in the sorrow, perhaps, but it is still there."

Acid burned in the back of Ava's throat. "You really believe that?"

"I believe the world is much bigger than our grief."

"And you believe that some god above ordains things like this? For my daughter to die inside me when I was seven-and-a-half months pregnant?" Ava heard the snarl in her voice and knew she should stop. Apologize. Yet she couldn't stand any platitudes about how her daughter's death had been for the best, or for some absurd purpose. It had been meaningless. Utterly, horribly meaningless.

"I don't have the answers you are seeking, Ava," Eleni said quietly. "But I don't believe our lives come together or apart by simple chance. There is something greater at work, even in our grief. In our pain."

Ava just shook her head. She swallowed and blinked hard. "I'm sorry," she said stiffly, "for seeming rude."

"Nonsense. I am the one who is rude, asking you these questions and telling you things you don't want to hear. I thought it might bring you comfort, to know it is not for nothing." Ava did not reply, and Eleni smiled sadly. "Let us eat."

The rest of the meal passed peaceably enough, although Ava felt a remnant of the strain between them. Parthenope joined them, and Eleni gave Ava another one of her warning looks. Perhaps after Ava's outburst she didn't trust her to leave her mother alone.

Yet Eleni's words came back to Ava as she walked in the quiet and the dark back to her grandmother's house. The village was silent, the air utterly still. She felt as if she were the last person on earth.

I don't believe our lives come together or apart by simple chance. There is something greater at work, even in our grief.

How could Eleni believe such a thing, when she'd seen so much suffering herself? Her entire country devastated and ruined for several generations. Her own lack of children. Her own mother refusing to talk about the past, for whatever painful reason. What greater purpose could there be in any of that?

In front of the house Ava stopped, tilted her head up to gaze at the fathomless night sky, inky black and spangled with stars. She tried to make out a few of the more familiar constellations, Ursa Major at least, but after a moment she stopped trying to make sense of it and simply stared at all that distant, endless beauty, impossible to fully understand.

Her grandmother had surely stood in this same spot, had perhaps tilted her head up in the same way and stared at these same stars. For the first time Ava felt a flicker of recognition, like an echo or a shadow, of her grandmother's life. Her grandmother herself. It was gone in an instant, but she felt it reverberate through her own soul. Slowly she lowered her head and blinked in the darkness. The cat, she saw, was on the railing of her grandmother's house, giving her its unblinking stare.

Ava stared back, and then with a swish of its tail the cat jumped down and stalked towards her, surprising her so much that she took an inadvertent step backwards.

In an instant it was gone, leaping elegantly over the wall and into the shadows, its tail having brushed her bare legs.

CHAPTER NINE

July 1942

Ever since her meeting with the stranger in the dark, Sophia had been counting the days. The hours, even, marking them as the sun rose and set in the sky, as the earth grew hot and then cool, light sliding into darkness, once, then twice. Two days passed. Just one day until she was expected to slip out into the night, a dangerous thing in itself, and meet a man named Perseus in the darkness of the Lethikos olive grove.

And if she didn't…?

The night of the proposed meeting Sophia went to the coffee-house. She could barely concentrate on the basin of dirty glasses, barely heard the rumble of conversation from the front room. Her stomach roiled, and for once it was not from the thick fog of cigarette smoke and oily paraffin.

"You are not yourself tonight, I think," Kristina said. She'd come into the kitchen and leaned against the table, her arms folded, her eyes narrowed shrewdly.

Sophia felt as if her heart were throwing itself against her ribs, almost as if it were separate from the rest of her body, desperate for escape. "I'm tired," she said after a moment, and heard how her voice shook. Mother of God, she was so frightened. And Kristina must surely know it.

"You work hard."

"Thank you," Sophia mumbled, her head down, her blurred gaze on the cracked basin of soapy water. Just a few more hours and then she would have to make her way alone in the dark, all the way to the Lethikos property, a distance of several kilometers. What would she find there? What if she was seen?

To her surprise she felt Kristina's hand heavy on her shoulder. "It will be all right, little one," she murmured. "Don't be so afraid."

Sophia jerked her head up and stared at Kristina in shock. *She knew.* She felt as if the world had tilted—and then righted itself again. *Of course Kristina knew. Of course she'd arranged it all.* Sophia had suspected something at the start, but then dismissed it. Now she was certain. Her working here, meeting the man in the back—Kristina must have had some part in it. Sophia had been naively stupid to imagine otherwise. And Spiro too, most likely, on those evenings when he disappeared and Sophia had to serve in the front room. It made sense now, terrible sense.

"Why…?" she finally whispered, her throat so dry the single word scraped it.

Kristina pressed her lips together in a hard line. "You're needed."

Sophia shook her head. "How? And why me? So many people want to help—"

"People with loud mouths and hot tempers." Kristina moved closer to her, her voice lowered to a vehement hiss. "Communists." The single word was a snarl.

Sophia swallowed. She had not realized Kristina was so against the communist *andartes.* So many people in the village supported them, listened to the stories of the guerrillas who raided Italian outposts and shot the Nazis in the streets of Athens. Loud, brave men, but all Sophia thought of was how your corn was as likely to be taken by an *andarte* as a soldier; you never knew who would be holding the gun.

"You are quiet, Sophia, and you keep your head down. That is what we need right now."

"But I…" Her throat ached and her eyes stung. "I don't want—"

Kristina grabbed her shoulder, her fingers digging into her skin through the thin cotton of her blouse. "Do you want to see this terrible war finished? Do you want to see your father smiling and your sister well and alive, married with a child in her arms, at the war's end?" Her fingers tightened, the nails sharp. "Do you think that will happen if we sit on our hands and let the soldiers saunter around, shooting good men like my Georgios?" Sophia said nothing and Kristina gave her a little shake. "Do you?"

Mutely Sophia shook her head. She saw the determined gleam in Kristina's eyes, felt the hard dig of her nails in her shoulder. She could not fight this.

"We are not talking about smuggling *psomi* to a band of bloodthirsty communists. Any fool can do that."

Then I am less than a fool, for I won't even do that. Sophia swallowed hard. "Then what are you talking about, Kristina?"

Kristina pressed her lips together once more and shook her head, releasing her grip on Sophia's shoulder. "It is not my place to speak of it. But you know what to do."

And then she was gone, leaving Sophia alone with her spinning thoughts, her shoulder stinging and a far worse ache in her heart.

Another hour passed, and she walked home slowly through the darkness, her mind still spinning, her heart thudding. Back in her father's house, all was quiet and dark, the only sounds the rustling of the animals in the shed and her father's soft snores from upstairs. Sophia walked up the outside staircase, each step taking as much effort as if she were climbing Mount Oeta. In the bedroom she saw her sister curled up on her bed, knees tucked up towards her chin like a child. She *was* a child. Silly and thoughtless, yes, but loving and affectionate, too. A child who deserved a full life ahead of her, a chance to become sensible, to have hope and happiness, a husband and children of her own.

Do you want to see your father smiling and your sister well and alive, married with a child in her arms?

Oh, yes, Mother of God, yes. She did. That did not mean she wanted to risk their well-being as well as her own in securing such a future. And yet she would do it, because she had to.

Slowly Sophia undressed, reached for the old, patched dress and work boots she would wear to walk the stony road to the Lethikos property. She twisted her hair up under a scarf, tying it tightly.

Why could she not be braver, stronger? There were men and women in this village and a hundred others who would leap at the chance she'd been given. Their hearts would sing with pride and joy at helping the brave *andartes*—whether republicans or communists—and thwarting the Nazis. Sophia's heart held only a lament.

I didn't want this. I never wanted any of this.

Taking a deep breath, she turned to Angelika. She could not keep herself from touching her round cheek, smoothing the soft hair away from her face.

"Stay safe," she whispered, even though she knew it was she who courted danger, not Angelika, for once sleeping safely in her bed. Then, with her heart still beating hard against her ribs, Sophia slipped from the room and down the stairs.

The breeze rattled through the olive trees of the Lethikos's grove, a sinister, skeletal sound, or so it seemed to Sophia as she made her way in the darkness, the light of the moon cutting a silver swath through the shadowy grove, illuminating the bent and twisted trunks of the olive trees. Her heart bumped unsteadily against her ribs and her throat was dry.

She'd walked in complete darkness, afraid to bring a light that might reveal and endanger her, and so she'd had to walk slowly, stumbling over the rock-strewn road, shrinking into the shadows when she heard a suspicious sound, even if it was only the bleat of a goat or the rustle of the wind.

Once she'd heard voices, the low, growling murmur of men, and she'd slipped off the road into the scrubby bushes at the side as they came towards her, her heart thudding. They weren't Nazis, of course; Sophia had yet to see even a single German soldier. Their Italian allies still controlled most of the countryside, although there were murmurs that the Italians would be forced out by the end of the year.

Yet if the men weren't soldiers, they could still be *andartes*. *Who else would be about at this time of night?* Sophia was almost as fearful of meeting one of Velouchiotis's men as she was of an Italian or even a full-blown Nazi in his gray uniform and jackboots.

The men, whoever they were, passed, no more than shadowy figures in the darkness, and Sophia counted to a hundred before she moved out into the road again. She breathed a small, shuddering sigh of relief when she came to the low stone wall that marked the border of the Lethikos's land.

She squinted through the twisted tree trunks, unsure how to find the man she'd come to meet. The olive grove was large, meandering over the hillside; he could be anywhere. A breeze rustled the trees again, rattling their branches, and Sophia shivered slightly even though the air was dry and warm. She walked a bit farther along the stone wall, away from the road, and then waited, unsure how far or long she should wander about in the dark. If she stayed for a quarter of an hour and then left without seeing anyone, would it be her fault? She could explain to Kristina, or the man she'd met in the yard, if she saw him again, what had happened. *I tried…*

"Sophia Paranoussis?"

Sophia jumped at the sound of the voice, for she had neither heard nor seen anyone approach her. She turned, and in the moonlight she saw a man's face, alarmingly close to hers. "Y-y-y... yes," she stammered. "That is who I am."

"What is my name?"

Startled, Sophia could think of nothing to say. How was she to know a stranger's name? Then, surfacing from the depths of her stunned mind, realization came. "Perseus," she whispered, and he circled her wrist none too gently and drew her to the hidden shelter of a nearby olive tree.

Sophia stumbled over the uneven ground, grateful when Perseus released her wrist. In the shelter of the tree, she could not see him at all, although she inhaled the faint scent of Karelia cigarettes, which she knew could be obtained only on the black market.

"The less you know, the better," he told her, his voice so low, Sophia had to strain to hear even though she was right next to him. "So, for now, I will only give you a few details." She nodded, even though he might not be able to see her, and he continued. "Within the next few weeks we are expecting a certain number of men. They will land near here, in several groups. You will be responsible for the aid and shelter of one group."

Sophia stared at him, her mind seething with questions she knew she didn't dare ask. What men? How would they arrive? What were they going to do? And how could she provide food for a group of strangers when there was barely enough to put on her own table?

"The man who contacted you in the coffeehouse will contact you again," Perseus said. "Wait for his message—and be on your guard always." Sophia swallowed, her heart hammering with a new fear. Suddenly her sleepy village seemed full of traitors and idiots. "Trust no one," Perseus warned her. "No one at all... not even those closest to you." A chill rippled through Sophia and she wondered whether he meant Angelika. Did he know about her sister's attachment to Dimitrios? "That is all you need to know now," he finished flatly, and the moon emerged from behind the clouds to illuminate his face. Sophia saw a long, thin scar curve down the outside of his cheek. He smiled grimly, the grove dark all around him. "God go with you, Sophia."

Sophia opened her mouth, but no words came out. She was icy with terror, unable to move. Think. Still smiling, Perseus took her elbow and led her back towards the road. His eyes narrowed, he glanced in both directions before sending her on her way with a none too gentle shove.

"Go. Quickly. And do not be seen."

Somehow Sophia managed to put one foot in front of the other, and walk in numb, mute terror all the way back to her father's house. As she climbed the outside staircase, she heard the gentle rumble of her father's snores. Her sister was asleep, still curled up on her side.

Sophia undressed, fumbling, her fingers blunt and clumsy. Now that the meeting was over, she felt her senses return. Her body began to shake. Mother of God, what had she agreed to? Except she hadn't even agreed. No one had even asked. It had simply been expected, demanded, and the price for disobedience could be in blood.

Angelika stirred and Sophia froze. "You're back? From the coffeehouse?"

With shaking hands Sophia reached for her nightdress. "Yes."

"Why did you wear that old dress?" Angelika asked, nodding at the dress lying discarded on Sophia's bed. "It's not good enough for feeding the goats in."

"I'm only in the kitchen," Sophia said, and was shocked to hear how quickly the words—the lies—came. "It doesn't matter."

"Oh, Sophia," Angelika sighed, sliding down into her bed once more. "You have no sense. Don't you want to be beautiful, noticed? Just a little bit?"

"No," Sophia whispered, "not at all."

But her sister had already fallen back asleep.

*

The days crawled by, and yet passed all too quickly, for every day that Sophia did not hear from her contact, whoever he was, she was one day closer to the day when she would.

She tried to say something of it to Kristina, but the older woman simply shook her head, her eyes flashing fire. Clearly the kitchen of the coffeehouse was no longer a safe place to talk. The thought terrified her.

Just as terrifying were the rumors and stories that swirled through the village, the men's mutters in the coffeehouse and the women's whispers by the fountain or in the field. Stories of how the Italians would be pushed out, stomped on by German jackboots as the Nazis swept through the villages of Greece's wild heart and broke it with their swift and brutal reprisals. Whole villages razed to the ground, hundreds taken into the square and shot like dogs. Men, women, even children, all with bullets in their heads, left to die, to rot.

Would Iousidous be next? Would she?

And what of Velouchiotis's men? She felt the danger, the threat of violence and even death from all sides. The guerrillas roamed in the mountains and, reckless and angry, shot anyone they liked; the Nazis marching in the towns were the same. Nowhere was safe.

A boy had gone missing one night; his body had been found with a bullet in it the next day. He was rumored to have worked with Velouchiotis. Angelika had been shaken by the death, yet Sophia knew her sister still flirted with Dimitrios when she could, still loitered by the fountain waiting for him, even if only to give him a smile and a toss of her pretty dark head. And Dimitrios had not learned any discretion, despite the new dangers, for he still stood up in the coffeehouse and bragged of his rifle and all the Nazis he was going to drive off with it one day.

Sophia suppressed a groan at the thought. *Angelika*, she implored silently, *don't you see what is happening? Don't you know what danger you're in?* Her dark gaze flitted to the doorway of the coffeehouse, as if Angelika might appear there, even though Sophia knew she would not. Women did not come to the coffeehouse. She only hoped her sister was at home, or with her aunt, or the other women of the village. Not, please God, courting troubles—and Dimitrios.

As her gaze rested on the doorway, she imagined another person entering, the thin, narrow-faced man who had accosted her by the water barrel before. How would he get in contact with her this time? She'd taken to hurrying through the streets and walking with other women, as if such childish ploys could keep her from being approached. She knew, with a chilling certainty, that the man would contact her whenever he liked, however he chose.

Yet how? And when? And what would she be asked to do? She was not a brave person. She was not reckless or daring or defiant, and the thought of having to call on a courage she was quite sure she did not possess filled her with a sick despair.

Yet as the days passed and August turned into September, Sophia started to nurture a faint, frail hope that she wouldn't be called on at all. Perhaps Perseus had changed his mind, or the plan had changed, or fallen apart completely. Perhaps she wouldn't be needed. With each passing day Sophia found herself beginning to unbend, that hope unfurling inside her like a seed planted in the soil of desperation. Each night she slept less fitfully and was spared the dark, bloodied dreams that had haunted her since she'd first gone to the Lethikos's grove.

*

The last of the men were emptying out of the coffeehouse one evening in late September as Sophia hefted a tray of empty glasses into the kitchen. She placed the tray next to the big stone sink and wiped her forehead. She was not looking forward to the washing up. Outside the sky glittered with stars, and she had not seen Angelika all day. Worry needled her as she pumped water into the sink and then turned to the glasses.

"Hello, Sophia."

The voice came from behind her, and her mouth opened in an instinctive scream that was silenced by a hand pressed firmly over her lips. Her whole body stiffened in shock and fear as a voice whispered in her ear. She felt the solid presence of a body only inches behind her, and the faint scent of Karelia cigarettes. It was strangely intimate, horribly invasive. She had never had her body so close to a man as to this stranger.

"Don't scream." After a second's pause he removed his hand from her mouth.

Sophia drew in a shuddering breath before she turned around. Perseus stood there, his face expressionless, his body relaxed despite the fact that he'd just scared her near senseless.

"I didn't hear you come in."

Perseus smiled faintly. "You weren't meant to."

She swallowed and wiped her now sweaty hands on her apron. "Why are you here?" she asked in a hoarse whisper, even though she knew. The knowledge pooled coldly in the pit of her stomach, and Perseus confirmed it with one terse sentence.

"You are needed."

Sophia swallowed. "How?"

"The men are scheduled to arrive in a few days. They will need food, shelter. You, along with some others, will meet them in the place you went to before."

"The Leth—"

"Shh." He held one hand to his lips.

"Who are you afraid of hearing?" Sophia asked in a whisper.

"Anyone. People talk, Sophia. Most cannot keep a tongue in their heads. They boast, they gossip, they whisper. But not you."

So she'd been told. It was horribly fitting, she supposed, that the quiet discretion she'd relied on to keep her safe was what had attracted these men to her and would put her in danger.

"When?" she asked, still whispering.

"The twenty-eighth of this month, at ten o'clock at night. Tell no one." He gripped her shoulder, his fingers biting into her flesh. "No one," he emphasized, and jerkily Sophia nodded. Her heart was hammering, the blood thundering in her ears.

Satisfied, Perseus turned away, and Sophia found enough courage to ask one last question.

"The man—the man who first talked to me. I thought he was meant to come—"

"He couldn't."

Dread plunged inside her. "Why not?"

Perseus's eyes were bleak as he smiled grimly. "He's dead. Taken out and shot three nights ago, like a dog. This is what we are fighting, Sophia. This is why we do it." He held her gaze for a long moment, and Sophia wondered what he would do if she refused to obey his orders. Would she be a threat, a danger then? From his dark eyes and cold smile, the man known as Perseus seemed capable of almost anything, including eliminating a reluctant spy.

Softly he said, "You believe. You are afraid, but you believe."

Sophia shook her head, desperate now. "But I'm too afraid."

"Then let the fear force you to act. It is the only way." With one last, hard look, he slipped silently from the room.

CHAPTER TEN

Now

Three days after her dinner with Eleni, Ava was surprised to find Andreas at her door. The top half of it was open to the sunlight streaming in, and when he'd poked his head in, she'd been attempting to access the internet on her laptop, a fistful of wires clutched uselessly in one hand. She'd had some of the rewiring done in the house earlier in the week, arranged by Eleni's cousin, but it seemed she still couldn't make things actually work.

"Oh, hello," she said, and then, for no real reason at all, blushed. Seeing him in the doorway, she was suddenly, surprisingly aware of how tall he was, how dark his hair and eyes were, and how blindingly white his smile in his tanned, weather-beaten face was. He ducked his head, and Ava dropped the wires and went over to the door.

"I was passing through the village," he said, still smiling, "and I thought I'd see how you are."

The line had the stiltedness of something that had been rehearsed, Ava thought, and then chastised herself for the thought. English was not Andreas's first language. Why shouldn't what he said be rehearsed? Yet she still felt a strange ripple of unease; she couldn't put her finger on it, or determine whether the unease came from Andreas's sudden visit or her own surprised pleasure at his arrival. She was still planning on having lunch with him on Saturday, although she hadn't really expected to see him before then.

"I'm having trouble with the internet," she said as she undid the latch on the bottom half of the door and ushered him in. "Someone from the power company told me I could have internet access starting today, but I've yet to see it actually working. It keeps saying it doesn't recognize the server—"

"Shall I have a look?"

Ava hesitated. She was tired of being rescued, but she'd been working on her laptop for a fruitless and frustrating hour. "Sure, if you wouldn't mind."

Three minutes later, Andreas clicked on a screen and her email popped up. He straightened. "There you are."

Ava suppressed a stab of annoyance. Why hadn't she been able to manage that? "Thank you. I don't know why I couldn't figure that out after an hour."

"You would have eventually, I am sure." Andreas smiled and Ava felt a sudden tightness in her chest. Simon used to tease her about being hopeless with computers. *You can't just start pushing buttons,* Ava, he'd say with a laugh. *You'll make it worse.* And she had; one time she'd turned all the text on her screen white and impossible to read, and no tinkering with the colors would change it back. Simon had ended up having to wipe her hard drive.

She had, she knew, made it worse in so many ways.

"May I get you a drink of something cold?" she asked, forcing her thoughts away from Simon. She'd been in Greece for two weeks and he hadn't called again; she hadn't called either, despite Julie's urgings. Stalemate, then.

Andreas hesitated, and then nodded. "Thank you."

Ava went to the tiny kitchen in the back, which looked marginally better with everything cleaned, if not precisely sparkling, and the new refrigerator humming away.

"Everything looks so much better since the last time I was here," Andreas said. He'd followed her into the kitchen and suddenly the small room seemed half its normal size. Ava's shoulder brushed against his as she opened the fridge.

"That's not saying much, though, really," she said lightly as she peered into the depths of the fridge. She was very conscious of Andreas behind her. "I have some orange juice or sparkling water. That's it, I'm afraid."

"Orange juice, please."

She poured a glass of juice and handed it to him. He took it with murmured thanks, and Ava, still feeling awkward and self-conscious, opened the back door and stepped outside.

"I've been doing a bit of gardening," she said, more to fill the silence than anything else. "Just a few plants. I'm not even sure what they are. I couldn't read the Greek on the tags—"

"Let me see."

Andreas stepped out into the little garden and crouched down on his haunches to inspect the few straggly little plants struggling up from the crumbly overturned earth. Ava took a step back, struck by how natural Andreas looked, sitting on his heels, the sun catching the threads of gray in his curly hair. How very Greek.

"This is jancaea," he said, pointing to a small flowering alpine with violet petals. "It used to grow only on Mount Olympus, in the wild."

"Oh—" Ava wasn't sure if that meant it was rather tacky to have it growing in her little patch of garden.

"And this is azalea. You have the same in England, I think?" Andreas turned to her, eyebrows raised, still crouching on his haunches.

"Oh. Yes. Azalea." Ava blushed. Again. "I'm not much of a gardener, actually. Back in England, anyway. So I'm not sure I'd recognize much of anything." Not even, apparently, an azalea.

"Perhaps you will learn here." Andreas rose, brushing the dirt from his jeans. "Perhaps you will like it."

"Perhaps," Ava agreed. "If I don't kill them all first by over-watering them or something." She felt a sudden, desperate urge to lighten the moment, even though nothing was happening. Andreas took a sip of juice, gazing around at the scrubby garden and the thick swath of pines in the distance, and Ava wondered why her heart was thudding so hard. Clearly an overreaction, and a ridiculous one, at that.

"They're both hardy, which is good, considering the soil here," Andreas said, his gaze coming back to rest on her. "I actually came to ask if you have any allergies to any food. I know one must ask these days. You hear things about peanuts." He smiled ruefully, and Ava shook her head.

"No, nothing."

"Good."

Had he really come all this way to ask her about that? He could have called or sent a text. She watched as he finished his juice. "I must go. It is a busy time of year for us."

"Oh—yes…" She had no idea, really, what went into olive oil production, but she supposed it was time-consuming. Did they stomp on the olives the way you did on grapes? Did anyone actually do that kind of thing any more, or had she just seen it in a film?

"I will see you on Saturday?" Andreas asked, and when Ava nodded, he smiled and she followed him back into the house before he went out the front door, swinging the bottom half shut behind him with one last whimsical smile.

After he'd gone, the house seemed very quiet. Ava went back outside, hoping to get some more gardening done, but weeding a flower bed when she had nothing to put in it seemed pointless. And how long would she really be here, anyway? She couldn't actually *live* here, could she? At some point she'd have to go back to her real life, what little was left of it, and pick up the broken pieces.

Her grandmother's house would fall back into ruin, first the garden and then the house itself. How long would it take for the fresh whitewash to start to flake or become covered in mildew? The weeds would grow back up in the storeroom, and the stairs would rust and fall apart. The wood would rot, the shutters once more hanging askew, if they didn't fall off completely. Perhaps the cat she was feeding would come back searching for food and find nothing. Perhaps it would have become complacent being fed on scraps and starve to death. In her kindness she would have killed it.

"Oh come on, Ava, get a grip." Her voice sounded loud in the empty house, but, honestly, she was being horribly maudlin. Without Simon to steady her, she could go right off the deep end into complete melodrama, even over a cat, or a bit of mildew.

Without thinking too much about what she was doing—or why—Ava grabbed her phone and pressed Simon's number in her contacts folder.

Her head beat with hard, painful thuds as the phone trilled, the sound tinny and distant. Once, twice, three times. Then, just when she expected it to click over to voicemail, someone answered.

"Hello?" Simon said, his voice giving nothing away. "Ava?"

Ava's fingers slackened around her mobile as Simon's voice echoed in her ears. She hadn't expected him to pick up, she realized; she hadn't prepared herself to actually talk to him.

"Ava?" he said again, and concern or perhaps just impatience sharpened his voice.

"Hello, Simon," Ava said quietly. It was good to hear his voice. Better than she'd expected, and yet more painful too. Her throat ached and she couldn't think of anything else to say. Simon apparently did not have that problem.

"Well," he said briskly. "You've arrived, then? How is the place?"

"Fine. Everything's fine." Ava forced herself to adopt Simon's practical tone. "There were a few mishaps with the electricity and things—"

"Mishaps? What kind?"

"The power wasn't turned on, and my hire car got a flat tire," Ava explained, speaking lightly, "but it's all sorted now."

"Is it?" Simon sounded dubious, or maybe even disappointed. Did he think she couldn't manage without him? "I don't like to think of you alone there, with no car or light—"

"It's sorted," Ava said firmly. "And I'm not alone. I've made friends—"

"Already?" Simon said incredulously, and now he really didn't sound pleased. Ava felt a sharp dart of satisfaction. Now he would know how it felt for someone to move on when you weren't ready to. Or perhaps he wouldn't; when she'd asked for a separation, Simon had hardly been reluctant to agree. *As you like* had been his exact words.

"Yes, a woman here knew my grandmother," Ava explained. "Or at least, her mother did. It's been interesting—I almost think something happened back then to make my grandmother emigrate."

"Something? What do you mean?"

As ever, Simon wanted facts. Practicalities. And as ever, Ava didn't have them to offer. "I don't know. It's just a feeling I have." She thought about telling Simon about Parthenope and her abject apology but didn't want to hear him sounding dubious. *She probably had no idea what she was talking about, Ava. She's in her nineties. She probably has dementia.* "I might learn more—there are a few survivors of the war still alive."

"And you plan on talking to them? Meeting them?"

Why, Ava wondered, *did he have to sound so skeptical?* Or was she just being oversensitive? "There's a schoolteacher here, Helena. She's interviewing them for an oral history project and she told me about it. Asked me to come along." Simon was silent, seeming to absorb this. "In any case, people have been friendly. I'm having lunch…" She stopped suddenly, not wanting to mention Andreas.

"You certainly sound settled," Simon said after a moment. His voice was very even, and Ava couldn't tell a thing from it. "Despite the problems with the car and the lights." He cleared his throat. "You do feel settled, Ava? You're happy?"

Happy, Ava thought incredulously. How could he even ask if she was happy, when in the space of a year her whole life—their life—had fallen apart? She felt the familiar feeling of helpless anger swamp her; Simon had never seemed to understand how his practical attitude hurt her. She'd tried to explain, after the stillbirth, how his ability to soldier on with seeming indifference had made her feel more alone than ever, as if he hadn't even cared, and Simon had just looked at her blankly. "What do you want me to do?" he'd asked, and she'd heard a weary sort of anger spiking his words. She hadn't attempted to explain that she wanted him to feel the way she did; she wanted him to share her grief. If it didn't come naturally, a manufactured emotion for her own benefit would hardly help. It would probably just make things worse.

Now she swallowed past the thickening of tears in her throat and said, "Yes. I'm settled." She didn't add the caveat *but not happy.* She'd been giving Simon every impression that she was doing fine; despite her initial flare of anger she knew it wasn't fair to be hurt simply because he expected her to be fine.

"Good," Simon said again. "That's good." What an awkward conversation they were having, Ava thought. It was as stilted and uncomfortable as anything she'd been afraid of. She opened her mouth to tell him she needed to ring off when Simon said quietly, "I miss you."

Shock raced through her like quicksilver, the kind of jolt she'd felt as a girl when she'd fancied someone and suddenly realized he might fancy her back. She hadn't felt that electric tingling in a long time. Years. A decade and a half, when she'd seen Simon in the university bar and he'd sloshed beer all over himself as he tried to hoist his glass aloft in a wave. He'd been so adorably incompetent for a moment; before then she'd seen only the stoic, capable Simon from the sailing club. That Simon, with his slightly scornful ease around a boat—Ava hadn't known a thing about sailing and had only joined the club to meet boys—had intimidated her. This Simon endeared himself to her, and she'd gone over and said hello.

And the rest, she thought rather bleakly, was history.

"Ava?" he prompted, and cleared his throat. "Say something."

"I'm… surprised," she finally said, and Simon let out a little huff of humorless laughter.

"Are you really?"

"I thought you wanted a break."

"A break?"

"From me." And her unending sadness, the tears that seemed to only irritate him, the grief he'd shaken off but kept swamping her.

"You were the one who said you wanted a break," he replied flatly. "I hope you're getting one."

She felt rebuked, even though what he'd said was true. She had been the one to suggest everything: the separation, her moving out, then going to Greece. It had all been her idea, and in that moment she knew she'd done it all because she'd wanted to provoke a reaction in him, something to pierce the indifferent armor he surrounded himself with. She'd wanted, Ava knew, for Simon to pull her to him and beg her not to leave. And of course he hadn't.

"It's good to be here," she said, because that was true, in its way. Yet she wished she could tell him other things, things she knew he didn't want to hear. *I went to church and I thought of our daughter's casket. Was it heavy when you held it? Or did its terrible lightness make you sad? Why did you never tell me anything about how you felt?*

"I'm glad," Simon said, interrupting her thoughts. He sounded formal, as if he were making a business call. *I'm glad your taxes are sorted. Is there anything else I can help you with?* "Do you think you'll stay a while?"

What was a while? "I don't really know. I'd like to find out more about my grandmother."

"By talking to the survivors?"

"If I can. I doubt they'll speak English, but Helena might translate for me."

"So your grandmother was in Greece during the war?" He actually sounded interested, and Ava felt a sudden rush of warmth. Perhaps they could talk about this, the distant past, without any awkwardness.

"Yes, as far as I know she left in 1946. She met my grandfather Edward and they married sometime after—1947 maybe? I honestly never really thought about her or any of it until I arrived here. To me she was always an old woman."

"I think most children think of their grandparents that way."

"Yes, I suppose. But then coming here…" Ava felt a thickening in her throat. Apparently she couldn't talk about the past without becoming emotional. "It suddenly struck me how different her life must have been. You should see the house, Simon…" Why had she said that? "It's rustic, to say the least," she hurried on. "And Eleni told me that when my grandmother lived here, there wouldn't have been electricity or running water or a tiled floor or anything."

"And that made you want to learn more about your grandmother?"

"Yes," she paused, then plunged on. "The first night I came here I met a woman—Eleni, whom I mentioned—she showed me my grandmother's house. I met her mother, Parthenope, as well, and when she saw me, she confused me with my grandmother and told me how sorry she was."

"Sorry? What for?"

"I don't know. She had tears running down her face and she kept saying *signomi*—I'm sorry."

She heard Simon breathing, could imagine the furrow between his eyes that he always got when he was thinking deeply. She used to smooth it away with her thumb before kissing him.

"How do you know she thought you were your grandmother?" he finally asked.

"She called me Sophia."

"Wow." Simon actually seemed impressed, and Ava felt another blaze of feeling—of hope, something she hadn't felt in a long time. "Sounds like a real mystery."

"If I can find any other clues."

"You said there were other survivors."

"Yes, and Iousidous is a tiny place. I don't know what the population was back in the 1940s, but I hope that someone I talk to, or really, Helena talks to, might know my grandmother. Remember her."

She lapsed into silence, and so did Simon. Ava felt the awkwardness again, the weight of all the things they weren't saying and couldn't talk about, and it hurt her afresh because this was her *husband*. Surely she should be able to talk about anything with him.

"Well, let me know if you find anything out," Simon said lightly, and it sounded like the beginning of a goodbye. *Glad you're safe. Nice to chat…*

"I will." Ava thought of all the things she wanted to say, now bottled up in her throat, bursting in her lungs. Somehow in that ensuing silence the words didn't come. It had been too long; she should have said it right away—*I miss you, too.* Yet she hadn't, even though she did. Desperately. "Well…" she began, uncertainly, and Simon took the opening.

"Yes, it's getting late there, isn't it? Thanks for ringing. I was wondering how you were."

Back to being brisk. Well, she could act the same. "Yes, fine, all right, thanks," Ava babbled, and then with another rather incoherent attempt at a farewell, she severed the connection. She sat in the living room of her little house, twilight falling softly around her. She rose and went to the window; the pine-covered hills were violet with shadows. Everything was silent save the breeze rustling through the trees, and the echo of Simon's words in her heart: *I miss you.*

Suddenly she remembered when she'd first told him she was pregnant, after so many years of fertility pills and then the endless injections and empty hope of IVF. His face had softened into the most wonderful smile, and he'd gathered her up into a spontaneous hug and kissed her thoroughly. She'd felt so cherished, so loved. She'd been so happy then… and so had Simon.

Happy and filled with hope.

Where had those days gone? Why hadn't their shared loss brought them closer together, instead of driving them so desperately apart? Was she being unreasonable, expecting something from Simon he didn't seem able to give? Or was he the unreasonable one, shutting her out without even realizing he was doing it? She'd asked all the questions before, again and again, and yet still they came pounding in her head, demanding answers she couldn't give.

Slowly she put the phone down and sat back on the sofa, drawing her knees up to her chest. Closing her eyes, she listened to the rustle of the breeze and felt as if that lonely wind was blowing right through her.

CHAPTER ELEVEN

Now

The day for her lunch with Andreas was bright and clear, with a sharp breeze blowing off the mountains. Helena had called just as Ava was leaving the house; the man she was interviewing tomorrow had agreed to see Ava as well. The news buoyed Ava's hopes so much that, as she climbed into her rental car, she heard herself humming under her breath, felt a smile bloom across her face. She was looking forward to lunch with Andreas and his daughter, although Kalista had done little so far to recommend herself. Who knew, Ava thought as she drove out of Iousidous, perhaps she could soften the teenager a little. She was good with kids, generally speaking. She'd been a teacher, after all. Perhaps she could help Andreas forge a stronger relationship with his daughter. It was the kind of day when almost anything felt possible.

Her thoughts occupied her all the way to the Lethikos property, and she turned up the long tree-lined drive, the sky high and blue above her, the lemony sunshine like a benediction.

Andreas came onto the veranda as she stepped out of the car, gave her a wave. Ava felt a funny little pang when she saw him, almost like a homesickness. What was she missing?

Simon. They hadn't spoken again since she'd rung him, and Ava had spent far too many hours dissecting every detail of that short phone conversation, every word, every moment's pause or sudden, awkward laugh. *I miss you.*

What had he meant by that, exactly? On the surface, of course, it seemed obvious. But Ava couldn't tell whether Simon missed who she'd been before they'd lost their daughter, cheerful, slightly crazy Ava who made him laugh, or did he miss the person she'd been when she left, miserable, mopey, prone to tears?

Nearly two months on, Ava was starting to accept that she might have been more than a little hard to deal with.

"Welcome, welcome," Andreas said, and he came down the steps to open her car door, a gesture Ava found both gentlemanly and the very tiniest bit annoying. "I thought we'd eat in the garden. It's so nice today, and not too hot."

"Sounds lovely," Ava said, and then pinned a smile on her face as Kalista came to the door. She was dressed in skinny jeans and a ripped T-shirt, and her long, dark hair streamed over her hunched shoulders. She gave both of them a sulky, defiant look that was halfway to a glare. "Hello, Kalista," Ava said brightly. "I hope I'll be of some use to you, practicing English." Kalista didn't reply, yet she still managed to convey her scornful incredulity that Ava could be of any use to her at all. Ava wondered whether she felt threatened by a woman's presence, and wished she could somehow reassure the girl—*but how? And about what?* She wasn't sure what Andreas's real intentions were in inviting her today, and she wasn't sure what hers were in accepting. She missed Simon, yes, but if her marriage was truly over... She put a stop to that thought before she could finish it.

"Shall we?" Andreas said, and he lightly pressed his hand against the small of Ava's back, urging her forward. It felt strange to have a man's hand there, the pressure warm. It wasn't unpleasant, but neither was it entirely welcome.

Andreas led their silent little party outside, where a wooden plank table was laid with a variety of dishes. A green glass bottle of murky olive oil and a blue jar of agapanthus were the proud centerpieces. As Ava sat down, she gestured to the bottle. "Your own?"

"Indeed," Andreas returned with a smile. "I could hardly serve a competitor's."

"I look forward to it," Ava said, and she held out her plate as Andreas served her salad and fresh, crusty bread, as well as pieces of succulent lamb cooked in a lemony garlic sauce.

"So," he said, once they were all served and had started eating, "are you feeling more settled, now you've been here a couple of weeks?"

"A bit," Ava replied. "The house looks more lived in, at least, and I've found a few things to occupy my time—I'm fortunate so many of you know English, since I speak very little Greek." She turned to Kalista, smiling, but the girl just looked down at her plate.

"Perhaps you will learn," Andreas said and Ava made a face.

"I did an online course, but it was slow going. I'm not sure I can learn so much at my age."

He let out a laugh. "You are not as old as all that, surely."

"I'm nearly thirty-seven."

"A child." He smiled at her, and Ava felt a prickle of annoyance. She was not a child. Her experience, her suffering, surely was proof of that.

He poured some of the olive oil onto a saucer and dipped a piece of bread into the golden puddle. Ava followed suit, deliberately letting the remark go. Had he been, in his Greek way, flirting? Ignoring it was surely the safer option. She didn't want an argument. And she didn't think she wanted to flirt.

"So I'm afraid I know nothing about olive oil production," she said as she dipped another piece of bread in the golden oil. "It's delicious, by the way, so much nuttier than the kind I buy in the supermarket."

"Bah." Andreas waved a hand in expansive dismissal. "Imitators. Idiots."

"So how do you make it?"

"It is very simple, really, although much work. We harvest the olives when they are not quite mature, not quite black. My family has used the old ways of making oil for many generations—presses rather than these new machines."

"So you do stamp on them with your feet?" Ava blurted out, and Andreas looked quite shocked.

"Our feet? *Signomi*, no. We grind them into a paste and then put the paste into a cold press to gather the oil."

"And that's the old-fashioned way?"

"It's the way," Andreas said, an inflexible note entering his voice, "to make the best oil." He glanced at Kalista as he said it, but the girl just tossed her hair and glanced away.

"So your family has had this place for a hundred years, you said?"

Andreas returned his gaze to Ava, looking, she thought, almost dispirited. He smiled quickly though and passed her more bread. "Yes. My great-grandfather first cultivated the land here."

"So your family was here during the war."

"Most certainly." He arched an eyebrow, clearly waiting, and Ava fumbled through her explanation.

"The house I live in, as you know, belonged to my grandmother's family. I'm trying to find out more about her."

"Have you had any success?"

"Not really," Ava admitted with a self-conscious laugh. "No one likes to talk about those days."

"No, indeed not. It was a hard time. Very little food, and of course the constant danger of the occupation, first by the Italians and then the Nazis."

"Yes, Eleni was telling me a bit about it. I'm afraid I know very little about Greece's history."

"As I said, people don't talk about it. It is too painful. But neither do we forget."

"No, you don't want to forget," Ava agreed quietly. "And even if you wanted to, you can't."

Andreas nodded, his gaze hooded and thoughtful. "You have some experience, I think, with sorrow."

"Yes." She took a sip of water, averting her own gaze, and Andreas took her cue and continued his explanation.

"The civil war that happened after the Germans left was in some ways worse than the occupation. Greeks fighting each other—very bloody."

"Who won?"

"The Greek governmental army defeated the communists in 1949."

"Right." Somehow she had a feeling she should have known that.

"But for many years, during the Second World War and immediately after, the communists were more powerful. They certainly had a greater Resistance force against the Italians and Germans during the war."

"So most people in the Resistance were communists?"

Andreas shook his head. "Not precisely. There were many communists, but most villagers in a place like Iousidous just wanted a better life, more food, more land, more comfort. Like most people."

"Yes."

"Some became quite—what is the word—strong about their politics?" He frowned faintly and Ava hazarded a guess.

"Militant?"

"I do not know that word, but it sounds right. They became so, whether communist or republican. Even when the country was occupied, they fought each other."

"Eleni mentioned that to me, I think."

"My grandfather wished to fight in EDES, the republican Resistance. But he was lame from an accident with his mule, and so he could not do as he wished and take a rifle and disappear into the mountains." He smiled, his eyes crinkling as he recalled the story. "The Resistance fighters from both groups hid in the mountains here. They fought each other a bit, but it wasn't until the summer of 1942 that it came to much."

Ava perked up at this. Her grandmother would have certainly been in Iousidous then. "What happened then?" she asked.

"The two groups worked together, with the British, no less, to blow up the Gorgopotamos railway bridge. I showed the river to you last time you were here."

"Yes—"

"The bridge was the only means of transporting supplies from Salonika to Athens. It was quite a good thing they blew it up."

"And what happened after that?"

"The Resistance groups never worked together again. They fought all the more, so by 1944 it was getting to be very dangerous. And by 1946 it was a full war." He sighed, shaking his head. "How could we fight each other, having endured so much? Yet that is the Greek spirit. Fight always. Resist."

Had her grandmother had that Greek spirit? She had certainly been strong-willed, in her own way. "And what of your grandfather?" Ava asked. "You said he couldn't be involved—"

"Not as a soldier, because of his leg. But he allowed the olive grove to be used for Resistance activities. He used to boast that the plans to explode the bridge were made right here…" Andreas swept his arm to the nearby twisted trunks. "Although who really knows? Neither Resistance group was going to say where they gathered!"

"No, indeed," Ava murmured. Her mind was spinning with all the new information. Could her grandmother have been involved in the Resistance in some way? When she thought of the rather stern, elderly lady she'd known in Leeds, it seemed hard to believe. Yet Sophia Paranoussis's life in Greece was far from anything Ava could have ever imagined.

After lunch Kalista excused herself, rather sullenly, and Andreas took Ava around the property. She admired the barns with their cold presses, cleaning system, and separator, and peeked into a dark cellar where Andreas stored the stainless-steel vats of oil.

"In another month I will bottle what we have," he said, and showed her a narrow-necked bottle of green glass. "And then begin shipping it out."

"It looks like a lot of work," Ava said as Andreas led her back out into the sunshine.

"It is. But I would not do anything else if I could." Ava glanced at him and saw he was frowning, and wondered why, for a moment, he looked so grim. Then his expression cleared and he turned to her with a smile.

"But let me show you the trees."

The sun was hot as they wandered through the grove of olive trees, their twisted trunks looking bent and misshapen against the bright blue sky.

"Some olive trees in Greece are thought to be thousands of years old," Andreas said as he led her through the rows of trees. "But the ones here are a few hundred only."

"That still seems quite old to me." Ava lifted one hand to shield her eyes from the sun. "Will you pass the business on to Kalista? Fifth generation?"

"Perhaps. If she is willing."

Was that what sometimes clouded Andreas's expression? Ava wondered. The possibility that his daughter had no interest in living in rural Greece and making olive oil?

"It is such a nice day," Andreas said as they returned to the house. "Would you like to drive out to the Gorgopotamos Bridge? It is a beautiful sight."

Ava hesitated. She'd enjoyed the afternoon, but she wasn't sure what Andreas wanted from her. Or, if she was honest, what she wanted from him.

"Perhaps you could talk English with Kalista," Andreas continued. "I know she did not speak much during lunch."

She'd been completely silent, and Ava didn't think going to see a bridge would turn Kalista into a chatterbox, but Andreas looked so hopeful, and she did want to see the Gorgopotamos. "All right," she said and went to freshen up while Andreas called Kalista.

A short while later the three of them drove in Andreas's truck to the park surrounding the Gorgopotamos River. As they got out of the truck, Ava felt a ripple of trepidation at seeing the steep, verdant sides of the gorge. A railway bridge, one rebuilt after the war, Andreas told her, spanned the river rushing fiercely far below.

"The original bridge was a bit farther down from that," Andreas explained as he pointed to the current bridge. "Twelve British Special Operations Executive agents and one hundred and fifty Greeks were involved, some of them just untrained villagers."

Ava turned to him. "Do you think people from Iousidous helped?"

Andreas shrugged. "Who can say? Some, I would think. We are a proud people. Not one of us liked being ruled." His glance slid to his daughter, who stood a few meters away, her shoulders hunched, her hair blowing in the wind. She kicked at the rocky ground with one sneaker. "She's been so unhappy lately," he murmured, his voice soft and sad. "I don't know what to do."

"It's bound to be difficult," Ava said hesitantly. "Since her mother—"

"Althea died two years ago. We both still grieve, of course, but it's not that." He let out a little sigh. "It's here. She wants to go to school in Athens and live with my sister-in-law there." He spoke with a new bitterness that surprised Ava.

"Perhaps that wouldn't be so bad," she offered cautiously. "A woman's influence can sometimes help—"

Andreas shook his head. When he spoke, his tone was vehement. "Never. If Kalista goes to Athens, she won't come back. I feel it here." He gestured to his heart. "I can't lose her like that."

He glanced at Ava, his expression softening. "Surely you can understand that?"

"Yes," Ava said after a moment. "I can." She knew about loss and fear; she also knew you couldn't hold on to people, or make them do or even feel what you wanted them to. That wasn't love. But Kalista was only fifteen, and Andreas surely knew what was best for his daughter. "Perhaps a weekend visit?" she suggested, but Andreas just shook his head again, and from the darkening of his eyes Ava knew he wasn't pleased by her suggestion.

"We should head back," he said, drawing her away from the side of the gorge. He gestured to some dark clouds roiling near the horizon. "It looks like rain."

Ava spared one last glance to the gorge, with the river churning furiously below, before climbing back into the truck. She would have to ask Helena about the Gorgopotamos Bridge when she saw her tomorrow.

CHAPTER TWELVE

Now

The house Helena led Ava to the next day was small and white-washed and immaculately kept. It was perched on one of the higher streets of the village, near the church, with a commanding view of the countryside.

The man who shuffled to the doorway was nearing ninety, his hair sparse and white, his cheeks sunken, but his eyes as bright as buttons. He spoke in rapid Greek to Helena, kissing her on both cheeks, before eyeing Ava curiously.

Helena introduced Ava while she waited nervously, conscious just how much she was presuming, coming into people's homes like this. No matter what Eleni said, she was still a stranger.

After a moment of silent consideration, the man, whom Helena introduced as Angelos Mallos, led them both inside. Ava and Helena both sat down on a small settee in the living room while Angelos brought them tiny cups of strong Greek coffee. Helena began to speak in Greek again, her notepad resting on her knees, and Ava sat silently and sipped her coffee as the conversation flowed around her. She found herself growing sleepy despite the coffee, for the room was warm and she couldn't understand a word of what either of them was saying.

Helena turned to her, giving her a sharp poke in the ribs, and Ava started, embarrassed to have been caught drifting. "Yes…?"

"Wake up, sleepyhead," Helena said with a grin. "Angelos has just said he knew your grandmother."

"Really?" Alert once more, Ava turned to the older man. He smiled at her, nodding in a friendly manner. He spoke rapidly to Helena, who frowned. "What?" Ava asked, anxiety needling at her at Helena's troubled expression. "What did he say?"

"He said he knew Sophia and Angelika… both the Paranoussis sisters."

Ava sat back, stunned. She'd had no idea her grandmother had had a sister. Had Angelika immigrated to England as well? Why had Sophia never mentioned her? *Her great-aunt.*

Helena and Angelos talked for a few more minutes, nodding and gesticulating so Ava had to keep herself from fidgeting from curiosity and impatience. Finally they took their leave, with Angelos kissing them both on each cheek.

Back outside the light was starting to fade, turning the horizon a dusky purple. A few birds twittered high above in the pine trees, but other than that the village was silent.

"Well?" Ava asked, and blushed at how demanding she sounded. "Sorry… I didn't realize how hard it would be for me not to understand a word! I should have thought about that."

"I can only imagine," Helena said, laughing. She slung her bag with her notepad and pens over one shoulder as she drew Ava along the steep street. "Perhaps you could come into school and teach the little ones English, and I will teach you Greek!"

"I'd like that," Ava said with sincerity. "I feel so slow some-times, not knowing a word of your language when everyone I've met knows mine."

Helena nodded. "It is understandable. In any case, Angelos didn't say much more than what I told you—there were two Paranoussis sisters, and they lived in the house you are in now, of course. He said Sophia worked in the café in the square, and something about Angelika being like a butterfly—which makes me think she must have been lazy or pretty or both."

"And what happened to them during the war?" Ava asked. "Does he remember?"

Helena shook her head. "He didn't know them well, and so many people left at that time. It was a dangerous place to be. He just said they both were gone by the time things were settled—so they must have left during the occupation, or perhaps during the civil war afterwards. Do you know when your grandmother came to England?"

"Not exactly," Ava admitted. "Around 1946, I thought, but I'm not sure. Just sometime soon after the Second World War."

Helena nodded. "You have to understand what an uncertain time it was. People fleeing in the night, or worse, simply disappearing. The Nazis had a habit of making people disappear." Helena smiled grimly, and Ava felt a ripple of foreboding.

"Do you think that is what happened to Angelika? That's why I've never heard of her?" The possibility gave Ava a pang of inexplicable grief, considering she'd only learned of her great-aunt's existence a few minutes ago.

"Who can say?" Helena put a comforting arm around Ava's shoulders. "But there are four other people in Iousidous who were here during the war, and perhaps they remember more of Sophia—and Angelika. You might be able to learn more."

"That would be amazing."

"I'll ask if you can accompany me to the next interview," Helena said. "Perhaps we will learn something then. But in the meantime, you could come to the school, maybe one afternoon a week? You could teach an English lesson."

"Teach—" Ava repeated in surprise. She realized she hadn't taken Helena's suggestion seriously.

"Why not? You were a teacher in England, yes?"

"Yes," Ava admitted somewhat reluctantly. "But I taught art—"

"And you speak English. I have been teaching them a bit, but I am so busy already. You would be very helpful if you came, and the children would enjoy getting to know you." Helena's smile held a certain compassion and understanding that made Ava blink rapidly. "And you might enjoy them, yes?"

"Yes," she said after a moment. "I would. Thank you for asking me, Helena."

Back at the house Ava wandered around the near-empty rooms, unable to settle to anything, her mind still spinning with the day's revelations. She knew more about Sophia, but it still didn't feel like nearly enough. The more she knew, she realized, the more she wanted to know. She tried to imagine her grandmother serving in a café, worrying about this unknown sister, the butterfly. *Angelika.* The images that danced through her mind were blurry and indistinct, for she had no real facts to base them on, yet they were more substantial than they'd been before. The ghosts were beginning to take shape.

Walking through those rooms, she felt the shadows of the past crowd around her, and she could almost imagine Sophia, moving around, sweeping, sewing, cooking—waiting and watching—yet for what? Whom?

Or was she just projecting her restless feelings onto her dead grandmother—and if so, just whom was she waiting for?

CHAPTER THIRTEEN

September 1942

Sophia walked through the main square of the village with her basket over her arm and her head tucked firmly down. Ever since Perseus had invaded the coffeehouse's kitchen and given his devastating news a week ago, she'd kept to herself more than ever. She didn't want to talk to anyone; she was terrified of saying the wrong thing, of secrets bubbling out from her because it was so frightening to keep it all locked inside.

In just four days she would slip out to the Lethikos property to meet Perseus and these men who were coming to do—what? Something damaging to the Nazis and Italians. Something dangerous. And she would be involved.

The fact that she didn't know what she was meant to do, or how, or to whom, made the prospect all the more frightening. There were so many unknowns, and she was forced to place her trust in a man she wasn't sure she liked, a man with a wicked scar and the coldest smile she'd ever seen. How could she trust a man like that?

How could she not?

"Sophia! You are walking so fast! What is the hurry?"

Sophia froze, wishing she could ignore the gay young voice, yet she knew to do so would draw more suspicion on her. Who knew who was watching, or why? She turned slowly. "*Herete*, Parthenope." She forced a smile for Parthenope Atrikes, Dimitrios's younger sister. She had her brother's dark curly hair and sparkling eyes, and even more arrogance. Sophia had never taken a particular liking to the girl, but she forced herself to appear natural and unconcerned now. Parthenope was just the type of girl to ask too many questions, and think she knew all their answers.

"You're in a rush," Parthenope said, flicking a glossy braid from under her head scarf. "Where are you going with your head tucked so low?"

"Nowhere," Sophia answered. "Just home." She was telling the truth, and yet she felt herself flush, conscious, so terribly conscious of all the secrets she was keeping.

Parthenope's eyes sparkled with curiosity. "Are you meeting someone?" she asked in a whisper that carried halfway across the square. She leaned closer to Sophia, although her voice was still loud enough for others to hear. "A man?"

"Of course not!" Sophia took a step back as if to distance herself from such a suggestion. *Stupid, thoughtless girl.* "I would not be so shamed."

Now Parthenope's cheeks flushed and she lifted her chin, the slight movement one of defiance. "You talk of shame? The war is changing things, Sophia. It gives us freedom—"

"Freedom?" Where was the freedom in fearing for your life, in having nothing but watery pottage to eat, and with all the decent men of the village dead or gone? Sophia just shook her head. She would not argue with someone as silly as Parthenope, although to look at her, the girl seemed to be doing all right. Her cheeks were round, her body still possessing the ripe curves of young womanhood, while most of the villagers were turning rail-thin from hunger, for the Italians took much of their food. She wondered if the ELAS was supplying Dimitrios's family with food.

"I must go," she said shortly, and without waiting for a farewell she turned and headed quickly back to the house.

*

Four days later Sophia lay in bed, feigning sleep for Angelika's sake before she stole out of the house and down the rutted road to the Lethikos's grove. She tried to calm herself with deep, even breaths, but her heart defied her by beating so fast, her chest hurt. The thin cotton sheet was damp with sweat from where she clutched it, even though the night was cool.

Finally Angelika's breath evened out in sleep and Sophia rose, dressing as quickly and quietly as she could in her old clothes and rough boots. There was no moon, and without a candle she could barely see her own hand in front of her face. She had no idea how she would manage to get to the grove, several kilometers away, without a light, yet she knew she dared not risk one.

Tying a scarf around her hair, she spared one glance for her sister; Angelika was sleeping like a child, one hand lying upturned against her pillow, looking utterly innocent. That evening she'd been full of laughter and fun, making even their father smile with her silly antics.

"Farewell, *koukla mou*," Sophia whispered, and then she slipped out into the night.

The village was still and silent save for the distant yowling of a cat, and the occasional breeze rattling through the pine trees. Sophia walked slowly, feeling for each step, as the moonless night offered no help or light. She wondered how these men, whoever they were, would come to the grove. Would they have torches, or something to light their way, or would they have to feel in the dark as she did, inching along, as good as blind?

It seemed as if she walked forever in this unending, unyielding darkness, one painstaking step in front of another, but finally the cluster of olive trees and the old stone wall that marked the border of the Lethikos property came into view, no more than shadowy masses in the darkness. Sophia glanced around to see whether anyone was about, but the night was empty and still and so very dark. Clumsily she clambered over the wall and slid down the other side, landing hard on the ground, her knees hitting the dirt.

"Quickly now." Within seconds Perseus had hauled her to her feet and was drawing her away from the open space towards a more sheltered area, the trees providing some cover. Sophia stumbled as she kept up with him; she felt blood trickle from the scrapes on her knees. He must have been watching for her arrival to get to her so quickly.

"Where… where is everyone?" Sophia whispered. As far as she could tell, she and Perseus were the only ones in the grove.

"There has been a complication." Although she couldn't see his face, Perseus's tone was grim. *Complications*, Sophia thought, *could never be good.*

"What happened?" she whispered.

"We received word that information about the drop-off had been leaked," Perseus explained tersely. "It was not safe to allow it to proceed."

The first emotion Sophia felt was relief, a sweet cold rush that left her weak in the knees so she nearly swayed where she stood. She could not think of a thing to say that would not betray her feelings, but Perseus seemed to guess them anyway, for he smiled grimly.

"You do not seem disappointed, eh, Sophia? Well, don't worry. There is use for you yet."

Sophia swallowed dryly. "Use…?"

"There will be another night," Perseus said. "A night with more moon, perhaps, so we are not as blind men feeling our way in the dark."

"You mean… another drop-off?"

"Of course." He thrust his face next to hers, and even in the darkness she could see the angry glint of his eyes. "Do you know how much planning and effort has gone into this, Sophia? How many men and hours? Do you think we will shrug our shoulders and forget it all, simply because one thing does not go according to plan?"

"But if the Nazis have heard—"

"It is not the Nazis," Perseus answered tersely.

"The Italians, then."

"No. The communists." He spat on the ground and Sophia jumped back. "They wanted to get to the men first and bring them to that ignorant butcher, Velouchiotis."

And that thought struck terror in her soul as much, or even more, than any of the alternatives. "ELAS is part of this plan?"

"They wish to be. And we may not have any choice in allowing them." He sighed and rubbed a weary hand over his face. "But not tonight, little Sophia. Tonight you rest easy, in your own bed… as long as you are able to make it back to your house alive."

Even though he smiled, Sophia didn't think he was joking.

Her head was spinning, trying to absorb this information about a plan she still knew nothing about. "So there will be another drop-off?" she finally managed. "When?"

"I do not know. Soon. But don't worry," his teeth flashed white in the darkness, "you will know when you are needed."

"And where are they coming from?"

Perseus blew out an impatient breath, then leaned closer, his fingers digging into Sophia's arm. "Twelve men are being dropped by parachute, in three different groups," he said in a low voice. "Or they were meant to be. Since we did not set out the signal fires, the group meant to drop here did not do so. I do not know where the others have landed."

"And then…?"

"They do not know the countryside," Perseus continued. "And since they dropped separately, they need to make contact with each other as well as our leaders. Once they do, they will be brought back here, to safety. You will be responsible for providing them with food, blankets. That is not too much to ask, is it?" She heard the barest hint of humor in his voice, but fear still clutched at her chest, rose in her throat.

"And where will I get such things?"

"I'm sure you are resourceful." *Resourceful?* Where could she possibly get food to feed a dozen men without anyone knowing? Even blankets were scarce. "There are others who will help as well," Perseus told her. "You are not alone, Sophia, even if you feel so."

"But you told me to trust no one—"

"And so you should not. It is better, safer that way. But you are not alone."

His words, Sophia thought bleakly, provided little comfort.

"But first," Perseus finished resolutely, "we must find the men. We have nothing if we don't have them. I will wait for news from our source. You will wait to be contacted."

She nodded, even though everything in her resisted. Why, she wondered yet again, uselessly, had they chosen her? And yet she knew the answer. She was quiet, discreet, talking to no one. She'd thought keeping her head down would keep her safe in this war, and yet it had put her into more danger than she could imagine.

"Go now," Perseus said. "And wait for my word."

Sophia made the journey back home with painstaking slowness. The night was impenetrably dark, and even though she couldn't deny the rush of relief she felt at the reprieve, she knew with a hollow feeling that it was precisely that: a reprieve. Perseus would contact her again; she would be needed again. She would have to, yet again, make the terrible, dangerous journey out to the Lethikos's grove, and who knew what would happen? Who would be there?

She almost wished it had gone ahead tonight as planned; at least one part of this treacherous experience would be over.

Instead, it loomed in front of her, as unknown and frightening as ever.

The stairs creaked as she tiptoed up them and into her bedroom. Angelika lay asleep in bed, yet she stirred as Sophia entered, rising onto her elbow as her forehead crinkled with concern. "Sophia, where have you been? You weren't working at the coffeehouse tonight."

Sophia stared at her sister, her mind emptying out of thoughts or possible explanations. Mother of God, she was no good at this. "I... I couldn't sleep."

Angelika stared at her in surprise. "So you went out? And you are always telling me how dangerous it is!"

"I know," Sophia said, her fingers trembling as she undid the laces of her boots. "I was foolish, Angelika." Her voice trembled along with her fingers. "So foolish," she whispered.

Angelika let out a little giggle as she settled back into bed. "As foolish as me," she teased, and Sophie stared at her as her sister's breathing evened out in the peacefulness of sleep even as her own mind spun and whirled more than ever.

CHAPTER FOURTEEN

Now

Ava stood outside the school gate and watched the children run in ragged circles on the dusty ground, their laughter ringing out over the mountains. It looked, from her brief glimpse, as if the girls were chasing all the boys, and both sides were loving it. She smiled at the sight, even as a pain in the region of her heart nagged her with its persistent ache. *When*, she wondered, *would it go away? Or did you carry grief with you always, a chronic condition you somehow learned to live with even as it debilitated you?*

Helena spotted her across the yard and waved a cheery hello. Waving back, Ava opened the gate and let herself into the friendly chaos of a primary school's recess period.

"Ava! I'm so glad you could come. The children are looking forward to their lesson."

"Your English is so good, you could give it yourself, I'm sure," Ava said, smiling. Several dark-eyed children clustered around her, quietly curious.

Helena rolled her eyes. "No, I do not think so! And I am so busy, as you can see—as I said before, I have little time for extra lessons. Niko!" Turning to give an impish boy a stern look, she issued an instruction in Greek that had even Ava quaking in her shoes. Although she didn't understand what Helena had said, she could certainly guess the gist of it. Nikos smiled sheepishly and hung his head before walking to the side of the schoolyard, scuffing his trainers through the dust.

"Come," Helena said once she saw to her satisfaction that Nikos was not going to cause any more trouble. "I'll show you where you will have your lesson."

Ava followed her into the school. It was a relatively new one-story building, and inside the corridors were painted a pale, cheerful blue, the walls lined with children's drawings. Ava breathed in the familiar smell of disinfectant and crayons and children, and realized how good it felt to be in a school again. Good and hard at the same time.

"Here we are." Helena led her into a small classroom with a few tables and chairs, and an old metal desk in the corner. "I'm sorry, it is very basic."

"It's perfect," Ava assured her. "I don't need much." In actuality, she wasn't even sure how the lesson would go. She'd taught art, not English, and she felt a flutter of nerves in her middle as she smiled at Helena. She'd spent some time planning a first lesson, but her head already felt as it if it were emptying out of all she'd planned.

A bell rang, and Ava heard the uneven troop of feet as the children all jostled and pushed their way back into the building. "This weekend I will take you out for a drink," Helena said. "There is no taverna in Iousidous any more, but we can go to Lamia."

"I'd love it," Ava said, and then turned to the line of children being led by a harried-looking teacher into her classroom. She decided to forgo the tables and chairs, and instead gestured for them to gather around her on the rug on the floor. They did so obediently, their faces alight with curiosity.

"Hello," Ava said, smiling. "My name is Ava Lancet, and I'm meant to teach you some English." By their blank looks, Ava knew the children probably hadn't understood a word of what she was saying. She thumped her chest caveman style. "Ava." Then she pointed to the child nearest her, a solemn-eyed girl with silky plaits. She raised her eyebrows questioningly and waited until the girl offered, in no more than a whisper, "Maria."

"Maria," Ava repeated, and then pointed to the next pupil. She knew she wouldn't remember all their names, but she soon had them in giggles with all the chest thumping, and that went a long way towards gaining their trust. Or so she hoped. It took ten minutes for the children to tell her their names, and then there were still thirty minutes left. *Now what?* Her lesson, she realized, had been planned for children who knew at least a tiny bit of English. These children, it seemed, knew not a word. She gazed at them for a moment, smiling rather helplessly, realizing how out of her depth she was, when a bright-eyed boy pointed insistently at her shoe.

"*Podi?*" he asked, and it took Ava a moment for to her understand.

"Foot," she said, wiggling her toes in her sandal. The children giggled. Another child, braver now, pointed to her head.

"*Kefali.*"

"Head."

They pointed to various parts of her body and Ava obliged them with the English names, which she made them repeat a couple of times each. They did so obediently, their young voices ringing out, each of them stumbling a bit over the pronunciations before gaining in confidence, and their wide smiles reached right inside her, felt like a fist squeezing her heart. She'd forgotten what joy children found in simple things, how much she loved being with them.

Then Maria, the shy little girl who had inched closer to her as the lesson went on, pointed to her finger.

"Finger," Ava said, but Maria shook her head and pointed to one of the two rings on Ava's finger. Her engagement ring.

Ava stared at the little cluster of emeralds, momentarily silenced. It had been a long time since she'd actually looked at the ring Simon had given her thirteen years ago. She'd become so used to having it on her finger, she'd taken it for granted.

Now suddenly she could remember how he'd bent down on one knee, joking that his joints creaked, as he'd presented the ring he'd designed himself because he knew emeralds were her favorite gemstone. She'd felt so happy and in love and sure of their future.

What had happened to that? What had happened to her? Was it really all ruined and lost, gone forever, just because of what they'd endured? Because no matter what Simon's reaction had been, they'd both endured it.

Maria tugged on the hem of her skirt, her eyes solemn as she gazed up at Ava, seeming to sense her teacher's disquiet.

"Ring," Ava finally said, managing to smile. "It's a very beautiful ring."

The bell rang then, thankfully, and the children trooped out. Ava was just gathering her things together when Helena came into the room.

"Was it all right?"

"I think so." Ava straightened, smiling as she tried to banish the ache that remembering Simon had caused within her. "They're new to this, but then so am I."

"You'll both learn, then," Helena answered. "Which is good. How about Friday for a drink? We can go in my car."

"That would be lovely," Ava said, and with a final goodbye she walked out of the school, waving to the children as she went.

The village was quiet in the heat of the afternoon sun, and Ava walked slowly down the winding street, past the village square with its fountain, to her grandmother's house. Her house.

She stood for a moment in front of the weathered door, the sky a bright, nearly blinding blue above the terracotta roof tiles. Slowly she walked inside.

Her heart felt full, yet in a different way than before, when all it seemed she could feel was grief and sorrow, when those emotions overwhelmed everything else.

Now, Ava thought as she stood inside this new home of hers, she felt a stirring of hope. Hope of what, she wasn't even sure. But she was tired of swimming in sorrow, drowning in grief. She didn't want to forget her daughter, but she felt, for the first time, a tiny, true flicker of desire to move on.

She spent the rest of the afternoon tidying up and working in her little garden; the cat came and stood at the edge of a flower bed, tail swishing as it watched her silently. Ava sat back on her heels and gazed back.

"You're getting used to me," she told it. "Even if you're still not sure about me. Even if you don't want to."

The cat swished its tail a few times more and then retreated haughtily back into the weeds. Ava couldn't keep from giving a little laugh as she called after it, "You don't fool me. I've got your number."

She was still smiling at the funny little interaction when she went inside to start making dinner. She'd been trying some recipes Eleni had given her and tonight was orzo with tomatoes and feta. As her meal cooked, she watched the setting sun turn the sky to flame and, with a sudden burst of determination, she reached for her phone and pressed Simon's number. It rang several times before he finally answered, sounding breathless and just a little bit harassed.

"Ava? Are you OK?"

Discomfited by how rushed he sounded, she retorted without thinking, "Yes, why wouldn't I be?"

Simon let out a tiny little sigh, but Ava knew the sound well. It was his I-need-to-be-patient sigh. "I was just worried," he answered in that oh-so-even tone. "I wasn't expecting you to call."

"Everything's fine," Ava said, and heard how brittle she sounded. *It was going all wrong already*, she thought, and that little flare of hope wavered alarmingly. How could they be arguing when they hadn't even started a conversation?

She took a deep breath. "Now that we've established that I'm fine," she said as lightly as she could, "how are you?"

"Fine."

So they were both fine. Ava closed her eyes. This was worse than their last conversation. "I just wanted to call you," she said in a rush, her eyes still squeezed shut. "To say—to say that I miss you, Simon. I wanted to say it before, but—"

"But you didn't," Simon finished when she'd trailed off rather miserably.

"No, I didn't. But I do. Miss you, that is."

Simon was silent for a long moment, long enough to make Ava wonder whether he'd regretted telling her he missed her. Maybe he'd got over it—her—already. Maybe he didn't miss her any more at all.

"Simon?" she prompted when she really couldn't stand the silence any more.

"Thank you for calling," he finally said, and he sounded regretful. "And for telling me that. But—"

But? There was a but? Ava opened her eyes, pinched the bridge of her nose. "But?" she prompted because he'd lapsed back into silence.

"But now's not a good time to talk. I'm going out and I'm running a bit late—"

And Simon was never late. "Where are you going?" Ava asked, and when Simon didn't answer she felt an icy panic drench her. Was he going out on a *date?*

"Just dinner with Julie," he finally said, and he sounded as if he were reluctant to tell her that much.

Icy panic turned to sudden, scalding jealousy. *Dinner with Julie.* They were friends, she knew that; they'd been mates in the university's sailing club before she'd joined. Even so, the very fact that Simon hadn't wanted to tell her made tears prick Ava's lids. "I see," she said quietly, and Simon didn't say anything. So clearly she did see. He wasn't jumping in and telling her it was just a friendly thing, or that Julie could wait if Ava needed to talk, or he wished she was there.

No, he was just silent. Stoic, silent Simon, giving her the message loud and clear.

He didn't miss her any more.

"Well," Ava finally said, and her voice felt as if it had to be squeezed from her throat, "maybe another time."

"Yes," Simon agreed quietly. "Maybe another time, Ava." And then he hung up before she could say goodbye.

Ava stood there for a moment, the phone still held in her hand. The silence all around her made her ears ring. So much for hope, then. So much for wanting to move past her grief, to make amends. She knew then what she'd been wanting to say, trying to say, in her own fumbling, useless way.

I miss you, Simon. I love you. I love being with you, and when I looked at my ring today, it made me realize I want another chance. I don't want to throw away everything we had together.

Too bad it seemed as if Simon already had.

She stood there another moment, a kind of comforting numbness spreading through her like Novocain. And then, again without thinking too much, she dialed another number on her phone.

"Ava?" Julie picked up on the first ring. "What's up?"

"Just felt like chatting." Ava heard her voice as if it were coming from another person, airy and light, almost careless. "Is now a good time?"

"Well…" She heard Julie fumbling with something, maybe her keys or a lipstick. "Actually, I'm just on my way out."

"Oh?" She sounded so interested, Ava thought distantly. So innocent. "Going anywhere nice?"

The slightest of pauses. "Just out with a couple of friends from work," Julie said, and then Ava's heart sank like a stone and all her airy lightness left her, so she felt both heavy and flat, and unable to speak a word. So Julie was lying about Simon. It really was a date. Something was going on between them, started, Ava supposed, by her own departure. Had Julie swooped in to comfort Simon when Ava had gone? Had her friend had a crush on her husband all along?

"Well, have fun," she said, and her voice sounded toneless. "Call me when you can."

"I will—"

Ava disconnected the call without saying goodbye, just as Simon had with her. She couldn't stand to lie any more, not with Julie, not with herself.

It's over. Your marriage is over.

In one violent movement she hurled her phone towards the huge fireplace; it bounced off the grate and lay silent and dark on the tile floor. Had she broken it? She hoped she had. She didn't want to call anyone any more: not Simon, not Julie, not even her mother, who had called several times to check in, always lightly concerned. Ava hadn't even told her about what she'd learned about Sophia or Angelika. She'd wanted to wait until she had some more definitive information, but suddenly it all seemed pointless.

Who cared what had happened to her grandmother seventy years ago? She was dead, and no doubt her sister was, as well. Who cared what had happened to anyone, anywhere, ever?

She let out a cry of despair and then whirled away towards the kitchen, ending up outside on the smooth stone stoop, her head in her hands.

She didn't know how long she sat there, the evening air cooling around her, everything in her aching. Eventually she heard the dry rustle of grass, and then felt something silky brush against her legs.

She jerked back in surprise, lifting her head to see the feral cat blinking up at her. It meowed once and then twined itself through her legs, its tail swishing against them. Amazed, near tears, Ava stroked its head, felt the fragile bones of its skull beneath her fingers.

"A feast for you tonight, I think," she said in a shaky voice, and her new friend meowed again.

CHAPTER FIFTEEN

October 1942

Three weeks after she met with Perseus, Sophia woke up to a stranger's hand pressed over her mouth. She went completely rigid, her pulse thundering in her ears, her mind blanking, as she felt another hand on her shoulder. Her sister's hand, soft and small.

"Don't scream, Sophia. It's all right."

Her eyes widened as panic raced through her veins. What on earth was going on? And how was Angelika involved?

"Promise you won't scream?" Angelika asked, her voice almost playful, as if this were a child's game. "We need your help, but you mustn't make any noise."

Her jaw bunching so hard her teeth ached, Sophia nodded, and the hand was lifted from her mouth.

She scrambled to a sitting position, swiping her tangled hair away from her face, and nearly forgot her resolution to scream when she saw Dimitrios Atrikes lounging nonchalantly on the end of her bed, hefting his rifle.

"What…" Sophia lowered her voice to a hiss. "What is he doing here? In our *bedroom*, Angelika!"

"I told you, we need your help."

Sophia turned to stare at Angelika, who was smiling at her, her eyes glinting with excitement. Mother of God, was this all just a game to her sister? Was she too young, too naïve, to understand? "My help with what?" she whispered, aiming her words at Angelika. She was determined to ignore Dimitrios, to pretend he was not sitting on the end of her bed, his insolent gaze wandering over her body, clad as she was only in a thin nightdress. How could her sister have brought this arrogant lout into their *bedroom?*

"With finding the soldiers, Sophia," Dimitrios interjected. "You know who we are talking about." His voice was a low growl, reminding Sophia of a thundercloud, and just as threatening.

Her tongue felt thick and swollen in her dry mouth. "What soldiers?" she managed and Dimitrios's face darkened.

"Don't be stupid."

"Dimitri—" Angelika began, pouting a little, and he waved a hand to silence her.

"Shut up, Angelika. Your sister is going to pretend she doesn't know she's been meeting with the republican army for weeks now, but I'm sure I can convince her to admit the truth." He smiled, and Sophia's skin crawled. What could her sister possibly see in this man? Oh, she knew he could be charming when he chose, but right now he looked ugly and menacing and mean. His breath stank of cigarettes and onions, and there was thick black dirt underneath his fingernails. He thrust his face close to hers, close enough so his beard brushed her face, and she could see the wildness in his eyes.

"You have been meeting with them, haven't you, Sophia? In the Lethikos's grove, if I'm not mistaken."

Her mind and heart raced and she could not think what to say. She had no idea what to do; she wished Perseus had given her instructions about what to do if someone confronted her. Dimitrios wasn't a Nazi or a blackshirt, but he was, in his own way, just as dangerous. More so, because he clearly knew what she'd been doing and he was in her bedroom, his sneering face thrust up close to hers, while the Nazis and Italians were kilometers away, with no idea of who she even was. Angelika stood at the end of the bed, her hands fluttering at her sides as a new, unwelcome uncertainty shadowed her childish face. Was she now beginning to realize the dangers?

"I have been meeting with them," Sophia finally said, and was thankful that her voice didn't tremble. "But it's been weeks since I've seen anyone. And as for the soldiers—I know less than you do. They are meant to arrive, but when or where no one has seen fit to tell me."

"Then I'll tell you," Dimitrios answered with a smile that looked and felt more like a leer. "They arrive tonight, by parachute, and you and I are going to take them to Zervas."

For a second Sophia's vision swam. She felt Dimitrios's fingers dig hard into her arm. "Is that understood, Sophia?"

"Why do you need me?" she whispered, trying not to wince at the pain of his hand heavy on her arm.

"Because you are my contact with Zervas, and Velouchiotis will thank me if I find these soldiers and bring them all together."

"You think I know the head of the republican army? I spoke with one man, and he never even gave me his name—"

"Even so. You're part of them. They'll recognize you."

"No, they won't—"

"Enough." He shook her arm, hard enough for her to gasp aloud. Angelika nibbled her lip in anxiety.

"Dimitrios, be gentle," she said, her voice sounding small, and he brushed her away as if she were no more than an annoying fly.

"Gentle? We are talking about a war, Angelika, although you've never bothered your head about it, have you? Never mind. You can stay here. Sophia comes with me."

"But where are you going? I thought you just wanted to ask her some questions. You didn't tell me—"

"She's coming with me to find these men," Dimitrios said grimly, his hand still gripping Sophia's arm. "And then leading us to Zervas."

"I don't know where Zervas is," Sophia cried, her voice rising in her panic. She couldn't go with Dimitrios. The thought of struggling through the forest on such a cold, dark night with this violent and ignorant man made everything inside her lurch with terror. Her stomach heaved and for a second she thought she might vomit.

"You'll find him," Dimitrios answered. "Or he'll find you. Don't you think they are watching you, Sophia? Or are you so stupid you don't realize even that?"

"Dimitrios—" Angelika tried again, and once more he waved her away, impatient, dismissive.

"Shut up, Angelika."

"If they're watching me, they're watching you," Sophia told him, and he just laughed.

"Oh, yes, but not tonight. Tonight they are looking for the soldiers who have fallen from the sky."

"If that's so, why didn't they contact me, then?" she challenged, reckless now with fear.

Dimitrios just shrugged. "No time. We only just heard. And now we go." He jerked her none too gently to her feet. "Dress warmly."

"This is madness," Sophia tried one last time. "I cannot help you, Dimitrios—"

He moved so quickly she didn't even see the back of his hand, just felt it hard against her cheek, tasted the metallic tang of blood on her tongue. Angelika let out a little shriek of dismay.

"Sophia!" she cried, starting forward, and Dimitrios pushed her back, hard enough so she stumbled as her eyes filled with tears.

"Get dressed," he said flatly, one hand resting on the rusty old rifle he had boasted about in the coffeehouse, and without another word Sophia reached for her dress and pulled it over her nightgown. She would need all the layers she could find on a cold night such as this.

She wore her oldest dress and thickest wool stockings, with two shawls wrapped around her. It was cold outside, and would be colder, she suspected, wherever they were going, whether mountain or forest. And, she realized bleakly, she had no idea how long she would be gone.

She turned to Angelika, who was gazing at her in silent misery. "Tell Father I'm safe," she said quietly and her sister wrung her hands.

"Oh, Sophia, I'm sorry," she exclaimed. "I didn't realize… oh, what shall I tell Father?"

For a moment, no more, Sophia wanted to slap her sister just as Dimitrios had slapped her. How could Angelika have been so stupid, to trust a man like this? She knew it wasn't really her sister's fault that she was heading into the forest with a man who was no better than a Nazi, hitting women as he did, threatening them with the rifle strapped across his chest, and yet for a bitter moment she was tempted to blame her.

"Tell him you don't know anything," she said with a despondent shrug.

"You'll think of something, 'Lika," Dimitrios said, patting the girl's cheek, and Sophia seethed as Angelika jerked away, her eyes flashing. How dare he touch her that way! Angelika, at least, did not respond to it the way she once might have. Perhaps her sister was finally gaining some sense.

Dimitrios turned to Sophia with a grim smile. "Let's go," he said, and prodding her in the small of her back, he urged her forward, down the rickety stairs, and out into the night.

CHAPTER SIXTEEN

Now

It was time, Ava decided grimly, to start living. To say yes to everything. She'd said yes to a drink with Helena in town that weekend, and yes to a shy and hesitant invitation to dinner with Andreas—no mention of Kalista—the following night. *Yes,* Ava thought defiantly. *Yes, I will move on, just as Simon so obviously is.*

She didn't want to be bitter; hadn't she been bitter long enough, in her grief? And yet she knew she was. She felt those sour seeds take root in the soil of her soul; it was as crumbly and rock-strewn as that on these ancient hills. Yes, she was bitter, more bitter than she'd ever been before. She forced it down when she went to meet Helena; their friendship was fragile and new and she wanted to forget her misery, not pour it out on someone else.

By half past five on Friday night Helena and Ava were settled at a corner table in one of Lamia's cheerful tavernas; a trio of musicians in the corner playing a lively tune on unfamiliar yet interesting-looking instruments.

Ava plucked an olive from the dish in the center of the table as Helena gave her a frankly appraising look. "So it is not very often we have English people move to a place like Iousidous. How are you finding it, really?"

"Really?" Ava repeated, swallowing. "It's been good to have a change." She paused, wanting to reveal more yet afraid to at the same time. "I needed a change." Helena nodded, accepting, and

Ava was glad she chose not to press. She didn't know whether she wanted to talk about the past or forget it for a night. A bit of both, she supposed.

"From what Eleni has told me," she asked Helena, "it's uncommon for young people to stay in Iousidous. Why have you chosen to live there?"

Helena grinned. "Well, not for the men I'll meet! Most of them are fifty years older than I am." She shrugged and reached for her drink. "I loved living in Iousidous as a child. I love how simple it is, and the…" She swept an arm out, impatient with her faltering English. "The sense of time—"

"And tradition?" Ava filled in, and Helena nodded.

"Yes. Sometimes change is good; sometimes it is not." She smiled wryly. "But I am glad you are here. It is good to spend time with a woman my own age. Have you found enough to keep you busy?"

"Yes, I think so." Ava thought of her little garden, the work on the house, her one English lesson at the school, her lunch with Andreas and Kalista, and her time with Eleni. It wasn't a life exactly, but perhaps the beginning of one. "I'm giving a local teenager some English lessons," she said, mostly just to make it seem as if she were more productive than she actually was. Helena seemed so confident, so competent. A bit like Simon that way. "Her name is Kalista Lethikos. Do you know her?"

Ava wasn't sure if she'd imagined the flash of emotion across Helena's face. She must have, for the other woman smiled easily and took an olive from the dish. "Oh, yes, I know the Lethikos family. Andreas and I were friends when we were children." She popped the olive in her mouth and gestured to a nearby waiter. "Now let's order some food. A day of teaching makes me hungry."

Ava nodded, yet she couldn't shake the feeling that Helena had just deliberately changed the subject.

*

The next night Ava drove to the Lethikos property for dinner with Andreas. As she made her way up the winding road, olive trees on either side, she thought back to what Andreas had said about the Greek Resistance using the grove to shelter the SOE agents before they blew up that viaduct. She wondered if there was any truth to the story.

The night was so peaceful, the first stars just starting to come out in an indigo sky, the only sound the rustle of the breeze through the trees, that it was hard to imagine this had once been a place of intrigue and danger, terror and violence.

How had her grandmother navigated through all of it? And when—and why—had she gone?

"Ava, welcome." Andreas had opened the front door and stood on the veranda, smiling. He wore a white linen shirt that was open at the throat and a pair of faded chinos, and Ava had to admit he looked attractive, the light color of his clothes setting off his olive skin and curly dark hair. She smoothed the swishy skirt in lilac cotton she'd finally decided to wear after changing outfits three times. She'd been worried about making it seem as if she were dressing up and yet she'd also wanted to make at least a little effort.

Now, as she came up the veranda stairs and Andreas placed his hand on the small of her back, she felt a jolt of alarm. This felt so date-like, so strange. She hadn't had a date, a first date, in over fifteen years. And no matter what she'd told herself about moving on, just being in a dimly lit room with Andreas as he handed her a glass of red wine felt like a betrayal.

Simon had gone out for dinner with Julie, she reminded herself. And Julie had lied about it. There was no way she should be feeling guilty now.

She took a sip of wine, defiance and dread both roiling within her. Not a great way to start the evening. "So, how are things?" she asked, her voice coming out a bit too loud, a bit too bright. "Where's Kalista?"

"Things are good. And Kalista is staying with a friend tonight."

They were completely alone? Ava's throat dried and she saw Andreas's cheeks redden slightly. "Were you expecting to practice English with her tonight?" he asked with an awkward little laugh. "I am sorry. I should have said. You can practice with me instead."

And now Ava was the one blushing, because even though she was quite sure Andreas didn't mean it like that, his words felt full of innuendo. Was the whole evening going to be this awkward and full of misunderstanding?

"Come into the dining room," he said, his voice little more than a mutter. Clearly he was as embarrassed as she was. "The food is already prepared."

The table in the dining room was laid with a snowy linen cloth, the porcelain and crystal glinting underneath the candlelight. Ava tried to swallow past the dryness in her throat. There could be no question now that this was a date.

And why shouldn't it be a date? she asked herself recklessly. She was separated, probably on her way to a divorce. The divorce papers might even be winging their way towards her already. The thought felt like a punch to the gut, but with effort she shrugged it off. She would enjoy herself tonight. She *would.*

"Come. Sit." Andreas pulled out a chair and Ava sat down, tensing slightly as he rested his hands on her shoulders for just a few brief seconds. His hands were warm, dry, the weight of them strangely comforting, and yet despite all that she still felt as if she were strung tight enough to snap. Break.

And Andreas didn't seem much better, she observed as he sat down across from her and began to serve out the food. Lines of tension bracketed his mouth and he concentrated just a little too much on simple things: pouring water, dishing out the salad appetizer.

"This is delicious," Ava said as she speared a cucumber. "Do you like to cook?" Her voice still sounded too high, too bright, too much.

Andreas looked up, smiling wryly. "What Greek male cooks? But since Althea died, yes. I have learned." He shrugged, a simple twist of his powerful shoulders. "I cannot say if I like it, though. What about you?"

"Do I like to cook? Sometimes." As with everything else, she and Simon had approached kitchen duty in two entirely different ways. She liked to dream up big meals: Chinese stir-fries accompanied by chopsticks and fortune cookies, Indian curries with homemade *naan* bread and onion *bhajis*, all of it without consulting a cookbook much. Simon was, of course, stolid when it came to cooking. He never deviated from a recipe, always measured things with mathematical precision. And, Ava had to acknowledge, he had more steady successes than she did with her madcap, wholehearted commitment to the endeavor.

"You are remembering something," Andreas said quietly, and she looked up to see him smiling at her in a kind of wry, understanding sorrow.

"Sorry. Yes, I was." She took a breath, made herself continue. "Just thinking about my husband and me, and how different we are. Were."

"How were you different?"

She shrugged, not really wanting to talk about Simon, and especially not with Andreas. "In all sorts of ways."

Andreas nodded, seeming to sense her reluctance to speak. "And you said you are separated?"

Ava nodded, her throat tightening.

"But you still love him?" he queried gently, and her throat tightened further so she could barely get the words out.

"I don't know." But she did know. She did love Simon, and she didn't want to, because she was wrenchingly certain that he was well on his way to no longer loving her. She wasn't about to say any of that to Andreas.

In any case he just nodded again, and then held out the little dish of olives swimming in seasoned oil. Ava took one, grateful that the intense conversation had stopped for a moment at least.

Things relaxed a bit between them after that, enough for Ava to sit back and feel the tension that had been tightening her body ease. She drank another glass of wine with the *moussaka* Andreas had made, and felt a little more of that tension slip away.

It was far more pleasant to chat about Andreas's work, and about her attempts at gardening, than the messy, painful past. Although perhaps the past always came round again, because as they were finishing the last of the wine along with sticky-sweet *baklava*, Andreas asked about her grandmother.

"Have you discovered anything more about her?"

"Not really. Only that she had a sister, Angelika. She never mentioned her to me, and as far as I know, my mother doesn't know about her, either." Which reminded Ava she needed to call her mother and tell her everything she'd learned, as well as deal with her mother's loving concern about how she was coping.

Andreas frowned. "Perhaps something happened to her? During the war?"

"Perhaps," Ava allowed. She didn't like to think of something terrible happening to Angelika, the unknown butterfly, although why it should matter, she wasn't sure. She hadn't even known the woman existed until a few days ago, and she'd most likely died—probably not recently. "I've been sitting in on some interviews of people who were here during the war," she told Andreas. "Helena, the schoolteacher in Iousidous, is trying to put together an oral history. Do you know her?"

Andreas's expression stilled for one tiny second before he smiled and nodded. "Yes, everyone knows everyone around here."

"So I'm realizing." Ava gestured to their plates. "Let me help you wash up."

"That is not necessary—"

"I'd feel guilty otherwise. If Greek men don't cook, I doubt they wash up either." She smiled, relaxed enough to have injected a faintly flirtatious note into her voice and not care. "Is that something else you've had to learn?"

"So it is." Andreas rose from the table and began stacking plates. "But I will accept your help."

They worked in companionable silence, taking all of the dishes to the kitchen, and then Ava scraped the dishes while Andreas loaded the dishwasher. With each dish she found herself moving more slowly, unwilling to let the evening end. It was so familiar, to clean up after a meal with a man, the night dark and silent outside, the kitchen a small oasis of warmth and light. Even though they barely spoke, she enjoyed the company, the lack of loneliness.

"This was lovely, thank you," she said as she hung a damp tea towel to dry on the oven's rail.

"You must come again."

"Yes…" She wasn't quite ready to commit to another evening like this one, enjoyable as it had been. Now that she was about to leave, the awkwardness had returned, and she felt the strain of her smile as she went to collect her things. Andreas followed her, his hands in the pockets of his chinos, and Ava was very aware of his presence, the size and strength and sheer maleness of him, so different from Simon's whippet leanness, gained from years of running and sailing.

"So…" Andreas stood on the veranda, holding the door open, so light spilled out onto the weathered boards, and Ava smiled again as she jangled her keys.

"Thank you for coming, Ava." He stepped closer, the door swinging shut behind him, his gaze steady on her. Ava didn't move; standing there, she realized she'd known this would happen, and now that it was here, she found she was almost anticipating it. How long since she'd been touched? Kissed? She couldn't even remember the last time she and Simon had touched each other with affection, much less desire.

He smiled slightly as he took another step towards her, and Ava waited, feeling the hard thud of her heart, her keys biting into her palm, uncertainty and anticipation waging war within her.

Andreas lifted his hands and slid them along her jawbone, his fingers stealing up her skull so he was cradling her face. Ava waited, her heart still beating hard, her lips slightly parted.

"Ava…" Andreas whispered, and he took her silence as assent, which it was, as he lowered his head and kissed her.

The first brush of his lips against hers was a shock, because they didn't feel like Simon's lips, cool and firm. They didn't taste like Simon, like minty toothpaste and tea; Simon never drank coffee. Andreas's lips were warm and soft and rather fleshy, and he tasted of wine and honey.

It should have been pleasant, but it wasn't. Instead Ava had to fight the deep-seated and instinctive urge to jerk away, to wipe her mouth. She remained still, and that only with effort, and after a moment Andreas pulled away, a rueful smile on his face.

"You are the first woman I've kissed since my wife."

"Andreas—" Ava didn't say anything else, because she didn't know what to say.

"It is too soon, I know," Andreas said quietly. "For both of us." He cupped her cheek with his palm, then stepped away. "Goodnight, Ava."

"Goodnight," she whispered, and then she hurried to her car, because she had a sudden, inexplicable urge to burst into tears.

She kept it together all the way back to Iousidous and into her cottage, checking her phone and then her computer: no messages or emails.

She sat on her sofa and rested her head in her hands and wished, quite desperately, that things were different. She just didn't know how to make them be so.

CHAPTER SEVENTEEN

October 1942

Sophia stumbled out of the house, Dimitrios's hand hard on her back. The cold air felt as sharp as a knife, cutting right through her. She pulled her shawl more tightly around her and gave Dimitrios what she hoped was a challenging look. She prayed he wouldn't see how she trembled, and not from the cold.

"So where do we go from here?"

"We look for the drop."

"The drop?"

"Where the SOE agents parachuted," Dimitrios answered impatiently.

"The SOE agents?"

"Do you not know anything?" He spoke sharply, yet she still had the sense he was enjoying her ignorance. "Soldiers, *Englezoi.*"

English. They were looking for Englishmen. Perseus really hadn't told her anything beyond the parachute drop.

She straightened, throwing her shoulders back. "And where are we meant to look for this—this drop?"

"We are looking for where they will go," Dimitrios corrected her, even though he'd just told her they were looking for where they dropped. Sophia knew better than to argue. "And I suppose you will now ask where they will go," he said, his mouth twisted into a sneer even though his eyes glinted. He really was enjoying this. Sophia didn't answer, even though she knew she risked

Dimitrios's ire. He just laughed, the sound harsh in the still darkness of the night. "We will go to the mountains, of course," he said. "It is the one place the Nazis don't go."

That was true enough, Sophia supposed. Mount Oeta loomed above the village, dark against a darker sky. Its densely forested peaks and freezing temperatures would keep any sane soldier from attempting to venture upon it. Even though it was only October, the mountainside was covered with snow. Sophia shivered just at the thought of following Dimitrios into that icy wilderness.

"Let's go," he said, and with another push in the small of Sophia's back he sent her stumbling towards the path at the end of their scrubby yard, the path that trailed to nothing amidst the dense pines.

It was a long awful night. After the first hour Sophia forgot the bite of cold in the mountain air and the gnawing of her fear; all she was conscious of was how tired she was, and how much her body ached. Dimitrios, thankfully, did not talk much; he was too concerned with finding these soldiers. *SOE agents*, he'd said, although Sophia did not know what that meant.

Her feet grew numb as they climbed higher up the mountainside, and the snow seeped into her boots. Her face and hands stung from the cold wind that blew down from the top of Mount Oeta. She recalled from stories that the demigod Herakles was meant to have died on the top of the mountain, having made a funeral pyre of trees. She hoped she did not share a similar fate.

Occasionally Dimitrios would stop and look around, as if searching for something, although Sophia knew not what. She didn't ask; they hadn't spoken in hours. *Were there men hiding in these mountains*, Sophia wondered. *The men Perseus was looking for? And what had happened to Perseus?* It seemed a terrible irony that she'd been so afraid of working for him, when all along something far more frightening was in store for her.

A pale gray dawn was lightening the sky when Dimitrios stopped suddenly, the trees dark and dense around them, so that

Sophia nearly bumped into his back. "Hush," he said, presumptuously, for she hadn't spoken.

Sophia waited, wondering if the thud of her heart was audible. *What had Dimitrios heard? Were there soldiers about? Nazis?* She heard the sweet, high trill of a bird, one she didn't recognize, and nodding in satisfaction, Dimitrios cut through the forest. Sophia hurried after him, the snow past her boots now, her body aching with exhaustion.

Just a few minutes later they came into a clearing; four men were crouched on their haunches on the ground, a small smoking fire in front of them. Sophia stared in surprise. So these four men with their plain, rough clothing and unshaven faces were the men they'd been looking for? The *Englezoi*? The sound of the bird must have been a signal, she realized, feeling completely out of her element. Perseus hadn't told her of signals; even more telling, she hadn't asked. She'd never even thought of such things.

One man straightened and strode towards Dimitrios. He spoke Greek, but he was the only one who looked as if he did. Dimitrios answered back in a low voice; Sophia couldn't hear what either of them was saying. She turned her gaze back to the three men around the fire; one of them had clearly hurt his wrist and was attempting to bind it with his good hand without much success.

Sophia watched him for a moment before she hesitantly approached him. In normal circumstances she would have never even thought of speaking to or even standing next to a man, any man, and certainly not a strange one. Yet these were not normal circumstances, and he clearly needed help.

He glanced up at her as she came closer, his brown eyes friendly, his face creased into a smile. Sophia smiled back, uncertainly, because this all felt so strange and in any case there seemed very little to smile about. She pointed to his injured hand

and then to herself. He clearly got her message for he chuckled ruefully and stretched his arm out.

"You think you can do a better job of it than me? Frankly, I think you're right."

Sophia didn't understand what he said, but she thought she took his meaning, for he held the bandage out and she bent to bind it more securely around his wrist, blushing as she did, for she'd never touched a man's skin like this before. His arm was brown and rough with dark hair. He winced and she mumbled an apology, blushing all the more. In return he smiled and patted her hand. Her skin tingled from where he'd touched her with his cold, bare fingers.

"Sorry, I'm a bit grubby," he said and then tried in Greek, "*Signomi*."

Surprised, Sophia stammered, "*Einai entaxei*." It's all right.

The man grinned and said in hesitant Greek, "I'm not very good, am I?"

Too discomfited by the simple banter to answer, she kept her head lowered as she wound the bandage around his wrist; the skin was red, the arm swollen, although not too badly.

"*Pos se lene?*" he asked, and she looked up warily. He pointed to himself. "Alex."

She swallowed dryly. "Sophia."

"Hello, Sophia. *Kalimera*." Good morning. He sounded like a schoolboy sounding out words, but Sophia appreciated the effort. She knew so little English, nothing more than a handful of words. And she saw that it was morning; a gray dawn had given way to sunshine, the sky pale blue above them.

The man who had been conversing with Dimitrios strode back to the fire and issued instructions to another man, who immediately dumped a bucket of snow on the flames. Then the men, save Alex, began to gather their things.

Sophia patted Alex's wrist and stood up. "Is—good?" she asked, as hesitant in her English as he had been in his Greek. He smiled at her, his straight white teeth dazzling her for a second.

"Is excellent," he answered. "Thank you very much. *Efharisto*." He stood up and began, rather clumsily, with his one good arm, to gather his things.

Sophia turned to Dimitrios, who was watching the proceedings with a rather satisfied smile, as if he had arranged everything. "Are we going back now?" she asked him, and heard the hope in her voice. Dimitrios saw it too, for he smirked and shook his head.

"Going back? What good would that do? No, we will go with the men. We will take them to the Major."

"The Major…?" Sophia stared at him in horror. "Major Velouchiotis?" she said in a whisper, and Dimitrios confirmed this with a terse nod.

"But—but I thought you wanted to take them to Zervas! To EDES!" The thought of heading into Aris Velouchiotis's camp was terrifying. He shot boys who hid a loaf of bread. What might he do to a group of British soldiers, men he could very well condemn as spies if he felt like it? And what of the Greeks who brought them? Sophia was under no illusion that Dimitrios Atrikes rated highly with the head of the communist resistance.

"After we see Velouchiotis, we will go to Zervas. The two groups are meant to work together."

"Work together?" Sophia thought of how Perseus had sneered about the rabble of communists. They were seen as the enemy as much as a blackshirt or a Nazi. *How in the name of God were they all meant to cooperate?* "That's impossible."

"And you know so much?" Dimitrios scoffed. His hand twitched by his side, and Sophia took a step backwards. She did not want to be slapped again, and she had a sense that it was only the presence of the *Englezoi* soldiers that kept Dimitrios from venting his frustration on her. This wasn't, she suspected, going according to his own foolish plan.

"I know the groups do not wish to work together," she answered in a low voice. "Is this a plan of the English? Can't you tell them otherwise?"

"There is more going on here than you or I know," Dimitrios snapped. "Now I've had enough of your woman's chatter. Make yourself useful and stop whimpering." He pushed roughly past her, and Sophia swallowed hard. Her fatigue had vanished, replaced by a clammy terror.

The man named Alex placed a hand on her shoulder. "All right?" he asked quietly, and Sophia understood that at least. She stared at him with a growing sense of despair, for she did not have the words—or the courage—to explain how she wasn't all right… and neither was he.

CHAPTER EIGHTEEN

Now

"Come in, come in."

Although her face was wreathed in smiles as she beckoned Ava into her home, Eleni looked worried. Ava noticed the dark circles under her eyes, the furrow between her brows, and wondered at their source. "How is the teaching?" Eleni asked. She'd invited Ava over for dinner, and the house was full of the spicy scent of a lamb stew. Ava perched on one of the chairs in the tiny kitchen while Eleni bustled around. Already the little house with its air of comfortable shabbiness felt familiar and loved, and the warmth of it banished the anxiety that had been eating away at Ava since her phone call with Simon, and that near-disastrous date with Andreas three days ago.

"Good… I think. It's been fun, anyway." She'd been to the school once more so far, and had progressed from her first day of pointing and miming to a slightly more advanced vocabulary drill. "The children seem to enjoy it."

"You are good with them, I'm sure."

"I miss teaching," Ava admitted. "It's good to be back in a classroom."

"You taught art before?" Eleni queried, and Ava nodded.

"They're cutting positions left and right, though. I don't think I could get a job teaching art again, at least not at the primary level."

Eleni arched an eyebrow. "You think of returning?"

"No—not yet," Ava said hastily. She felt a sudden surge of confusion, as if she'd missed the last step in a staircase. She wasn't thinking of returning; she'd been here only a few weeks. And yet the ache of loneliness, of missing Simon, had intensified, so she felt as if she had an emptiness inside her. Yet returning to England wouldn't do anything about that. *Would it?*

"Ah, well." Eleni shrugged. "I wondered." She set a crusty loaf of bread on the table and Ava noticed there were only two places set.

"Will your mother be joining us?"

Eleni shook her head, and the furrow between her brows deepened. "No, she is sleeping. She has not been well."

Ava felt a little lurch of alarm. "I'm sorry to hear that."

Eleni nodded and began to ladle out the stew. "She is nearly one hundred years old, of course her health is bound to fail. Every day with her is a blessing." She pursed her lips, frowning, and Ava waited, sensing that Eleni had more to say. "She has seemed so distracted lately," Eleni continued after a moment. "As though something is distressing her, and she won't tell me what it is."

Once again Ava thought of Parthenope's desperate apology. Had her arrival in Iousidous, her likeness to her grandmother, brought up painful memories for the older woman? "How long has she been like that?" she asked.

"A few weeks. Since—" Eleni stopped abruptly, but it was easy to guess what the older woman was reluctant to say.

"Since I arrived?" Ava asked quietly. "She was distressed to see me, I remember. Because I look like my grandmother."

Eleni nodded slowly. "Yes, although she won't speak of it at all."

"Maybe if you asked her—"

"No." Eleni spoke with the same firm finality as before. "I do not wish to distress her further. The past is finished."

"But maybe she needs to talk about it, whatever it is," Ava pressed, trying to keep her voice gentle. "Maybe talking about it would help her with her distress."

Eleni stared at her for a moment, the furrow deep between her brows, and for a moment Ava thought she might agree. Then she shook her head resolutely. "No. It's better to forget."

But Parthenope clearly couldn't forget, Ava thought, and for a moment she wondered if it was Eleni, rather than her mother, who did not want to speak about the past. *But what on earth could Eleni possibly be afraid of? She hadn't even been born then.*

"Have you learned anything of your grandmother?" Eleni asked, and it felt like a peace offering. Ava accepted it as such and she began to tell Eleni about the interview with Angelos Mallos as they started to eat.

"He said she had a sister, a sister like a butterfly."

"A butterfly?"

"Yes, I suppose that means she was a bit scatty—"

"I don't know this word 'scatty.'"

Ava gave a little laugh. "Lazy. Easily distracted—"

Eleni nodded, pursing her lips. "Or he could have meant something else. Angelos taught literature before he retired. Do you remember when I told you about Zorba?"

Ava's throat tightened. "The man who danced."

"Yes." For a moment Eleni's voice softened with compassion. "There is something else in that book. In one part Zorba talks about a butterfly. He found a cocoon on a leaf and he breathed on it to make the butterfly come out, but of course it came out too soon, and its wings were too wet and it died. Zorba realized he should not have rushed it, and he learned patience." Eleni paused, lost in thought. "I wonder if your grandmother's sister was a bit like that—the war breathed on her, and she was forced to grow up too soon." She shook her head sorrowfully. "Who knows what the young men and women of that time could have been, if not for the war."

And Ava knew she was not thinking only of Sophia's sister, but of her own mother. What had happened to Parthenope back then to make tears course down her cheeks over seventy years later? Whatever it was, Eleni didn't seem to want to find out.

"But enough of that," Eleni said briskly. "Let us talk of the future. Have you heard from that husband of yours?"

"Simon?" Ava blurted, startled, and Eleni glanced at her curiously.

"Is that his name?"

"Yes."

"It is not good for you to be so far apart."

Although Eleni spoke gently, her words still stung. "It's... it's not like that," Ava said quietly. "I told you before, we're separated. We're... I suppose it's likely we'll get a divorce now." Why did saying that aloud hurt her so much? It felt as if she were being sawn in half.

"It is likely," Eleni returned, "if you remain here and he is there."

Ava flushed and put down her fork. "If you think we could just work it out if we were together, that's not possible. That's why I came here in the first place. I needed a change, and it was clear that we were not working it out when we were together. It just made things worse. And in any case, I think Simon's glad to be shot of me. He seems to have moved on, at any rate."

Eleni frowned. "Moved on?"

"He's seeing my best friend. I think they're just friends... at least I hope they are. But they're spending time together."

Eleni looked startled, but then she pressed her lips together, her expression seeming to harden. "He wouldn't if you were there."

"How can you say that!" Ava exclaimed. She rose from the table, her whole body trembling. "You know nothing—nothing about it! I know you've been kind, welcoming me into your home, but..." She broke off, her voice choking, and Eleni leaned over to lay a placating hand on her arm.

"Ava, I'm sorry. I should not have spoken so. But I can see how unhappy you are, and I wish for you and your husband to—what is the word?"

"Reconcile," Ava filled in dully. Her rage, like a flash flood, had come and gone in a matter of seconds. Now she just felt drained. She sat back down and picked up her fork, toying with her stew, for her appetite had vanished.

"Reconcile," Eleni repeated quietly. "But now you say it is not possible?"

Ava didn't answer for a moment. Everything in her wanted to deny what she'd just told Eleni, to insist that it was possible—and yet how? She closed her eyes. "I don't think so."

Eleni cocked her head, her eyes warm now with compassion. "Why not?"

Now that her anger had gone, Ava found she could talk about it. She almost wanted to. She hadn't really talked about her marriage problems with anyone, and there was so much kindness in Eleni's face now that Ava suddenly found herself practically tripping over her words to explain. "I'd known Simon wasn't very expressive, of course I had. But we'd been trying to have a baby for years and when I finally fell pregnant..." She bit her lip, the memories flooding through her. "I was seven months along and I hadn't felt any movement for a day or two, so I went in for a scan. Even then I wasn't really worried." She pressed the heel of her hand against her eyes. "I was so stupid. Simon used to tease me about how I panicked about the most pointless things. But when I should have panicked, I didn't. I felt like something that terrible couldn't happen to me." She dropped her hand, gazed dully at Eleni. "When I had the scan, there was no heartbeat. No explanation why the baby—my daughter—had died. Just one of those things." She offered Eleni an awful, twisted smile. "That's what the technician said. 'Just one of those things.' As if it was a rainy day or a long bus queue." She drew a shuddering breath. The eerie stillness on the scan's screen still haunted her dreams, caused her to wake with her face wet with tears. "It was devastating. After trying for so long and then to lose it… lose it all…"

Eleni covered Ava's hand with her own. "I am so sorry."

Ava nodded jerkily. "Anyway, afterwards I was a wreck. And Simon just seemed to soldier on. It was like he didn't even care. He didn't want to talk about what happened. He didn't even hold her when she was born." Ava heard the accusation ringing in her voice. "He just asked them to take her away, like she was so much rubbish." Tears stung her eyes, and she felt the kind of great, choking sobs she hadn't given into in months tug at her chest. She gulped down a breath and blinked hard.

"That must have been very painful," Eleni said quietly. "But perhaps he was not comfortable telling you how he felt. Men are like that."

"I know, and I know Simon, and he's never been emotional, but I needed more from him than he was willing to give. I wanted to talk about it, but he just shut down when I tried. Then he seemed impatient, as if he expected I should be over it all just weeks afterwards and was annoyed that I wasn't. That hurt as much as anything else. I just got more and more depressed, and he got more and more angry. It was a terrible cycle, and the only way I knew of breaking it was to leave." Ava swallowed down the sobs, forced herself to continue. "My whole life started falling apart. I couldn't keep up with work—I was an art teacher, but with the proposed budget cuts my job was scrapped anyway. When I learned about this place, I thought it seemed like the best solution. Time apart to really think about what we wanted out of life."

"And do you think time apart will draw you close together again?"

"Not any more." Ava gave a twisted smile. "Even though that's what I still want. I think." She thought of that painful conversation when she'd asked Simon for a separation. *I think it's best... for a little while... we don't seem to be getting on, do we?*

Simon had stared at her for a long silent moment before he'd given an indifferent little shrug. "If that's what you want," he'd said, and Ava had wanted to scream that of course it wasn't, but she was running out of options. Out of hope.

Eleni patted Ava's hand. "Why don't you ask him to visit you here?"

"I think he's moved on, Eleni."

"You don't know that."

"He went on a date with my best friend." Yet even as she snapped out the words, she questioned them. Simon hadn't actually said it was a date, and Julie might not have told her simply because she didn't want to make her upset, as she had been before. And she had, more or less, gone on a date with Andreas...

As if she could sense the nature of Ava's thoughts, Eleni spoke again, patting her hand. "Ask him, Ava," Eleni advised. "Ask him to visit. Don't throw it all away simply because of disappointment. Everyone will disappoint you at some time or another. It is not the same as betrayal."

Even, Ava thought sadly, if it felt the same.

CHAPTER NINETEEN

October 1942

The soldiers trudged silently through the woods as day broke all around them with a chorus of birdsong and pale shafts of sunlight filtering through the trees. Dimitrios and the one Greek SOE agent, whose name Sophia knew now was Marinos, walked ahead, sometimes slowing to confer quietly between themselves. Numb with fatigue, Sophia could barely manage to put one foot in front of another. She was even too tired to feel the fear that lurked in the corners of her heart and the fringes of her mind, knowing they were walking right into a nest of communist agitators, including the volatile Velouchiotis himself.

After half an hour of walking, the soldier called Alex fell into step beside her. Sophia snuck a sideways glance at him, noticing again his friendly eyes and ruddy complexion. He seemed so... ordinary, and yet so foreign at the same time. She felt very conscious of his close presence, and her heart raced. She looked away again.

"What brought you into all this?" he asked in slow, hesitant Greek. She was startled by it, and he gave her a cheeky grin. "I do know a little of your language."

His pronunciation, she thought, was awful. Still Sophia smiled and nodded her thanks.

"So? How did you come to be here?"

She shrugged. She could hardly explain that she'd had no choice. "We must do what we can," she finally said, and Alex nodded.

"My thoughts exactly."

She gazed at him, and saw that he was smiling, whistling tunelessly under his breath. Anyone would have thought he was going for a stroll around the village square rather than tramping through enemy-occupied forest, on his way to a mission that could mean the end of his life. "Are you scared?" she whispered in Greek, and Alex turned to smile at her, his eyes crinkling at the corners.

"Yes, very much so." He switched to English then, speaking slowly in the hopes that she would understand. "But I'm used to it. I'm an explosives engineer."

Sophia shook her head, the words meaningless.

Alex grinned again. "I make the bombs."

"Bombs?"

His eyes twinkling, he leaned closer and whispered so his breath tickled her ear, "Boom!"

Sophia clapped a hand to her mouth as she gazed back at him. She understood that. If she took Alex's meaning, not only was he at risk of being found and killed by the Nazis, but his very profession could end his life most horribly. Another thought slid into her mind.

Boom.

They were going to blow something up. That was why the men were here, that was why they had come. *What could it be? What was their target?*

She glanced back at Alex; he was still smiling, still whistling under his breath. He saw her looking at him and winked, making Sophia blush and quickly look away. No man had ever been so forward with her. In her village, she would have been insulted and shamed, yet here she felt an unfamiliar and wary thrill, a surprising frisson of pleasure.

"Don't worry," he said in a low, laughing voice, switching back to Greek again. "I haven't blown anyone up yet."

Sophia glanced back, smiling shyly, his cheer and humor impossible to ignore. She felt her own spirits lift. Some would think him a fool for not being more cautious, more afraid.

And yet wasn't this a kind of courage? It was so far from what Sophia felt she was capable of herself but realizing that Alex must know what he was facing and yet he still chose to smile and joke made her heart swell with a surprised admiration.

The man was no fool.

They walked for most of the day, through rugged hills and dense pines, deeper into the mountains where Velouchiotis made his camp. Still aching with fatigue and numb with cold, Sophia could not keep the fear that had been crouching in the corners of her heart from threatening to overwhelm her completely as they drew closer to their destination. She had no idea what lay ahead; she knew only that Perseus had not warned her about this. She wondered if he'd even known about it.

It happened suddenly. One minute they were walking slowly, steadily forward, the next they were surrounded. The men melted from the trees, emerging from the shadows, rifles held in their hands. Rifles, Sophia saw, that were pointed at the SOE agents. At her.

Everyone stopped, and when one of the guerrillas barked for them to put their hands in the air, no one hesitated, not even Dimitrios. Sophia's heart started to thud with hard, heavy beats.

"We come in peace," Dimitrios said. He sounded both irritated and afraid, and Sophia silently prayed that he would show more sense than swagger for once. "Velouchiotis is expecting us."

"Major Velouchiotis to you, boy," one of the guerrillas sneered, and Sophia closed her eyes. God help them all if they had to entrust their lives to Dimitrios Atrikes.

"Major Velouchiotis," Dimitrios said, a bit sulkily. "He is expecting us. He knows of these men. They come to help."

"We'll see what he knows," the leader of the group said, and with a brusque nod at his men, they started forward. Sophia felt the cold, hard butt of a gun in the small of her back, and she stumbled forward, stifling a cry, her whole body numb with terror.

The guerrillas surrounded them, rifles still aimed, as they herded them towards Velouchiotis's camp. Sophia glanced at Alex; he wasn't smiling now. Yet he saw her glance and quietly, stealthily, he reached out his hand and touched her fingers with his own, squeezing briefly, imparting strength.

Tears stung Sophia's eyes and she nodded once, accepting his encouragement even as her body and mind roiled with fear. *Was this going to be the end of them all?*

They walked for half an hour with guns at their backs; it was the longest thirty minutes of her life. When they finally came to Velouchiotis's camp, nothing more than a few tents pitched around an old, half-abandoned dwelling in a clearing on the mountainside, she nearly fell to her knees. Surely her legs could not hold her up much longer. They both ached and trembled.

With the men surrounding them and the guns still trained on their backs, no one dared move or speak. Then a man strode into the clearing. He had a bushy black beard and surprisingly sad, thoughtful eyes; he wore a leather coat over a wool blazer, and a rifle across his shoulder. He glanced at the sorry little group, his eyes narrowing.

"Who is this?" he demanded, and the head of the guerrillas answered.

"We found them in the woods. British men—they say they come to help us."

"Help us?" Velouchiotis sneered. "What British men help us? They bow the knee to the king-in-exile. I have no need or want of them." He spat on the ground, and then moved his gaze over each one of them; as he did so, his eyes no longer looked sad.

They glittered coldly, like the eyes of a snake. "How do I know they're not spies?"

Sophia glanced at Dimitrios and saw that his face had turned a terrible chalky white. She realized yet again how young and foolish he really was; he'd probably never even met Velouchiotis before. He'd acted with his usual reckless bravado, and now she and these *Englezoi* would pay the price. She wondered hollowly just how high that price would be.

Velouchiotis turned back to his man, nodding once. "No need or want," he repeated, spitting the words out with a kind of vicious satisfaction. "Execute them."

CHAPTER TWENTY

Now

Ava opened the front door of her house and kicked off her shoes with a grateful sigh of relief. She'd been out at the school teaching again, and the hike back home made her feet ache.

She sank onto her sofa with another sigh and reached for her phone. She was checking for messages far too often these days, and she couldn't pretend it was for any other reason than Simon. She wondered how she could expect or even hope he would call after their last conversation. She didn't even know what she would say if he did call, or if she'd be able to speak past the lump of anger and pain that always rose up in her throat when she thought of him.

The phone, pressed against her chest, emitted a buzz that vibrated all the way through her. Her heart seeming to leap right into her throat, she checked the screen. It was her mother.

"Hi, Mum."

"Ava!" Her mother's warm, cheerful voice flooded through her, and strangely made that lump intensify. She closed her eyes, tried to swallow and speak. "Sorry I haven't called—"

"I've been worried about you." Her mother spoke with concern rather than reproach. "Wondering how you're getting on. And of course I want to hear all about the house and the village—your grandmother would never even say where she was from, you know. She wouldn't speak of Greece at all."

"I can believe it. No one here seems to want to talk about the war."

"No one? You've met people, then?"

"Yes, quite a few people. Everyone's very friendly..." She stopped suddenly, because the lump in her throat had grown again, and she couldn't speak at all. Tears stung her eyes and she wiped them away with the back of her hand.

"Ava? You're all right, aren't you?"

"Yes. Yes, I'm fine." She managed to squeeze the words out, and thankfully her voice sounded normal. Almost.

Her mother let out a sorrowful little sigh. "Is it very difficult, being on your own?"

"No, it's not that."

"Sweetheart..." Her mother's sympathetic murmur made Ava straighten, take a clogged breath.

"I'm OK. Just a bit emotional."

"That's understandable."

Is it? Ava wondered. A year later maybe she did need to move on. Maybe she needed to let go, as terrifying as that prospect seemed. "Actually," she said, almost brisk now, "I've found out quite a bit about your mother. Well, that's somewhat of an exaggeration. But a schoolteacher here is putting an oral history together, and she's talked to some people who remember Granny."

"Really? What do they say?"

"Well..." Ava paused, wondering if she should tell her mother about Angelika. The truth could hurt, and if her mother had never even known she had an aunt...

"Ava?"

"Did you know she had a sister? Angelika?"

"A sister?" Her mother sounded shocked. "No, she never said—she never said anything except that her mother had died young and there was no one left in Greece."

"Maybe Angelika had died then too. I don't know what happened to her. Only that someone said she was like a butterfly."

"A butterfly," Susan repeated, her voice sounding distant in a way that had nothing to do with the kilometers separating them. "How strange."

"I know."

"And what is the house like?"

"A bit—rustic. But livable."

They chatted for a few more minutes, with Ava telling her a bit about Iousidous. She left out any mention of Andreas, and neither of them spoke of Simon.

"Ava," her mother said as they were finishing the call. "Be careful."

"Careful? I'm not in any danger, Mum—"

"I know that, but digging into the past can be... painful. And you've had enough pain, haven't you? There's a reason why my mother never spoke of Greece. Discovering it might not be the cozy little mystery it seems."

"I know that." She thought of Parthenope's tears, her agitation since Ava had arrived. "I know that," she repeated quietly. "But sometimes you need to talk about what happened, whatever it was, to move on."

"But your grandmother's dead—"

"There are other people who remember her, Mum. Other people who might need to move on."

Including her.

Yet how did she begin, Ava wondered after she'd finished the call. She sat for a moment, her chin resting on her drawn-up knees, the house silent all around her. Then, faintly, she heard a scratching sound from the kitchen. She went to look and found the rail-thin cat with the yellow eyes mewling by the back door.

"Have I actually tamed you?" Ava asked as she opened the door and the cat came in, swishing its tail as it wound through her legs. She emptied some of last night's chicken into a bowl and put it on the floor. The cat fell upon it greedily, eating every morsel and cleaning its whiskers afterwards as Ava crouched on the floor next to the bowl.

Then suddenly it jumped up on her bent knees, rubbed its bony head against her shoulder and purred. Tears stung her eyes and she stroked its head, scratched behind its ears. A moment later the cat jumped off her lap and slipped through the open door, disappearing into the tall grass with a last swish of its tail.

Ava sat there for a moment, still smiling, wondering if she needed to worry about fleas, when she heard her phone ring from the sitting room.

Simon...

She hurried to answer, felt a flicker of disappointment when she saw it was Andreas.

"Ava? Have you seen Kalista?"

"Kalista? No, why?"

Andreas's voice was gruff with worry, his accent more pronounced than usual.

"She's missing," he said. "She didn't return from school, and when I called her teacher, she said she has been absent all day." His voice rose in a father's anguished cry. "I have no idea where she could be."

Kalista... gone? Could she have bunked off for the day in Lamia? When Ava suggested as much to Andreas, he rejected the idea.

"That's not like her. None of this is like her. I'm worried..." He stopped, but Ava thought she knew what he'd been going to say. He was worried she'd run away, perhaps all the way to Athens. She forced herself to think logically. Reasonably. As Simon would.

"Does she have a phone?"

"No, she doesn't. I didn't want her calling her friends at all hours..." He sounded both defensive and apologetic, and Ava wondered if he was realizing just how controlling he'd been. She'd known Andreas was strict, but a mobile phone for a fifteen-year-old made sense right about now, when he so desperately needed to contact her.

"How did she get to school?"

"She didn't go to school today—"

"I know," Ava said, her calm somewhat restored, "but you thought she went to school, so how does she get to school usually?"

He let out a ragged sigh. "I drove her, right to the school gates, as I always do. She got out and waved and I drove away before she even went in." He let out another sigh, this one an angry huff. "She didn't go in, I see that now."

"And how does she get home, usually?"

"The bus. It lets her off on the main road, about half a kilometer from home. She walks the rest of the way."

Ava was silent, wanting to comfort Andreas in his worry and fear, yet not knowing what he wanted or needed to hear. She knew all about the fear of losing someone precious: the hollow feeling in your stomach, the disbelief that this could actually be happening to you. That bad things, the worst thing, were possible.

Yet Kalista was fifteen, not a baby, and she was only missing. She might already be on her way home, happy to have played truant for the day.

"Where do you think she would go if—"

"If she ran away?" Andreas filled in bitterly, his accent so pronounced in his distress that Ava could barely make out his words. "I don't know. She has a few friends in Lamia. I don't know their names or addresses. I don't know anything."

Ava heard the recrimination in Andreas's voice. She knew all about that too. Blaming yourself could feel productive; sometimes it felt like the only thing you could do.

"She might have just wanted some time by herself—"

"She's fifteen—"

"Which is old enough to get around by herself," Ava pointed out, trying to stay practical. Someone needed to be. Funny it was her; that was usually Simon's role. She was the one having fits. "Have you rung the police?"

"Yes. They are not interested until it has been twenty-four hours."

Which, Ava knew, had to feel like a lifetime to Andreas. She knew all about that, the endless waiting, just wanting it to be over even as you desperately wished for it never to have begun.

This is not about you. She closed her eyes, willed herself to focus. "Would you like me to take a look around the village?" Ava asked. "Or I could drive to Lamia—"

"I wondered whether she might come to you," Andreas admitted in a low voice.

"Me?" Ava could not hide her surprise. She thought it had been fairly obvious that she and Kalista hadn't hit it off the few times they'd met together.

"You are young and glamorous," Andreas said, and Ava bit her lip to keep from laughing outright. She was thirty-six years old and far from glamorous in her own estimation. "She admires you."

That had most definitely not been apparent to Ava. "I'll look in the village," she said. "I'll go out right now; it's not even dark yet. And I'll ring you as soon as I've had a look round."

"Thank you," Andreas said, his voice ragged and heartfelt. "I am very grateful."

Ava rung off, slipped her aching feet once more into her shoes, and retrieved her coat and a torch in case she was out late. Then she opened the front door and almost tripped over the rather forlorn figure huddling on the stoop.

It was Kalista.

CHAPTER TWENTY-ONE

October 1942

Execute them.

Velouchiotis had barely given his men the order before they were pushing the SOE agents and Sophia along, clearly intent on carrying out his orders as quickly as possible. Sophia felt the butt of a rifle in her back and a disbelieving panic rose in her in an icy, unstoppable tide. She bit her lips to keep from crying out, felt the metallic tang of blood on her tongue.

The worst was happening. The thing she'd dreaded and feared was taking place right now, and everything in her sought to deny it.

She turned to Alex, as if he could help her now, when he was being prodded along with the others, his face set in lines of resignation. He caught her wild glance and smiled sorrowfully; it felt like a farewell.

Everything in Sophia rose up in an angry howl, a defiant refusal to believe that it could end so abruptly, so awfully.

"Wait!" The word burst from her lungs like a bullet, shattered the taut stillness of the forest.

No one paid any attention to her, of course. The guerrillas barely looked at her, and Velouchiotis was already turning away. He'd just ordered a mass execution and he couldn't even be bothered to watch it being carried out.

Driven by a force and strength she'd never felt before, Sophia lurched forward and grabbed the ragged hem of Velouchiotis's coat, falling to her knees. "*Parakalo*." Please.

He kicked her in the stomach with his boot, and she felt the breath leave her body in a painful rush as she doubled over. "So you, little maid, are going to defend your king on your way to your death?" He sounded only scornfully amused. "*Porni*." Whore. He spat in her face and Sophia blinked the gob of spittle away, still clutching his hem.

"I know nothing of a king, and neither do these men." Her voice came out in something between a gasp and a whisper. She could feel Velouchiotis's spittle trickling towards her mouth. "They've come here to perform an act of sabotage against the Nazis and blackshirts—they want to work with you."

A small, cruel smile played about Velouchiotis's mouth. "You mean they want to use my men as fodder. I know how those British bastards work." He spat again, smiling when it hit her full in the face.

Tears threatened and she blinked them back, furious with herself that she could succumb to crying when everything was so urgent, so important.

"No, Major," she said, purposely using his title in a reckless appeal to his vanity. "They want your help. They were brought here to ask you for help." She didn't know that precisely, but her mind was scrambling for sense even as words spilled from her in a thoughtless, desperate rush. "This man," she pointed at Alex, who she saw was looking at her with an almost blazing light in his eyes, "works in explosives. He is going to make bombs that will blow the Nazis to the other side of the Gorgopotamos!" As soon as she said the words, Sophia thought *of course*. They must be planning to blow up the Gorgopotamos viaduct. As the main railway link to Athens, it was surely the most strategic target in the area.

Velouchiotis must have been thinking similarly, for after an endless moment when he stared at Sophia with eyes as black as pits, he raised his hand. "Lower your guns."

Sophia let go of his coat and eased back on her heels. She was shaking so badly that she nearly keeled over, and Alex reached out to steady her, his uninjured hand reassuringly warm and firm on her elbow.

"Amazing," he whispered in her ear, his voice low and heartfelt. "You are a very, very brave young woman."

Sophia let out a strangled laugh, halfway to hysteria. *Her— brave?* She was always so afraid, so afraid that she'd never wanted any of this.

And yet here she was.

Velouchiotis summoned Dimitrios and Alex's commander with an arrogant jerk of his thumb, and Sophia watched them disappear into a derelict shed, its stone walls crumbling. The guerrillas herded the rest of them to a stand of pine trees, the ground patchy with snow, and Sophia sank onto it, heedless of the cold or wet. She rested her head on her knees, her stomach churning with nerves, the aftereffects of her heedless confrontation of Velouchiotis. Alex handed her his canteen.

"Water."

She looked up in surprise. "You need—"

"No," he said wryly, his eyes crinkling, "you need it. Take it."

After a moment, awkwardly, Sophia took the canteen and unscrewed the lid. She drank thirstily, for her throat was parched and her stomach empty. She was conscious of Alex's gaze resting on her, and she thought, bizarrely, of the fact that she was putting her mouth where he had once put his. Embarrassed now, she lowered the canteen and handed it back to Alex. "*Efharisto.*"

He smiled, and for a moment Sophia wanted to say something else, something more, but she didn't know what. In any case she did not have the English; perhaps she didn't even have the Greek for the feelings churning inside her. Exhausted in more ways than one, she closed her eyes and leaned her head back against the tree. Eventually she fell into a doze, despite all the fear and uncertainty that bubbled inside her. She was startled awake some time later, dizzy and disoriented, by the return of Dimitrios and the SOE commander, as well as Major Velouchiotis. Sophia waited, tension coiled in every muscle and tendon of her body. They could very well, she knew, still be executed.

Dimitrios didn't look at her as he spoke to the British SOE agents. "We take you to another shelter," he said in hesitant, disjointed English. "Better for the target. We leave soon." He turned on his heel, going to join the other ELAS men with an obvious swagger. Sophia watched him, felt a weary derision at his childish behavior. Her outspokenness might have saved the SOE agents, but Dimitrios was clearly going to take the credit. She hardly cared about such things even in the best of times, and so with a sigh she sank back against the tree. Alex crouched down next to her, his hand cradled against his chest.

"Saved," he said softly, "for now. And it is thanks to you, Sophia."

She smiled shyly, but his words echoed disturbingly in her head. *For now... for now...*

For how long?

CHAPTER TWENTY-TWO

Now

"Kalista…" Ava gazed down at the girl in surprise and more than a little concern. She was sitting on the stone slab that served as the stoop, her arms hugging her knees. Her hair was tangled in front of her face as she looked up at Ava with both hope and defiance, but she offered no explanation or apology for her presence. "Come in," Ava finally said, opening the door wider. "You must be freezing."

Kalista grabbed her rucksack and slouched inside. Ava closed the door and wondered wearily what on earth to do now. "Your father is very worried about you."

"I don't care."

Not a great beginning, Ava thought. "I should call him—"

"Don't!" Kalista whirled around to face her. "I came here because I thought you were the one person who *wouldn't* call him."

Ava stared at her in surprise. "Why would you think that?"

She hunched one shoulder. "You fought with him, out at the bridge. You're the only person who has stood up to him."

"I didn't mean to stand up to him," Ava said quietly. "Not like that. I just didn't realize the topic was so volatile."

Kalista looked at her sulkily. "I don't know that word."

"Difficult, then," Ava said, and Kalista just shrugged. "Are you running away then?" she asked after a moment.

"I don't know." Kalista sat on her sofa, her skinny arms wrapped around her knees. "I just wanted to get away."

"And go where?"

Kalista looked up at her, scowling. "I don't know! I came here, didn't I?"

Ava nodded, dropping down next to her on the sofa. "So you did. But perhaps you could have told him where you were going—"

"He wouldn't have let me go."

"Not even here?" Ava asked, trying to hit a teasing note. "All the way to Iousidous?"

"Probably not," Kalista said sulkily, and Ava sighed. The girl was most likely right; Andreas didn't seem to let her do much of anything, or go anywhere.

"Even so," she said after a moment, "you need to tell him where you are. He just called me in an absolute panic. He's already contacted the police."

Kalista looked startled, her eyes widening and her mouth parting, and then, for a moment, scared. She masked it quickly, shrugging as if she didn't care, but Ava had seen it and her heart twisted in both understanding and compassion.

She knew what it was like to be desperate to get away. To run away.

Was that what she had done? Run away from her marriage and her grief?

Just like Kalista, she needed to go back. The thought filled her with a fear similar, she suspected, to Kalista's. How did you manage that? How did you try?

Awkwardly she patted the girl's bony knee. "Kalista, I know things are difficult between you and your father. But running away and making him worry are hardly going to make him see you as someone responsible—responsible enough to live in Athens, as I believe you've wanted."

Kalista hunched a shoulder. "I wasn't thinking about that," she mumbled. "I just wanted to be alone."

Ava frowned. "Doesn't your father give you time alone?"

"He always wants me to study, to go outside, to do this or do that." Her mouth twisted, the words coming haltingly, her English broken, yet the sentiment all too understandable. "He thinks he can make me like it here, but I won't. Never!" She buried her head on her knees, her thin shoulders shaking.

"Oh, sweetheart." Ava pulled the girl into her arms, and Kalista came willingly, sobbing as she pressed her face against Ava's shoulder. Ava could feel the girl's shoulder blades under her sweater, as bony as chicken wings. Kalista's dark hair streamed over her shoulders and Ava patted her back, clumsily, her own heart aching.

Andreas had a child, a beautiful daughter, and he was wrecking the relationship without even realizing.

A relationship, she acknowledged, that she had so desperately wanted. A relationship that had been taken from her. From her and Simon.

How would Simon have been with their daughter? Would he have been too strict, or would her blond curls and blue eyes—that was how Ava had always imagined her—*have made him unbend?* She pictured her daughter's little face with tendrils of corn-silk hair and rosebud lips, and everything in her ached, but it was a different ache, a cleaner one somehow. Instead of the sprawling mess of grief, she felt the quiet pulse of sorrow and knew it was something she could live with. She would have to.

"Kalista," she said after a moment, when the girl's muffled sobs had turned to sniffles, "I do need to ring your father and let him know where you are. He really is worried."

Kalista eased back from Ava and wiped her face with the ragged sleeve of her sweater. "Fine."

Sighing, Ava reached for her phone. Andreas answered on the first ring.

"Ava? Have you learned anything?"

"Kalista is here with me, Andreas."

She heard his breath come out in a long, ragged rush. "Thank God. I'll be right over." He severed the connection before Ava could suggest an alternative, although what that would be she didn't know.

She turned back to Kalista, who eyed her anxiously. "Your father is on his way."

"Now? I don't—"

"Perhaps it will help if we all sit down and talk together," Ava said, although she wasn't sure it would. "In the meantime, let me get you something to eat."

Kalista stared at her with wide eyes, and Ava knew she was dreading the confrontation with Andreas. "Look, it won't be so bad," she said, trying to smile. "And maybe this can help you two to talk more."

Kalista looked rather doubtful, and with a sigh Ava went to the kitchen to find some bread and cheese.

They didn't talk much in the twenty minutes it took Andreas to drive to Iousidous; Kalista was too busy wolfing down as much bread and cheese as she could manage, as if this was to be her last meal. The wash of headlights through the front window and the following sharp rap on the door made them both jump. Ava hurried to open it.

"Andreas—"

Andreas brushed past her to address his daughter quite furiously in Greek. Ava watched as Kalista shrank back, her eyes glittering with both tears and defiance. She couldn't understand what Andreas was saying, but none of it sounded good. After several minutes of this incomprehensible diatribe, she laid a hand on his arm, the muscles tensing under her touch. "Andreas— perhaps we should all talk—'"

"All?" Andreas repeated, swinging around to face her, still furious. "She is my daughter, not yours."

Stung, Ava snapped, "Then treat her like one."

"Don't tell me how to treat my own child," Andreas retorted, his voice rising. "You don't even have a child—"

He couldn't know how much that hurt, Ava told herself. She blinked back angry tears and forced herself to stay calm. "No, I don't, which is why I could be of help here. I can see you've had trouble talking to each other properly—"

"You know nothing about it," Andreas answered shortly. "This is not your business, Ava. I appreciate Kalista came to you, but this is a family matter. And as I said, you know nothing of raising a child."

Ava flinched under the onslaught of his words. She knew nothing. He was right; she didn't. She'd held her daughter in her arms once, but that was all. That was nothing.

She wished, suddenly and fiercely, that Simon were there. He would have stood up to Andreas. He would have stayed calm, and so wonderfully firm. He would have told Andreas that Ava did know what it was to have a child, to love her.

"You're right, Andreas," Ava said stiffly when she trusted herself to speak. "I know nothing of raising a child. Perhaps you should take Kalista home and deal with the matter there, instead of in my living room."

"I want to stay here." Kalista's voice was no more than a thread of sound, and Andreas turned to her sharply. Ava braced herself for another furious and foreign scolding, only to hear him sigh and see his shoulders sag.

He turned back to Ava, and she saw regret shadow his eyes and etch lines in his face. "I'm sorry. In my anger and fear I have behaved badly." He shook his head. "Not as I would have wished."

"It's all right," Ava said, her voice still stiff from his rebuke. *You know nothing of raising a child.* No, she didn't. And God only knew how much she wished she did, that she'd had the opportunity.

No, not only God. Simon knew. He might not have seemed as if he understood, but he'd known.

"Your offer to talk is kind," Andreas said after a moment, choosing the English words with stilted care. "Does it still stand?"

"Of course."

He smiled at her, the curve of his lips both wry and sad, and then at his daughter. "Then perhaps we should talk. But not tonight. Tonight, Kalista, you come home with me. And tomorrow we will both talk with Ava."

*

The next afternoon Ava went with Helena to the house of another war survivor, Agathe Boulos. The elderly woman lived alone in a small house at the top of the village, a neat garden out in front and three baleful-looking cats taking up residence in the sitting room.

She turfed one out of its chair before gesturing for Ava and Helena to sit down. Ava sat, watched as Agathe reached for a tin on a high shelf above the television stand, her arthritic fingers curling carefully around it.

Smiling in satisfaction, she opened the tin and offered them sweets of rosewater jelly. Ava accepted one diplomatically; she'd had them before and thought they tasted like soap. Yet she could hardly refuse Agathe's hospitality, and in any case, the tin of sweets reminded her, rather poignantly, of how her grandmother would give her a sweet every time she visited her in Leeds.

"Sophia Paranoussis?" Agathe mused after she and Helena had chatted in Greek for half an hour. Ava sat up straight, her mouth still tasting of the soapy sweet.

Agathe leaned back in her rocking chair and surveyed both Helena and Ava with surprisingly shrewd eyes. "Yes," she said after a moment in careful English, "I knew her."

Hope leaped inside her and Ava leaned forward. "You did? How?"

Agathe glanced at Helena. "My English. It is not so good."

Helena nodded in understanding; Ava waited eagerly as Agathe spoke and Helena translated into English. "'Iousidous has always been a small place,'" she began. "'Everyone has known everyone else, and all their business.'" Helena smiled wryly in acknowledgement, and Agathe grinned before resuming her story.

"'I have not seen Sophia since the war,'" Helena translated. "'She disappeared right after the bridge was blown up—you know it?'"

Helena glanced at Ava, who nodded quickly. "You mean the Gorgopotamos viaduct? The Resistance bombed it in 1942."

"You've been learning the local history, I see," Helena told her teasingly, and Ava smiled.

"It's the least I can do, considering I don't really know the language."

Helena turned back to Agathe, who began to speak again, her Greek rapid, almost agitated. "'The Nazis came to Iousidous after the bridge was bombed. They were furious—they believed some of the villagers helped the Resistance.'"

Ava stilled; she could feel the thud of her heart in her ears. "And do you think Sophia had something to do with it? With the bombing of the bridge?"

Helena repeated the question in Greek, and Agathe shrugged. "'Who knows?'" Helena translated back. "'But the Nazis had her name somehow. They were looking for her and her sister too. Angelika. They both disappeared, and I never learned what happened to either of them.'"

Ava sat back, her mind spinning with this new information. Had her grandmother really been involved in the Resistance? She remembered her grandmother reigning over a tea of weak squash and dry biscuits in her stuffy sitting room in a semidetached house in Leeds and could hardly reconcile the image with a young woman who could help to blow up a bridge.

"How would the Nazis get her name?" she asked Helena. "Could someone have been an informer?"

Helena shrugged. "I have no idea. Many villagers helped the Resistance back then. They gave food and shelter to the guerrillas, at least in the beginning. Then the fighting became too ugly and showing loyalty to one side or another was dangerous."

"Do you think my grandmother might have been allied to one side or another?"

"It is impossible to say. But perhaps someone else will know more."

Agathe spoke again, and Helena listened intently before translating. "'I remember it well. One day all was peaceful, or as peaceful as it could be in such times, and the next the bridge was blown up and the Nazis were marching through the main street here, in their jackboots. They dragged out some of the villagers,'" Helena's voice hitched. "'Shot them right in the square—'"

Agathe's face crumpled and she reached for a tissue, dabbing her eyes. "*Apesio*," she said. "*Apesio*." Terrible.

And it was terrible, terrible to imagine the village's sleepy street filled with Nazis, the villagers dragged out to the square, the gunshots echoing through the mountains.

Where had Sophia been then? And Angelika? Had her great-aunt died in the square by the fountain?

Ava shivered suddenly, for while it was terrible, it was also unbearably vivid: Sophia fleeing for her life, her sister dead, her house abandoned and empty…

Fifteen minutes later she took her leave with Helena and they walked down the twisting road back to the school.

"At least you have learned more," Helena said, "even if it leads to more questions."

"I wonder if we'll ever know the whole truth."

Helena shrugged with cheerful pragmatism. "There is one more person to talk to. His name is Lukas."

"I'll live in hope," Ava said with a wry smile. "Why don't you come down to my house?" she asked impulsively. "I've learned how to make a half-decent cup of Greek coffee. If you're not busy…?" She felt that sudden flutter of insecurity that you often had with a new friend, that such an invitation would not be welcome.

"I'd love to," Helena answered, and a few minutes later they were settled in Ava's sitting room, two cups of thick Greek coffee before them.

"This is quite good," Helena told her, sounding surprised, and Ava laughed.

"Eleni taught me. I've actually developed a taste for the stuff, although I've never boiled coffee in a saucepan before."

"It takes some time to learn to like it," Helena acknowledged. She took another sip of the thick, bitter brew. "You are well?"

"Yes—"

"You do not sound certain."

Ava thought of the revelations of the last week: wanting to see Simon, wanting finally somehow to let go of her grief—or at least not clutch it quite so tightly—and then Andreas's difficulties with his daughter. Andreas and Kalista, at least, seemed to have come to some understanding; they'd come over that morning and talked awkwardly, with Ava acting as an unofficial and decidedly inexperienced mediator.

"I'm certain," she told Helena with a wry smile. "It's just been a bit busy. Do you remember my friend Andreas?" Helena nodded a bit guardedly, and Ava remembered how it had seemed as if Helena had been hiding something when it came to Andreas. She'd told Ava they had been friends as children, but it had almost sounded as if they weren't friends now. "Well," Ava continued, not wanting to betray Andreas's confidence but thinking she could use the advice, "he's having a bit of trouble with his daughter."

"Kalista."

"Yes. She bunked off school last week—"

"Bunked?"

"Skipped a day. Didn't go."

"Ah." Helena nodded knowingly.

"Anyway…" Ava sipped her coffee, wondering how much she should divulge to Helena. "It seems Kalista wants to go to Athens," she finally said. "See a bit of the city."

"A natural desire."

"Yes…" *Not according to Andreas, though.* Ava still remembered the stony look he'd given his daughter when she'd begged to be allowed to visit her aunt. His reaction seemed extreme considering Kalista had been proposing nothing more than a weekend away, but after an hour of back and forth he had, rather grudgingly, relented to a day trip… with one proviso.

Ava had to accompany Kalista.

"Well," she continued, "Andreas asked me if I'd take Kalista to Athens, just for the day. And I thought perhaps you could go with us." She hadn't told Andreas this, but she could hardly see how he'd object. Surely Helena, a schoolteacher who had chosen to return to Iousidous, would be considered a safe companion for Kalista.

Something like pain flashed across Helena's face and then was gone. She placed her cup of coffee back on the table and shook her head. "I do not think that would be wise, Ava."

"Not wise?" Ava repeated. She'd wanted Helena's company because she wasn't looking forward to an entire day alone with Kalista, but she'd also thought Helena would get along well with the girl. She hadn't expected this certain and quiet refusal. "Why not? That is, if you want to tell me—"

Helena sighed, pain shadowing her eyes. "I told you that Andreas and I were childhood friends, but that was not quite true. Or at least not the whole truth. We were childhood sweethearts—that is the English term, yes?" Ava nodded, and Helena continued. "I was eighteen and he was twenty-five. He wanted to marry, settle down, but I was young, so young…" She trailed off, lost in memories, and Ava waited, not speaking. She'd suspected some sort of history between Andreas and Helena, but not as much as this, not broken hearts and betrayal. She thought of her awkward kiss with Andreas and flushed.

"I wanted to live a little," Helena continued after a moment. She took a sip of coffee. "Experience life." She paused, meeting Ava's gaze with sober honesty. "I moved to Athens and left him behind. A few months later Andreas married his wife. I think they were happy together for a while, but I know that she grew tired of this country life. She wanted more. She died in a car accident—on her way to Athens." Helena paused, then added, "She was leaving him."

"Oh. Oh, no." Ava sat back, sifting through all she'd learned. *No wonder Andreas was so reluctant to let Kalista go to Athens.* If she'd known all that, she would have been far more understanding of Andreas's strict ways.

Yet she knew Andreas couldn't keep Kalista here through rules and restrictions, at least not forever. If she didn't want to stay, she wouldn't. You couldn't force someone to feel the same way you did.

How many times had she confronted and even baited Simon? She'd been trying to make him feel the same sharp grief she'd been feeling, using methods as futile as Andreas's. She'd thought that if he'd shared her pain, they would have been drawn closer together; she certainly would have felt some comfort and relief.

But her ugly jabs and angry accusations had only made him retreat all the more. Stoic Simon, more silent than ever.

Just as she hadn't been able to change Simon, neither could Andreas force Kalista to love the land the way he did. He could try, and as her father he could forbid her to leave, but in the end it would only create more bitterness and resentment. Ava realized the day trip Andreas was offering was an olive branch, and she knew she needed to help his daughter grasp it.

"In any case," Helena resumed quietly, "Andreas and I parted badly. I said some things… they were unfair. Unkind. And it has left this," she waved an arm through the air, as if to encompass a yawning and empty space, "distance," she finally said, "between us. Even though I have been back in Iousidous for years, we haven't seen much of each other in all that time. Kalista had already started secondary school in Lamia when I began teaching here. In truth, we have little reason to see each other any more."

"Maybe this could be a way to change that," Ava suggested, although considering how set in his ways Andreas was, she didn't hold too much hope.

Helena shook her head. "If I thought Andreas would be open to such a thing, I might agree. But accompanying his daughter to Athens would only anger him, I know. And his temper can be short."

"Yes, I know… although I think he's trying to change that."

Helena smiled sadly. "We're all trying to change, aren't we?" She paused, gazing down into the dregs of her coffee. "I sometimes regret the way things happened," she admitted in a low voice. "And my own stubbornness."

Ava nodded, felt her insides twist with her own regret. Had she been stubborn with Simon, insisting on trying to change him in ways he couldn't be changed?

Maybe she should have just accepted him and his reaction, or lack of it, to the death of their daughter. Yet even as she considered this, she dismissed it. Such a thing would have been impossible for her then, caught in the throes of deepest grief.

And now? Was it possible now? What did you do when your supposed soul mate disappointed you?

CHAPTER TWENTY-THREE

October 1942

An hour after Velouchiotis rescinded his execution order, they began a long, exhausting trek through the mountains in heavy snow. Once Sophia tried to ask Dimitrios where they were going, but he merely grunted. She wondered if he even knew.

The Englishman Alex walked next to her for most of that exhausting journey, chatting in his halting Greek or sometimes slowly in English, and when she didn't understand, he'd act out the words with rather ridiculous gestures that made Sophia laugh. She knew he was trying to distract her from her own fear, and despite everything, the cold and the snow, the hunger and the terror, she found she enjoyed his company, and she felt a tiny, surprising flicker of disappointment when they reached their destination, a makeshift camp at the foothills of Mount Oeta, only a few kilometers from Iousidous.

One of Velouchiotis's men dismissed her with a kind of rough indifference once they'd reached their new destination, and Sophia hurried away through the darkened forest, tripping on tree roots and fallen branches, the space between her shoulder blades prickling as if she expected one of the guerrillas to shoot her as if she were a deserter.

She arrived home near dawn, cold, wet, and utterly exhausted. As she crept into her bedroom, Angelika rose from her bed with wide, frightened eyes.

"Oh, Sophia! You've been gone for so long!"

Sophia stared at her sister and said nothing; she was too tired to address the reproach in Angelika's voice or remind her that the only reason she'd gone at all was because Angelika had stupidly brought Dimitrios into their house, into their lives. She just shook her head and with fumbling fingers undid the knot of her wet shawl.

"Where were you?" Angelika asked. "What did you do?"

Sophia glanced at her sister's childlike face and felt a weary resignation that Angelika would never understand the danger she'd been in, the danger she herself had put her in. "Go to sleep, Angelika," she said, and sulking a bit, her sister turned over on her side and tucked her knees up to her chest.

Sophia did the same, her back to Angelika, her whole body throbbing with exhaustion.

As she tumbled into that thankful oblivion, she thought, in the moment before sleep finally claimed her completely, of Alex.

Sophia woke up slowly just a few hours later, blinking in the morning light, listening to the familiar clump of her father's boots on the staircase. She should be downstairs, Sophia knew, making the coffee, starting the bread. Her eyelids fluttered closed again and she slept.

She woke when the sun was high in the sky, although the room was still cold. Angelika was gone, and Sophia could only hope her sister was making herself useful. She dressed and washed quickly, found that the fire downstairs had burned dangerously low and the bread, clearly begun with the best of intentions, had been left to rise for far too long.

Sighing, Sophia began to set things to rights, wondering where Angelika had gone. *Surely not in search of Dimitrios?* Now that he was firmly in Velouchiotis's camp, Sophia had even less desire for Angelika to chase after him.

She wondered what the *Englezoi* soldiers were doing, when they might blow up the bridge. And if they did…

Alex might die in the explosion, or at the hands of Italians or Nazis. She shouldn't think of only Alex of course, but he was the only one of the *Englezoi* she'd talked to, the only one who had told her she was brave and made her laugh.

How would they blow up the bridge? She wondered now. There were guardhouses with armed soldiers on either end of it. *Would they attack the soldiers? Kill them?*

She knew she was being naïve and maybe even stupid in not knowing the answers to these questions; she had not even known to ask them until now. But she was out of it, she told herself; Velouchiotis had no more use for her, thank God, and she had no idea where Perseus was, or whether he was even involved in the operation any more. Perhaps Velouchiotis would now claim it for his own.

She had two days' reprieve, and then, as she was fetching water from the fountain in the square, Kristina approached her.

"You have not been to the coffeehouse."

Sophia hoisted the heavy wooden bucket, her back already aching. "Do you need me?"

Kristina eyed her in that calm, deliberating way that made Sophia look away. "Yes, but not to serve drinks or wash glasses."

Sophia's hand clenched on the bucket's rough rope handle. "I've done my part."

"Is the war over?"

"What do you mean?"

"That is when your part ends, Sophia. Not before."

She shook her head, a sudden desperate fury rising up in her. "Do you know he almost killed us?" she demanded in a hiss. "That butcher Velouchiotis—he ordered our execution!"

Kristina's bland face remained unimpressed. "You are here, are you not? You are still alive."

"Yes, but—"

"Then you do not complain," Kristina said fiercely. "Very little is asked of you, Sophia. Only to bring food."

"Why can't someone else—"

Kristina shook her head contemptuously. "Do you think you are the only one helping? The men would have little hope, then, if they relied only on you!"

Stung, Sophia nearly replied that she'd saved all their lives once already. She said nothing, for she saw the grief as well as the anger glittering in Kristina's eyes and knew the older woman was right. She had no cause to complain. She would do what was asked of her.

She worried at first about finding food for the soldiers; there was little enough to go round as it was. Yet nearly every day since she spoke to Kristina, there was some anonymous gift left for Sophia: a wrapped cheese by the door, a loaf of *psomi* left by her washing mangle. Sophia was strangely touched by these gifts; they made her feel less alone, knowing that others were helping, were giving out of their poverty just as she was acting even in her fear. You could, she supposed, rise above your circumstances, above the events and emotions that so often dictated the crooked course of life, and she was humbled by the villagers who gave and risked so much, so silently. Another kind of bravery.

The air was sharp with cold when Sophia set out one evening three days after her return to the village, to deliver food to the camp. As she tramped through the heavy, wet snow that had come even to the foothills, the forest dark and quiet all around her, she realized, with a jolt of something almost like alarm, that she was looking forward to seeing Alex again.

She'd been afraid she wouldn't find the little camp again, but as she continued deeper into the forest, a soldier emerged from the shadows and, after seeing the food she brought, silently led her the rest of the way to the makeshift camp, no more than a few miserable tents around an abandoned stone hut once used by goatherds. A single fire sputtered and smoked; the wood the soldiers had used clearly had been damp.

More of Velouchiotis's men appeared behind her, emerging from the shadows like wraiths, their rifles drawn. Her heart pounding, Sophia held up the basket. "Bread. Cheese." The man who had led her to the camp gave a brief nod of approval, but even so one of the men prodded the basket with the butt of his rifle before he let her pass, tearing a hunk of bread off for himself. Sophia saw Alex rise from where he'd been sitting by the fire. "You're saving us once again, Sophia," he said in clumsy Greek, and she smiled, ridiculously pleased.

"With a bit of bread?"

Alex's white teeth flashed in his tanned and weathered face. "We are very hungry."

Sophia blushed, glad for the cover of darkness. What about this man unsettled and affected her so? It was utterly foolish, she knew, to think that anything might happen between them. He was English, a soldier, and after they blew up the bridge—or failed in trying—she would never see him again.

And yet she'd never met anyone who made her laugh and blush, who made her heart beat so hard it hurt her chest, and not from fear. She had never felt this way before, and it both frightened and thrilled her.

Keeping her gaze averted from Alex, she began to unpack the provisions. "It is not only me," she told him as she took out the loaves of *psomi* and rounds of cheese. "Many people from the village provided food. I could not provide this all on my own."

"You must thank them for us."

She looked up at him, shaking her head with a smile. "But I do not know who they are!"

"Then I hope they learn somehow how appreciated they are." Alex looked down at the food she'd unpacked. "What do we have here?"

"Very simple. Bread and cheese. Olives, some dried plums."

"A feast." Alex looked up, and his gaze seemed to linger on her, his smile so warm that Sophia felt her own body heat. She looked away quickly, unsettled and almost ashamed by her own reaction. She was being as brazen and reckless as Angelika in her own way, and with a man whom she could never marry.

"May I take it to the others?" Alex asked, nodding towards the other *Englezoi* sitting around the fire. Sophia nodded, still unable to look at him.

She watched him, covertly, as he distributed the food, knowing she had no real reason to stay any longer, yet feeling strangely, stupidly, reluctant to leave. After he'd distributed the food, Alex turned back to her. "Come eat with us."

Sophia shook her head. "No, there is not enough—"

"There is," Alex said firmly. "And you must be hungry. It is at least three kilometers back to your village."

Still Sophia hesitated, because she had never sat down with strange men before, not even to eat. Then Barba Niko, the old goatherd who had become a guide and cook for the soldiers, beckoned her over. "Come, little maid. There is enough."

Smiling shyly, she joined them, sitting down next to Alex and accepting a hunk of bread and cheese.

He smiled back at her. "That's not so bad, is it?" Sophia just ducked her head in reply. "Tell me about yourself," he invited. "Do you have brothers? Sisters?"

"One sister."

"Is she is as brave as you?" Alex gave her a teasing smile. "Or as pretty?"

Sophia stared at the smoking fire, her cheeks hot. She could not think of a thing to say; no one had ever spoken to her so.

Alex laid a hand on her arm. "I'm sorry. I did not mean to embarrass you."

She shook her head, still tongue-tied. Despite her embarrassment, she felt a flicker of pleasure that he thought she was brave—and pretty. Of course, she told herself quickly, it was just foolish talk; it meant nothing. Yet it still warmed her from the inside.

"I shouldn't have said anything," Alex said, and from the corner of her eye she saw him smile crookedly. "I just wanted to say how I… I like you."

As if her skirt had been singed by the fire, Sophia sprang up, tucking her shawl more firmly around her. She could not look anywhere, it seemed, and so her gaze darted wildly around. "I must go—"

"Of course." Alex stood too. "Of course. You will come again?" Sophia just nodded and Alex rubbed a hand over his face. "I've made it worse, haven't I?"

She stared at him rather miserably. "I am just a simple Greek girl."

Alex took a step closer to her. "I think that's what I like about you," he said, his words slow and halting. "You—you don't know how special you really are."

She felt a smile bloom across her face before she turned away, embarrassed yet again to have shown so much to this man. What did it even mean that he liked her? What did it even matter?

She hurried from the little camp, making her way through the forest as quickly as she could, heedless of the snow that wet the hem of her skirt and soaked her boots. As she emerged from the trees, she realized she'd gone too far and was coming out on the main road into the village, rather than behind the house as she had hoped.

"Stupid," she muttered, shaking her head. It was after dark, and dangerous to be out at all, much less alone. "Stupid."

She turned down the rutted road towards the village, huddling under her shawl as the wind swept down from Mount Oeta and the stars twinkled coldly above. She kept her head tucked low and shock blazed through her as she suddenly collided with another person, who from her gasp seemed as surprised as she was.

"Sophia! What on earth are you doing out at such an hour?"

Sophia blinked in the darkness, and saw Parthenope blinking back at her. Silly, nosy Parthenope Atrikes, who just like her brother could not keep her tongue, or even a thought, in her head.

"I could ask the same of you, Parthenope," she said tartly. Although Parthenope was Dimitrios's sister, Sophia had never seen her among the guerrillas or SOE agents. Did she know what was happening? Judging by her question and her curious stare, she did not.

Parthenope bit her lip and looked away. "I was just… visiting. The hour got away from me."

Visiting, Sophia wondered. *Who could Parthenope be visiting at such an hour?* The answer came quickly, obviously: *a man.* Parthenope was a stupid girl indeed to risk so much for a man.

And aren't you as well?

Everything in her stilled at the thought. "We should hurry back, then," Sophia said, trying to sound cheerful instead of afraid. "It's foolish to be caught out so late."

Parthenope let out a high laugh, the sound half wild. "Oh, I'm not afraid," she said almost defiantly. "Not any more. Not of blackshirts, anyway."

Sophia just kept walking; she had no wish to reveal anything to Parthenope, and if the girl had secrets, it was surely better not to know them.

CHAPTER TWENTY-FOUR

Now

Loneliness was a strange thing. One day Ava would feel cheerful and fine and maybe even happy, and then in a sudden moment the loneliness landed on her with a thud, enveloping her with an emptiness that left her breathless and near tears.

She was tired of the seesaw her emotions had been on since the stillbirth and separation, and yet she also realized that this loneliness was different to the endless, aching sorrow she'd felt before. This loneliness had a specific, single source: Simon.

She missed him.

She missed his dry sense of humor and the way his mouth quirked upwards on one side when he smiled. She missed the way they'd stretch out on the sofa after dinner, their feet propped on the old coffee table, while they exchanged sections of the newspaper and pointed at the articles that interested them. She missed having someone there to talk to and laugh with and hug, and it wasn't just having someone she missed, but having *Simon*.

The only problem was, she was more and more afraid that he did not miss her, at least not in the same way. He'd said he missed her, but he'd also said he was having dinner with Julie. He hadn't called in a week, and she hadn't either.

It was so childish, Ava thought, this to-ing and fro-ing, wondering who should call first, an absurd kind of power play after over a decade of marriage. She wanted it to stop.

One evening after a busy day of visiting Eleni and teaching at the school, she sat on the sofa in her little living room and stared at her phone, willing for it to ring. She wished she had the courage to dial his number and tell him all the crazy thoughts that were swirling around in her mind. Once she would have; once it would have been easy and simple. Now every move, every word, felt loaded and fraught with danger, the possibility of getting hurt.

She thought of Helena still regretting her parting from Andreas, even though so many years had passed. Would she be the same? Would she live the rest of her life in grief and regret because she'd been too stubborn or too afraid to tell Simon how she really felt?

I miss you. I need you. I love you. I know I haven't shown it, I've been more or less impossible, but it's true all the same.

Taking a deep breath, Ava punched in Simon's contact. Her fingers trembled, and she took a deep breath. She could do this. She needed to do this. And then to her surprise, the phone rang before she could make the call, its tinny trill seeming to echo through the room. She stared at the glowing little screen on the phone and saw that it was Eleni, felt a stab of disappointment that it wasn't Simon.

"Eleni?"

"Ava?"

Ava frowned, for in just the single word she heard a surprising anxiety in her friend's voice. "Is everything all right?"

"No, it's why I am calling. It's my mother, Parthenope. She lay down this afternoon—she was tired and when I went to wake her up she… she wouldn't." Eleni's voice trembled. "She is still breathing, she's not…" She stopped, gulping, and then said, "I called the ambulance and they're coming to take her to hospital in Lamia. But I wondered if… if you would come? With me?"

Ava's heart twisted and she swallowed hard. "Of course, Eleni," she said. "I'll come right away."

*

An hour later Ava and Eleni were both sitting on hard plastic chairs in the waiting room of the hospital's emergency department.

Eleni knotted her hands together, stared down at her lap. "I know she is old. No matter what happens now, the end for her is near." She looked up, her face looked almost ghostly under the hospital's fluorescent lights. "I will grieve, of course, but it isn't that."

"What is it, then?" Ava asked, for Eleni had been barely able to contain her distress as they waited for the doctors to examine Parthenope.

"I told you she has been anxious lately," Eleni said, her voice low. "Something—some memory of the war has distressed her."

"Yes—"

"What I didn't say was that she has wanted to speak of it," Eleni confessed, her voice thick with misery. "She would speak of it, saying your grandmother's name, tugging on my sleeve. I always put her off. I didn't want her to tell me."

"You didn't want to distress her," Ava said, covering her surprise at this admission. "That's certainly understandable, Eleni."

"No—it's not just that. I didn't want to distress myself." She bit her lip, tears pooling in her eyes. "I am a coward, Ava. A selfish coward. I am afraid of what my mother might tell me. I am afraid it might change things, make me think differently of her. Of myself."

Ava stared at the older woman and wondered what she suspected, or even knew. "How could something from so long ago change things now?"

But Eleni just shook her head, pressing her lips together, and didn't answer.

Another cup of lukewarm coffee and an hour later, the doctors emerged to report on Parthenope's condition. After they'd left again, Eleni turned to Ava.

"It's not good," she said wearily. "But my mother is over ninety. How could it be?"

"What did they say?"

"She had a—a what do you call it?" Eleni closed her eyes as she tried to remember the English.

"A stroke?" Ava suggested gently, and the older woman nodded.

"Yes, that is it. She wakened, but is not speaking, and she cannot move on one side. They say they will know more tomorrow. She is sleeping now." Eleni reached out to touch Ava's hand. "Thank you for coming with me."

Back in her house Ava dropped her keys on the table and stared round at the home she'd patched together for herself. Except it wasn't a home, not really. Not for her. It was a sofa and table and a couple of chairs, a huge fireplace she hadn't even used. It was a bolthole, a stopover, a lay-by in her life.

Taking a deep breath, she reached for her phone and pressed Simon's contact. The phone rang and rang, trill after trill, and then switched over to voicemail. Ava felt disappointment like a leaden weight inside her. She'd been gearing up for a big conversation, even if she hadn't actually thought of what she would say. A message felt like a poor substitution, but she was still going to try.

"Simon? It's Ava. But you probably know that, since you have my number programmed in… if you still do, that is…" She stopped abruptly, knew she was wittering on in her nervousness. "Anyway I just wanted to call because—because I miss you and I never said. I mean, I really miss you." She swallowed hard, forced herself to go on. "I didn't want to say this in a message, but maybe it's better this way because I never seem to say the right thing when we're together. I get so angry, but it's really just me being hurt and I just wanted you to realize that…" She stopped again; the last thing she wanted this message to be was more blaming.

"So I guess I just wanted to talk to you. And know what you were thinking, if you're thinking anything, I mean. About me. Us." Another breath, and then she made herself say the words that she should have said a long time ago. "I lo—"

The message clicked off, and a smooth, imperturbable recorded voice said, "I'm sorry, but you've exceeded the time allotted for a message—"

With a groan, Ava disconnected the call and threw the phone on the sofa. Why hadn't she started her message by telling Simon she loved him? Why had she waited—again?

She only hoped Simon would know what she'd been about to say.

*

Two days later Helena stopped by to tell Ava of the final interview with Lukas Petrakides. "I only heard about him recently. He lives in Lamia. He says he was in the Resistance."

"In the Resistance? Really?" Ava felt a frisson of excitement mingling with all of her other emotions: worry about Parthenope, concern for Andreas and Kalista, and need for Simon. Simon still hadn't called, and with every passing hour she felt her frail, fledgling hopes plummet a little further. Why wouldn't he call, after hearing that message? She was afraid it could only mean one thing, that he really didn't care.

"Do you think he knew my grandmother?"

"He might have. Of course, quite a few villagers helped the Resistance, especially with the bombing of the Gorgopotamos viaduct near here. They supplied the *andartes* and the British SOE agents with food for weeks while they planned the sabotage and hid from the Italians and Nazis."

"And my grandmother might have been part of that," Ava agreed, a note of wonder in her voice. "But why would the Nazis have had her name, and no other?"

"Perhaps Lukas Petrakides can help us," Helena answered. "You can certainly come with me on the interview. And fortunately for you, he speaks English."

"I look forward to it." She made a slight face. "More than my trip to Athens tomorrow, I have to admit, with Kalista."

Helena smiled in sympathy. "Teenagers can be difficult, but perhaps you'll have fun."

"She's barely spoken two words to me, aside from on the night she ran away." Ava had hardly seen Andreas or his daughter since that awkward conversation the day after Kalista's attempt at running away, but they'd spoken on the phone and arranged this trip.

"We're having lunch with her aunt, Iolanthe, and then visiting the shops. Andreas asked her to show me the Acropolis, but I have a feeling Kalista would rather spend the whole time shopping."

"Understandable," Helena answered with a laugh. "So would I!"

A knock sounded at the door, and Ava glanced towards it in surprise.

"Are you expecting someone?" Helena asked.

"No, but perhaps Eleni stopped by with some news about her mother."

With that thought in mind, Helena followed Ava to the door, and then they both froze as Ava opened it and saw Andreas on the threshold.

He stared at them both, his eyes widening as he struggled for something to say. "Helena," he finally said, and nodded stiffly.

"Hello, Andreas," Helena said quietly. Her cheeks were flushed and she couldn't quite look at him. Andreas looked equally awkward, and Ava felt a flicker of curiosity. Clearly these two were not completely immune to one another, despite the passage of time.

Andreas turned to Ava. "I just wanted to check on the arrangements for tomorrow," he said, his voice still sounding stiff. "I was in Iousidous anyway, so I thought I'd stop by."

"Of course." And now she was sounding awkward too. "Won't you come in?"

Andreas glanced again at Helena and then quickly looked away. "No… no, I should get home. I just wanted to say Kalista is very excited about tomorrow. I told her she could visit the shops after you've seen the Acropolis."

Ava exchanged an amused glance with Helena; they both knew the shops would be the highlight of the trip for Kalista. "That sounds lovely. Thank you, Andreas."

"Thank you for taking her. I—I hope this will be a new beginning. For us. I mean…" His cheeks reddened and he glanced again, somewhat inexplicably, at Helena. "I mean for Kalista and me."

"Of course," Ava murmured. It seemed a lifetime ago that Andreas had kissed her, and thankfully it seemed to be something that neither of them wished to remember.

"I've said she could buy something… a dress, perhaps? You'll make sure she picks out something suitable?"

"I'm not sure I'm an expert on teenage styles, but I'll do my best," Ava replied. She wondered whether her and Andreas's idea of *something suitable* would be the same, never mind what Kalista thought.

"Thank you," Andreas said, and then they both lapsed into silence. Andreas's gaze once again swung, seemingly of its own accord, towards Helena. She gazed back at him steadily, saying nothing, although the tilt to her chin was proud. "You're well?" he finally asked, speaking in English for Ava's benefit, and Ava saw surprise flicker across Helena's features.

"Yes. Very well." Helena hesitated. "And you?"

Andreas nodded rather brusquely. "Fine. We're… fine."

Ava watched this exchange with a growing fascination. Surely she wasn't imagining the undercurrent, the tension between the two of them? She didn't know what Andreas and Helena felt for each other, but surely it wasn't dislike or even indifference. It was something else entirely. Something that made it easy for her to believe they'd once been in love, had thought to marry.

They'd all lapsed into yet another silence, simply staring at each other, and finally Andreas roused himself. "I should go," he said, jangling his keys, and ducking his head in farewell at the pair of them, he left.

Ava closed the door slowly, then turned to Helena, who seemed in as much of a daze as Andreas had been. "Well," she said with a touch of mischief, "that was interesting."

Helena glanced at her rather sharply. "What do you mean?"

Ava shrugged, not wanting to press. She already knew that Helena was sensitive about her relationship, or lack of it, with Andreas. And she knew how prickly she was when anyone asked her about Simon.

Simon. Why hadn't he called her back? Maybe he really just didn't care any more. Maybe her rambling message had annoyed him. She thought of calling him again, but something in her resisted. She didn't want to pester him, and yet she was desperate for some kind of contact. For as she'd just seen with Helena and Andreas, time didn't heal all wounds. It didn't even make you forget.

If anything, it made you realize all the more what you might be missing.

*

The next day the sky was a bright, hard blue, and a fresh breeze blew off the mountains; it was perfect for sightseeing. Ava drove down the road towards the motorway with the windows down and the wind blowing through her and Kalista's hair.

Kalista had been quiet since Ava had picked her up, twisting a strand of hair around one finger as she glanced at the passing scenery. Ava decided to let the girl have her peace. She was lost in her own musings, remembering how just six weeks ago she'd been driving through these darkened hills, feeling close to despair as the fog rolled ominously in. She felt different now, she knew, content in a way she had not experienced in a long time, and yet restless too, ready for change. Finally ready to move on.

But to what?

She glanced over at Kalista. "Have you seen the Acropolis before?"

Kalista hunched one shoulder. "School trip." Her tone did not invite further inquiry.

"Your father said we could do a bit of shopping afterwards," Ava tried again. "Are there any shops you'd like to visit?"

Kalista brightened visibly and rattled off the names of several shops Ava had never heard of. "Good," she said, her voice light and teasing. "I like when a girl knows what she wants."

After parking the car, they walked up Theorias, the road that circled the Acropolis, and then made the final ascent on steep, stone-cut steps to the top of the rock. Ava gazed out at Athens spread like a map before them, amazed at all the buildings and cars, the signs of busy urban life. She hadn't left Iousidous except to go to Lamia since she'd arrived.

Kalista, she saw, was gazing almost hungrily at the city below them, utterly uninterested in the ancient sites around them, scattered on the hill.

"It's an exciting place, isn't it?" Ava said quietly, and Kalista glanced at her with something like suspicion before she nodded. "Papa hates it."

"He's a country person at heart, I suppose."

Kalista shook her head. "It's more than that. He thinks if I spend time in Athens, I won't want to live with him, do what he does." She made a face.

Ava was impressed by how perceptive Kalista was; weren't most teenagers completely self-absorbed? Kalista had certainly given that impression before. "Are you interested in taking over the business one day?" she asked cautiously.

Kalista hunched her shoulders and dug her hands into her pockets. "I don't know what I want," she said. "I just want to live my life and see things." She gave Ava a surly, resentful look. "I'm only fifteen."

"True enough," Ava replied lightly. She felt sorry for Kalista; clearly this teenaged girl carried the weight of other people's choices on her shoulders. Andreas needed to see Kalista for who she was now, not who she might become given time and opportunity, or who her mother, or Helena, had been. Yet Ava knew how hard it was to see and accept people for who they really were.

Hadn't she burdened Simon with her own expectations? She'd expected him to grieve the same way she had grieved, and when he hadn't, she'd turned away from him. Yet if only he'd said something…

Sighing, she checked her phone again, even though she hadn't heard it ring. *No missed calls. No messages.*

"I think it's time for lunch with your aunt," Ava said. "And then shopping!"

Kalista's Aunt Iolanthe was not the wild child Ava had been half-expecting. She worked in a bank, dressed sedately, and hugged Kalista to her as soon as they arrived in the restaurant in Athens's business district.

"It's been too long," Iolanthe said as she kissed Kalista's cheeks. She turned to Ava. "Thank you for bringing her to me."

The rest of the day passed happily enough. Iolanthe and Kalista spoke mostly in Greek during lunch, with apologies to Ava, who waved them away. She could see that they were both hungry for a proper talk, and not the kind of halting chitchat they'd have to make in order to include her. After their dishes were cleared away, she excused herself, saying she'd like to have a stroll around while Iolanthe and Kalista had dessert.

Outside, Ava walked past Athens's disconcerting mix of old and new: crumbling stone and frosted glass. She checked her phone several times, and each time the blank screen mocked her. Maybe he hadn't got the message. Maybe it had been automatically deleted because she'd gone over the time limit. Maybe—

With a sigh of impatience for her own dithering, Ava quickly thumbed through her contacts for Simon's. She'd call him again. Forget pride, forget being stubborn. She just wanted to call him. Hear him.

Yet the call switched straight through to voicemail; Simon's phone had to be turned off.

"Damn it," Ava said, well and truly frustrated, and yes, a little hurt. Was his phone turned off because he was trying to avoid her calls? A paranoid thought, but one at this point she couldn't help but think, considering his silence.

After lunch with Iolanthe, Ava took Kalista to the promised shops; the girl spent several happy hours trying various outfits on before settling on a pair of skinny jeans and a colorful top that Ava thought Andreas would accept. At least she hoped he would.

Twilight was settling over the mountains as they drove home, and Kalista glanced shyly at Ava. "Thank you for taking me," she said, the words hesitant yet heartfelt. "I had a good time."

Ava smiled back at her. "So did I," she said, and meant it. "Thanks for asking me."

"Do you think you're going to stay in Greece?" Kalista asked, and Ava tensed. The question felt loaded, although from Kalista's tone she couldn't tell if her continued presence in Iousidous would be welcome or not. "I don't know," she said after a moment. "I think I need to return to England at some point. I need to go home." Because it was still home, and always would be. "This has been more of…" Ava paused. "An extended break, I suppose."

"Oh." Ava couldn't tell whether Kalista sounded disappointed or not. The girl twisted a strand of hair around her finger. "I thought maybe you and my dad…" She stopped, blushing, and looked out the window.

Ava flushed and shook her head. "No, nothing like that. We've just been friends, Kalista." *Friends and one very awkward kiss.* "I'm married," she added for good measure, and the words felt right. "But I hope your father finds someone again," she added, and Kalista nodded.

"So do I," she said, ducking her head.

Perhaps if Andreas married again, Ava mused, he might relax a little bit with his daughter. It could be a positive situation for everybody… perhaps even Helena.

Later that night, after dropping Kalista off, Ava rang Eleni again to check on Parthenope's condition. There was no change; she was conscious and had tried to speak, but nothing was intelligible. Eleni sounded both worried and weary, and Ava's heart ached for her. Not knowing was sometimes worse than knowing, she thought.

She finished the call and sat there, alone in the living room, mobile phone in hand, and wondered what Simon was doing. It was eight o'clock at night back in England; was he relaxing with one of his nerdy IT magazines, his spectacles perched on the bridge of his nose, that wrinkly frown appearing between his brows as he concentrated? He'd have made himself a cup of tea and forgotten to drink it, and then when he discovered it, he'd make himself drink it cold so as not to waste it.

Just the thought of him there, lying in bed by himself in the house they'd chosen together, sent such a wave of longing and homesickness through her that Ava nearly doubled over from it.

At that moment, more than anything, she wanted nothing more than to return to England. To Simon.

And what if she did? What if she just packed her bags and left? Showed up at her own front door, told Simon she was back if he'd have her?

She couldn't do that, Ava knew, at least not yet. Eleni needed her, and she was still accompanying Helena on her last interview. Her life in Greece was not yet at an ending point, even if part of her felt as if it were.

CHAPTER TWENTY-FIVE

November 1942

Sophia knew something was going to happen soon. She felt it the way you felt snow in the air, a sharp awareness, a tense expectation. None of the SOE agents or guerrillas had said anything, but there had been more activity at the little camp in the foothills of Mount Oeta. *Andartes* came into the camp and then melted back into the night; more villagers had left her food to bring to them. Then she'd found a note under her pillow, of all places, telling her to stay away from the camp until she was called for again. She had no idea who had left it there, only that she was being watched even more closely than she'd realized.

She found she missed her daily visits to provide the SOE agents with food; she knew, stupid girl that she was, what she missed most was Alex. Every time she'd arrived at the camp, he'd greeted her, taking the basket from her and letting his hand linger just a little on her arm. His smile had always been so warm, his eyes so friendly, and even though she'd known it was foolish, she'd sought him out, had sat next to him by the fire and had lingered longer into the night.

And now, in a day or two perhaps, it would all be over. They would blow up the bridge; Alex would leave. Perhaps he would die. The knot of anxiety in her middle tightened and grew, so it made it impossible to eat or sometimes even to swallow. She felt as if she carried a stone in her stomach.

She felt it in the village as well, the expectation, the tension. People hurried past in the street, and no one dallied by the fountain in the square. Even her father, so stolid and silent, seemed to feel it. To Sophia's surprise he grabbed her by the arm one morning before he headed out into the fields, half pulled her towards him.

"Stay safe," he muttered, and with a cold ripple of shock Sophia realized he knew. He must have always known she was involved with the *andartes.*

And then it began.

She didn't have time to scream; the hand closed over her mouth before she was even awake, and strong hands held her arms down so she didn't flail as she instinctively tried to. In the darkness of her bedroom she smelled the faint aroma of Karelia cigarettes.

"Quiet," Perseus murmured into her ear. "And listen. The hour has come; it is now. You must rise from this bed without a sound. Dress warmly and meet me outside as quickly as you can."

Sophia managed to jerk her head in a nod of acceptance, and Perseus released her. He melted from the room and in the bed next to her Angelika sighed and turned over. Sophia let out a shuddering breath that was halfway to a sob. What use could she be now? When would this end?

Quickly, on trembling legs, she swung out of bed and dressed. It was late November now, and the air was sharp with cold; her breath came in frosty puffs. Sophia dressed in as many layers as she could, wrapping two shawls around her before she plunged her feet into her old leather boots and tied a scarf over her hair. She looked as stout as a grandmother in all of her bundled layers, but it hardly mattered now.

Perseus stood by the old iron washtub in the yard outside the house, calmly smoking a cigarette. The moonlight silvered his scar, so it looked like a sickle carving the side of his cheek. Sophia resisted the urge to shiver, and not just from the biting cold.

"What is happening?"

Perseus dropped his cigarette and stubbed it out with one booted foot. "We move," he said brusquely. "To a camp closer to the target."

"The bridge."

"Hush." He nodded at her bulky attire. "You dressed well."

"Why do you need me now? And how long will I be gone?"

"So many questions, Sophia." Perseus's mocking smile gleamed in the darkness. "Remember what I told you about questions? Better not to ask. Not to know. If all goes as we wish, you will be back in your bed tomorrow night."

Sophia swallowed, felt the acid taste of fear in her mouth. So the attack was to be tonight, or perhaps tomorrow night. It was time again to be brave. She lifted her chin. "All right," she said. "Lead on."

They didn't speak on the three-kilometer journey back to the camp; the only sound was the crunch of their boots on the snow that was now hardened into an icy crust. A new snow started falling soon after they set out, a needling, wet kind of sleet that stung Sophia's skin and soaked her layers of wool.

The camp, when they arrived, was bustling with people, bristling with guns and *andartes*. Everything had been packed up and was now shouldered by a couple of mules. Men Sophia had never seen before strode around, blustering to their comrades and clapping each other on the shoulder. There was a feeling of intensity, of energy, that both scared and excited her; it was so different from anything she'd known or felt.

Then she saw Alex coming towards her, smiling as always, and she felt a wave of something so strong, her knees nearly buckled.

"What is happening?" she asked and he took her hands in his.

"You're freezing. And wet."

In answer she pointed to the sky, the needling sleet still falling fast. "Tell me what is happening, Alex."

"We're moving out, to a place nearer—well, you know where nearer."

She nodded, gulping. "Then it will happen soon?"

Alex held a finger to his lips, his eyes gleaming, and nodded.

Sophia swallowed, words spilling from her. "But it is guarded on both sides. Soldiers…" *So many soldiers, ones who would shoot to kill.*

Alex touched the bare expanse of her wrist between coat and glove, shocking her with the intimacy of the touch. His fingers were surprisingly warm against her skin.

"There has always been danger, Sophia."

"Yes." Sophia swallowed; her throat felt tight. "I know."

Someone shouted an order, and the *andartes* and British soldiers began moving, the mules shuffling behind. Still trying to quell her fear, Sophia began to move along with them, Alex at her side.

The march up the mountain to the assembly point was arduous. The snow began to fall heavily, cloaking everything, even the men and the mules, in white. At the front of the line a dark-bearded man was singing cheerfully, rousing his men with jokes and songs, as if they were on a holiday.

Sophia shook her head, glancing at Alex. "That man—singing—"

"Yes, he's good at keeping our spirits up, isn't he?" Alex answered with a smile. "That's General Zervas."

"It is?" She eyed the man with his smiling eyes and bushy beard with wary respect. This was the man she had, in essence, been working for. "And what of—the other? Velouchiotis?" Even though she had thankfully not seen him since they'd moved from his camp, she could still picture his cold eyes and the indifferent order he'd given: *execute them.*

Alex's smile turned grim. "He's been delayed. Apparently there was trouble in a nearby village, and one of his men was accused of thievery."

Sophia shivered. She knew how Aris Velouchiotis dealt with trouble. And yet soon he would be here, and the different factions of the Greek Resistance would work together to blow up this bridge. That, at least, was the aim. Sophia still could not see how everyone would get along; the two Resistance factions had always been enemies. Perhaps they would end up blowing themselves up as well as the bridge. Perhaps she would never see Alex again.

Of course you won't see Alex again, you stupid girl, no matter what happens.

They lapsed into silence, too worried and weary to talk any more. The night seemed endless, the snow never stopping. Sophia's whole body ached.

Finally they arrived at their resting place: a derelict sawmill nearly hidden by the trees. Sophia glanced at it dubiously while all around her men unloaded packs and stripped the mules of their supplies. Sophia glanced at the growing pile of what she knew must be explosives, and swallowed dryly.

"Come." Barba Niko tapped her on the shoulder. "The men must eat."

Nodding, Sophia followed him and began to unpack the food supplies while Barba Niko set about making a campfire. The men would need hot food to sustain them tonight.

The camp descended into a grim, focused silence as they ate the simple stew Sophia and Barba Niko had prepared, then stretched out and prepared to get a few hours' sleep before they moved again. Sophia huddled against the side of the sawmill, wondering what would happen next and feeling frozen to the bone.

As the sky lightened to a leaden gray, the snow still falling, Alex found her. "We are moving to a closer point," he told her. He looked different now, Sophia saw; he looked like a soldier. A rifle was slung across his chest and a knife was strapped to his thigh. His features had become harder somehow, and the friendly gleam in his eyes was gone.

"We are moving again?" she said, struggling to sit up. Her shawls crackled as she moved; the wet wool had frozen.

"No." Alex shook her head. "You will stay here with Barba Niko and wait for our return. It is too dangerous for you."

Sophia stared at him, his words penetrating the tired fog of her brain. "What are you going to do?" She saw Alex shake his head, and she grabbed his arm. "I know you are going to attack the bridge, blow it up—but you, Alex. What are you going to do?"

Alex hesitated, then bent his head close to hers so his lips nearly grazed her ear. "Just my job, Sophia," he said softly. "I'll place the explosives on the viaduct and then I'll get out of there. Trust me." He smiled, but it lacked the endearing crookedness Sophia had come to know, to need. Her fingers tightened on his arm.

"I'm afraid for you."

"I'm afraid for me too," he said, his tone light even though she knew he meant it. He reached out and brushed a tendril of hair away from her cheek. "But you will be safe here, and for that I am glad."

Tears stung Sophia's eyes. She had not prepared herself for this moment, for how much she would feel. "God go with you," she managed, hardly able to speak. Alex's fingers lingered on her cheek.

"Sophia…" His voice had turned hoarse and his eyes seemed to blaze. Sophia waited, hope and fear filling her right up to overflowing.

Someone shouted an order, and the men began to move once more, shouldering their packs. A mule brayed piteously. Still Alex just stared at her, and then, almost desperately, he pulled her into his arms and kissed her.

His lips were cold, and felt hard and soft at the same time. His whiskers, for he hadn't shaved in weeks, scraped her cheeks. She breathed in the scent of him, her arms coming round him, her fingers brushing the cold metal of his rifle.

She loved him, she realized then. She loved him, even after such a short time, but could he possibly love her? Or was this simply the kiss of a man who knew he might die that very night, in the next few hours?

"Come on!" Someone beckoned to Alex, and slowly, reluctantly, he released her. He fished a scrap of paper from inside his jacket and handed it to her.

Sophia looked down at the scrawled English and shook her head. "What—"

"It's where I live in England. Just in case… in case I don't see you again. When this war is over…" He took a breath. "You could find me. Or I will try to find you. I want to. I… love you, Sophia. I know it hasn't been very long, but…" He reached for her hand and squeezed it. "Do you love me?"

Sophia clutched the scrap of paper in one hand, the other held tightly by Alex. "Yes," she whispered. "*S'agapao.*"

He smiled, squeezed her hand one last time, and then let go. Sophia watched him walk out of the camp, the memory of his kiss still imprinted on her lips, his words in her heart. She stood there watching until the snow swallowed him up and the camp was empty except for her and Barba Niko.

Now it truly had begun—and soon, Mother of God, soon it would all end.

CHAPTER TWENTY-SIX

Now

Ava's phone rang just as she was getting ready for bed. She snatched it up, her heart beating wildly, only to feel a tiny flicker of disappointment when she saw it wasn't Simon.

"Eleni…?"

"My mother is finally able to speak, praise God," Eleni said, her voice rough with emotion.

"Oh, I'm so glad—"

"And," Eleni continued, "she's asking for you."

Ava blinked. "Me?"

"Yes, she said she has something she must tell you. And this time I will let her speak. Perhaps then we will find some peace. Can you come?"

"Now?"

"I know it is late, but she is distressed and won't settle. Whatever it is, it must be spoken."

Ava nodded, already reaching for her shoes. "Of course."

Half an hour later Ava was at the hospital in Lamia, being ushered by the ward sister to Parthenope's room. Ava was shocked at the sight of the older woman; in just a few days she already seemed slighter, more fragile, barely making a bump under the starchy hospital sheet.

"Hello, Parthenope," Ava said softly as she sat next to the bed. "I'm so glad you're feeling better." Even though Ava knew she didn't understand English, she thought Parthenope grasped her meaning.

She managed a smile and reached for Ava's hand. Her skin felt like tissue paper, yet her grip was surprisingly strong. She spoke in Greek. Ava shook her head helplessly, glancing at Eleni. "I'm sorry; my Greek isn't good enough—"

"I will translate." Eleni stepped forward. Parthenope spoke again, and Ava looked expectantly at Eleni. "'When I saw you,'" Eleni translated for Parthenope, "'I thought you were Sophia. It shocked me because for so long I have tried to forget.'" Parthenope broke off, her eyes bright with unshed tears, and Ava patted her hand encouragingly.

"It's all right now," she said. "Whatever it is, it's all right now."

Parthenope, seeming to gather the gist of what Ava had said, shook her head with vehemence. She started speaking again, hesitantly at first, yet with growing determination, and Eleni translated once more, her own expression shadowed with apprehension. "'I did not know Sophia very well, or her sister, Angelika, although I knew Angelika had always liked my brother Dimitrios. She flirted with him terribly, at least terribly for those days. But one night I saw Sophia on the road. It was late, and she should not have been out. I should not have been out.'"

Parthenope, quite suddenly, dropped her head into her hands and wept with the kind of deep desperate grief that Ava knew only too well.

"Mama," Eleni exclaimed brokenly, and she sat on the edge of the bed to take Parthenope into her arms. Parthenope wept against her daughter's chest, her thin shoulders shaking with the force of her sobs.

"*Thimamai*," she said over and over. I remember.

All that grief, Ava thought, her eyes stinging with tears of her own. All that grief kept in for so long, and it was only now finding its way out.

"What do you remember, Mama?" Eleni asked once Parthenope's sobs had subsided a little.

"I am ashamed to say this," she said in Greek, and Eleni translated for Ava, her voice wobbly with emotion. "'I am ashamed, and so I have never spoken of it. Of the war, and what I did.'"

Parthenope leaned back against the pillows, her eyes closed, her cheeks sunken. She spoke with a slow, weary resignation now, and Eleni translated. "'I was a foolish, stupid girl once, Ava. I made such selfish choices, such stupid mistakes.'"

Eleni broke off, her face pale, and impulsively Ava leaned forward. "Don't translate, Eleni. Not if you don't want to."

"But it is you she is telling this to," Eleni answered. Her voice was choked, her eyes bright with tears. "It's you whom she wants to know."

Parthenope continued speaking, and resolutely Eleni resumed her translation, her voice halting as she struggled to find the right words in English. "'I cared more for pretty things back then. Dresses and trinkets and nonsense. And so I did a terrible, foolish thing. I took a lover.'" Parthenope took a deep breath, and then spoke a word that needed no translation. "A Nazi."

Eleni let out a little cry and pressed her fist to her lips. Parthenope opened her eyes, tears trickling down her wrinkled cheeks as she gazed at her daughter. "*Signomi*," she whispered. "*Signomi*."

Eleni shook her head, still shocked, and Ava squeezed the older woman's hand. After a long moment, her voice heavy with unspoken sorrow and regret, Parthenope resumed her story and with effort Eleni continued to translate.

"'He was in Athens, but he came to Lamia once in a while. I caught his eye during a patrol, and he invited me to a party. I was so excited at the thought. He bought me a lipstick, and silk stockings, and sometimes—sometimes he asked me questions.'" Parthenope closed her eyes again, her breathing labored and ragged. "'I was such a stupid girl. I thought nothing of his questions. I felt clever, for knowing things, and I was happy to please him. The war was so distant to me then. People spoke of terrible things, but I hadn't seen them.'" She opened her eyes, clutching at Ava's sleeve, her eyes wide with remembered horror. "'I hadn't seen them yet.'"

"What happened?" Ava whispered.

"'I told him—the Nazi, my lover—that I'd seen Sophia, late at night, coming back from the forest. It was right before the *andartes* blew up the bridge.'" Eleni translated as Parthenope dabbed at her eyes. "'I told him my brother had a gun. I thought he was a kind man. He gave me things.'" She let out another choked cry, then shook her head and forced herself to continue, speaking quickly. Eleni lapsed into silence as she listened, her eyes wide and dark. Ava longed to know what Parthenope was saying but waited until she'd reached the end and sank back against the pillows once more.

Eleni let out a shuddering breath and turned to Ava. "After the bridge was blown up," she began, "my mother says the Nazis marched through Iousidous. They took people out of their homes and shot them like dogs. They shot Sophia's sister."

"No—"

"And my own uncle, my mother's brother, Dimitrios. Sophia was never seen again."

"She made it out alive," Ava whispered.

"Yes… but as for the others…"

Parthenope struggled to sit up, her hands stretched out to Ava imploringly. "*Signomi…*"

Ava clasped the older woman's hands and tried to smile. She knew the guilt the older woman felt could never be truly erased, yet she hoped the sharing of it gave her some peace. Parthenope had finally been able to grieve for her own losses, her own terrible choices.

"My grandmother survived the war," Ava said, "and lived a long, happy life in England. She only died recently, as Eleni told you before."

Eleni translated, and Ava watched as Parthenope smiled through her tears and nodded, seeming finally to understand and accept.

Afterwards Parthenope fell into a doze, and Eleni turned to Ava, her expression grave. "I think I was afraid of something like this."

"How did you know?"

Eleni shook her head. "I don't know. It was just a feeling. A burden I sensed she carried, all these years. A guilt. And as for your family, Ava… I am so sorry. As sorry as my mother."

"It was a long time ago, and I never even knew I had an aunt." Ava squeezed Eleni's hand. "I hope you are able to find some peace, along with your mother."

"I hope so, too." Eleni brushed at her eyes, a smile trembling on her lips although she still looked grieved. "It is good she spoke of it, yes? It helps."

By the time she returned to Iousidous, Ava was exhausted both emotionally and physically. Her mind had spun with Parthenope's revelations for the entire drive from Lamia. She tried to imagine her great-aunt, the poor butterfly, being pulled out of her house, shot in the street. And her own grandmother fleeing the Nazis, in fear of her life. She'd been so brave, so strong, and Ava had never known. Sophia had never said.

And Ava had never asked, not about anything, not about Greece or the war. She wondered how her grandmother had escaped after the explosion, how she'd managed to get all the way to England.

"She must have been so brave," she said aloud. She felt a lump of emotion rise in her throat. "I wish I'd had a chance to tell you that," she said softly. "I wish you'd had a chance to tell me."

All of her emotions were still close to the surface as she pulled up in front of her grandmother's house. There were no streetlights, but by the light of the moon she could see that someone was standing on her doorstep, and she felt a flicker of alarm. Who would be waiting there at this hour?

Cautiously she climbed out of her car, the closing of the door as loud as a gunshot in the quiet of the sleepy village.

The person on the doorstep turned towards her, a man. Ava still couldn't recognize his features, but she knew that voice.

"Hello, Ava."

It was Simon.

CHAPTER TWENTY-SEVEN

November 1942

The snow continued to fall all night, cloaking the world in whiteness and obliterating any signs that the SOE agents had even been at the camp. Sophia tried to busy herself tidying away the remnants of the meal that the SOE agents and *andartes* had eaten, but that didn't take very long and it left her mind still free to wander—and fear.

She touched her lips, as if she could still feel the imprint of Alex's kiss. Her first kiss, perhaps her only kiss. He loved her—*loved* her! And yet the future had never been so uncertain. She knew Alex would be laying the explosives along the viaduct. She pictured him crouched in the cold and snow, his hands full of danger and death, and her heart seemed to freeze right in her chest. *What good was his love if he died tonight?*

And if he did not...

Sophia could not bear to dream of a future they could have. Hope was as seductive as a siren, and just as dangerous. How on earth could she marry an Englishman? And after the excitement of a single night when he'd skirted so close to death, perhaps he would not want her anyway.

And so she waited, and tried to keep herself busy—and not to think.

The snow had made everything eerily quiet and still. The night was moonless, and Sophia could hardly see anything at all as she moved around the remnants of the camp. It was hard to believe that just a kilometer away, men were about to lead an attack—or had it happened already? Barba Niko had told her, after the men had all gone, that they were hoping to secure the Gorgopotamos garrison in an hour or less; the placing of the explosives would take only ten minutes. It was a quick operation, by necessity. It would not take long for the enemy to mobilize once they realized they had been attacked.

"Shh!" Barba Niko stopped in the middle of slicing onions for the grand meal he was preparing for the men's return, a feast for the victors—should they be victorious. "Listen," he whispered, and frozen with both shock and terror, Sophia heard it—a sound like thunder, ominous and unrelenting, but she knew it was not merely thunder. It was gunfire.

"They're taking the garrison," she whispered back, and Barba Niko nodded and crossed himself.

"God be with them."

Sophia nodded fervently. The SOE agents and *andartes* were surely in need of divine protection now. The gunfire seemed to go on forever, an endless, distant, awful thunder. Sophia and Barba Niko continued chopping and peeling, pausing every now and then to listen to the staccato sounds that told of death and destruction.

And then, finally, the gunfire stopped, and Sophia sagged in relief even though she didn't know what had happened, or if Alex was still alive. Perhaps they'd been captured or killed.

"They will place the explosives now," Barba Niko said, his wrinkled face creasing into a smile. "In just a few minutes we shall see it, I know!"

They both hurried to the edge of the camp, their feet cold and wet in the freezing snow, and waited for the reddening of the horizon that would indicate that the explosives had been successfully placed and set off, and the bridge would be blown up.

Except nothing happened. Sophia stamped her feet and blew on her hands as the icy cold penetrated to her very marrow. Next to her she could hear Barba Niko's breath rattle in his chest and he craned his neck, as if by just trying a bit harder he would able to see the reddening sky, the proof of their success.

The sky remained dark and still, the night's silence turning ominous, perhaps deadly.

"Something's wrong," Sophia whispered. "It must be. It's been too long. They should have laid the bombs and got away already…" She stopped abruptly, biting hard on her lip to keep the panic and terror from spilling over. *They'd failed. They must have…*

Barba Niko nodded and sucked his teeth. "Something has gone wrong," he agreed somberly. "But it is in God's hands now. Come." He pulled gently on her shoulder, leading her back to the camp. "Let us continue our own work. We shall make a feast… for whoever comes back."

Sophia nodded, knowing that keeping busy was best. Yet her hands shook as she reached for an onion, and her heart thundered inside her. Something had gone wrong with the explosives— which meant something had gone wrong with Alex.

And then they heard it. First it just sounded like a few pops, and then louder booms that Sophia felt reverberate right through her chest. The sky glowed red on the horizon, a violent sunset in the middle of the night. Barba Niko nodded in satisfaction.

"There it is."

But it was at least twenty minutes later than the soldiers and *andartes* had planned, and as they continued to prepare the meal, Sophia wondered bleakly just who would be eating it—and who would not.

Another hour passed, cold and endless. The sky was just beginning to lighten with dawn when the first men returned. Sophia hurried to the edge of the camp, watching as the *andartes* strode through the snow, exhausted yet jubilant. Their faces were streaked with dirt, their eyes bright, and Sophia could hear them exchanging jests, clapping each other hard on the back or shoulder.

The mission had clearly been a success, but Sophia knew better than to ask questions. The men would not give details to the girl who warmed their soup.

Barba Niko hugged and kissed them all, and then began to dish out the stew that had been bubbling over the fire. Sophia heard snatches of conversation: the battle for the garrison, the problem with the explosives. They'd been nailed to boards in the wrong shape, an L instead of a U, and the engineers had had to rip them apart with their bare hands and reassemble them right there on the bridge.

The *andartes* laughed about it now, as if it were all a good joke, but Sophia could feel only a hard clench of terror as she thought of Alex kneeling on that bridge in the dark, realizing with only minutes to spare that their plans had gone so terribly wrong. She searched among the milling men for Alex, but she saw no sign of him or any of the other SOE agents.

Then another man came into the camp, his face familiar from the long, wicked-looking scar, visible even from a distance. *Perseus.* Sophia had never seen him at the camp before, and the sight of him brought a sudden wave of foreboding. *Why was he here?*

His hard gaze took in her obvious uncertainty and concern, and he jerked his head.

"You must leave."

She stared at him, uncomprehending. "What—"

"Someone has informed on us," Perseus answered brusquely. "Your name was spoken to the blackshirts. They are looking for you even as I speak. And if they find you…" He did not finish that sentence. He did not need to.

Sophia could only stare in response; she felt numb and icy with shock, her brain buzzing with the words. *Your name was spoken…*

"How?" she whispered. Who would inform on her? She thought of the gifts of food left on her door, by the mangle; it seemed as if everyone in Iousidous had known what she was doing, even if no one had spoken of it.

Except someone had now. To the blackshirts, no less. "What will I do?" she whispered. "Where will I go?" She couldn't return home, she realized sickly, not if they were looking for her.

Another realization following on the heels of the first caused her to gasp aloud. "My father, Angelika—"

"You cannot save them," Perseus told her. A flicker of sympathy passed over his face, gone quickly. "You can only save yourself."

But I wanted to keep us all safe. That's all I wanted. Sophia bit her lips to keep the useless words from spilling out. She could not bear to think of her stern father, sweet Angelika, in danger. And as for her…

"But I have nowhere to go," she whispered. She felt tears tremble on her lids, a howl rise in her chest. "I have nothing!"

"One of the *andartes* will take you to safety." He laid a hand on her arm. "That is all I can offer you. I'm sorry."

It was so very little. Sophia shook her head, hating the finality in his tone, the unbearable gentleness that hinted at things he had not yet told her. "Has something happened to my father? My sister?"

Perseus stepped back. "Go," he said, and his features were implacable once more. "Go, and quickly. We will all move from here as soon as we can, but your presence in particular is a danger."

She was no use to them now, Sophia thought. They wanted only to be rid of her. She wondered if she would ever see her father and sister again, or if they were even alive. What if they'd been harmed? She imagined the rough knock at the door, the sound of boots, screams…

A surly-looking *andarte* approached, his rifle strapped across his chest as he jerked a thumb towards the still-dark mountains. "Let's go."

Wildly Sophia turned back to Perseus. "What of the soldiers?" she asked, her voice ragged. "The *Englezoi*?"

Perseus stared at her, stony-faced. "What of them?"

"Are they—are they all safe?"

"The mission was successful," Perseus answered. "That is all you need to know."

Sophia knew she would never get another opportunity to ask about Alex; everything had happened so quickly, so terribly. She would most likely never see Alex, or perhaps anyone she ever knew, again. The thought was too terrible to contemplate, a great big chasm of unknowing opening in front of her, inside her, endless and empty. "What of Alex... the explosives engineer? He is safe?"

Perseus hesitated, his gaze assessing, and Sophia wondered how much he'd guessed. Still he didn't speak, and she knew he was debating whether to tell her the truth. She flung out one hand, tears trickling down her cheeks. "Please... please tell me," she whispered.

Perseus's expression hardened once more. "He's dead," he said flatly. "Now go."

CHAPTER TWENTY-EIGHT

Now

"Simon," Ava said faintly. She blinked rapidly, as if her vision might clear in a moment and he would be gone. And yet still he stood there on the stone slab in front of the house, his coat and hair both rumpled. The car keys slipped from her hand, landing on the ground with a clatter.

Simon smiled crookedly. "Surprise."

She felt a welling of emotion, a pressure in her chest, making it impossible to speak. She just shook her head, and Simon moved forward to pick up her keys. He handed them to her, his fingers brushing hers, and even that small contact made everything in her ache.

"Come inside," she finally managed, and she unlocked the door to the house. She stepped inside the living room, flicking on the lights.

She saw Simon take in the few furnishings, the enormous stone fireplace. "Rustic," he said, and she managed a rather shaky laugh.

"You should have seen it before." She put down her bag, feeling as awkward as if Simon were no more than a passing acquaintance, come to pay a sudden social call. "Are you hungry? Do you want something?"

Simon hunched one shoulder, his hands shoved in his pockets. "A cup of tea would be nice," he said, and Ava nodded and went to the kitchen. After a moment Simon followed her.

"This is quite a place," he offered hesitantly as she switched on the kettle. It took her a moment to realize he sounded nervous. It was so unlike him; Simon had always been the steady one: stoic, often silent, unemotional, and completely confident in himself. Yet now he shifted from foot to foot, smiling awkwardly as Ava bustled about the kitchen. Her hands trembled as she got out the mugs. She was nervous too.

"Sugar?" she asked, before belatedly remembering that he never took sugar. How could she forget such a thing? She must have made him at least a thousand cups of tea over the years. She gave a little laugh and shook her head. "Sorry."

"I suppose—I suppose it's been a while."

"Yes."

"You're wondering why I'm here," he said as he took the cup of tea and Ava nodded. "I should have called first."

"I called you," Ava blurted. "A few days ago. I left a message—"

"I know." Simon gave her another crooked smile. "I think I've listened to it a hundred times."

Surprise had her blinking, realization trickling slowly through her. "Then why... why didn't you call, Simon?" She heard the broken note in her voice and realized this encapsulated so much of what had gone wrong between them. He cared, but he hadn't called. Hadn't done or said anything, *ever*—

And yet he was here.

"I was going to call," Simon said, his hands, those slender, long-fingered hands Ava had missed, cradled around his mug, "but then I thought it would be better to see you in person. Talk face to face."

Ava took her own cup of tea back into the sitting room. "So you just hopped on a plane?"

"That's about the size of it."

It was so unlike him, so impulsive. Ava glanced up at Simon, knowing there were so many things they both needed to say. "And now that you're here?"

"I miss you. I never wanted you to go in the first place."

"You didn't seem as if you minded so much," Ava answered, and heard the sudden tautness in her voice. She'd thought she was ready to let go of all her hurt, but apparently she wasn't.

"What was I supposed to say? You were clearly determined to leave. It was your idea to separate, not mine."

"Only because I was so clearly making you miserable!" Ava closed her eyes against the sudden sting of tears. "And what about the other week, when I called? You were having dinner with Julie—"

"As friends! Ava, you don't think I've been interested in Julie? I've been moaning to her about how unhappy I am and she's been trying to get us to talk, to make up…"

Ava sniffed loudly. "I spoke to her after I called you, and she didn't tell me you were going out. She as good as lied—"

"She just didn't want to upset you." Simon shook his head. "I can't believe we're arguing about *Julie.*"

"I'm sorry." She realized she'd never really thought anything was going on between Simon and Julie, but even the fact of their friendship had stung when she'd been feeling so raw. "I don't care about that, not really," she admitted with a sniff. "It's just all coming out now because we haven't actually spoken in so long."

"And that's my fault?" he asked evenly.

Ava let out a tired sigh. "We're just going to go round in circles again, aren't we, Simon?"

"No." Simon came to sit next to her on the sofa, his thigh nudging hers. "At least, I don't want to go round in circles. I came here because I want to make it right between us, Ava. I want to be a couple again. I want to try."

She opened her eyes, stared down at her tea. "It might not be that simple."

Simon let out a rush of breath, and she knew what he was thinking. *Why can't it be that simple?* She wished it could be, and yet she knew she held too much hurt and sorrow inside to just go trotting back to England, hand in hand with Simon, as if her trip to Greece had been nothing more than a solo holiday.

Simon fumbled for her hand, lacing her fingers through his. "I've never stopped loving you," he said in a low voice, and everything in her clenched with both longing and grief.

She drew a shaky breath. "I never stopped loving you, either. But we were still making each other miserable, Simon, for the better part of a year. I don't want that to happen again."

Simon sighed. "I know it wasn't easy—"

"It wasn't not easy," Ava corrected sharply. "It was awful. Unbearable. Every day felt like a year."

Simon pressed his lips together and nodded. "I know."

Ava gazed at him, saw the seriousness in his eyes, the stubborn set of his jaw, and wondered if even now, when they were both trying, they could understand each other. Make it work. She thought of all the months when she'd been prostrate with grief, struggling with severe depression, and Simon had just seemed impatient. Irritated. *Stop moping,* he'd said.

"Ava," he said now, prompting her—to say what? Did he just want her to shrug away the last year and start over? Could she do that?

"Why didn't you hold her?" Ava blurted. The question emerged from the deepest part of her, surprising them both. It wasn't what she'd expected to say, and it clearly wasn't what Simon had expected to hear. And yet she knew then that she needed to know—it had bothered her, without her realizing, ever since that awful day when she'd looked down into the beautiful, still face of their daughter.

He stared at her for a long moment, his face expressionless, and then he turned his head so she couldn't see his face. "Do you think I don't regret that?" he asked, his voice wooden.

"I have no idea, Simon, because you never told me. Do you?"

"Yes." He passed a hand over his face and then dropped it. "Yes, I do."

Ava wanted to touch him, although whether to shake him or hug him she didn't know. Even now he wasn't giving her anything; his voice had been completely flat. "So why didn't you?" she asked. "When they offered?" She still remembered the kindly face of the midwife, offering up her little girl wrapped in a pink blanket like any other newborn, but so still. So very, very still. The midwife had left them alone with her for a little while, and Ava had cradled her to her chest. Their daughter had still been warm; she'd been *perfect*. But Simon hadn't even looked at her. When she'd asked, her voice choked with tears, if he wanted to hold her, he'd just shook his head and looked away. And then the midwife had come back and taken Charlotte away forever.

"Simon?" Ava prompted. His face was still turned away from her.

"I don't know." He turned back to her, and to her shock she saw tears glinting in his eyes. He blinked them back rapidly. "I know that's not much of an answer, but it's the truth. I just… couldn't handle it, I suppose." He drew a shuddering breath. "It felt so unreal, so awful. I just wanted it all to be over as quickly as possible, to move on, to be able to, and then when—when she was actually gone…" He pressed a hand to his eyes, framing them with his thumb and forefinger. "It was too late."

"Oh, Simon." Tears spilled over onto her cheeks. "I wish you'd told me that before. It always seemed to me like you didn't even care. Like you were indifferent."

"I know it did, Ava." He dropped his hand, hunching his shoulders as he turned away from her. "Trust me, I got that. You made it abundantly clear. Your grief always trumped mine."

"What?" She stared at him in shock. "It wasn't like that, Simon. I *wanted* you to grieve. I wanted you to grieve with me."

"No," Simon corrected, "you wanted me to grieve like you. But I couldn't. I'm not like that, Ava. I never have been. I thought you knew that, understood it. Just because I wasn't in floods of tears didn't mean I didn't feel anything."

I'm not a stone. "But if you'd just *said*—"

"I suppose I thought my wife would know I grieved for our child, the child we'd been trying to have for five bloody years." He stood up suddenly, knocking his tea over, the mug shattering on the stone floor, the sound echoing through the room. He stared down at the mess of broken china and puddling tea. "Sorry."

"For a broken cup?" Ava shook her head, tears still slipping down her cheeks. She thought she'd cried all her tears for their daughter, but she realized she'd never wept for Simon. She'd never thought about the nature of his grief, the reality of it… only that it hadn't felt like enough. "Don't be," she said softly.

He looked up at her, and for once the emotion was naked on his face. "I'm sorry for everything, Ava. I really am. I know I didn't handle things right. I should have spoken up, suggested counseling, something. I knew you were struggling, but I still just wanted to get over it, move on. Not because I didn't care…" His voice wobbled and he looked down again. "Maybe because I cared too much. Because I was afraid of losing you. Losing us."

Ava dabbed at her tears. "I thought you were annoyed with me for still grieving."

"Not annoyed. Just… frustrated, I suppose. With the situation more than anything. And with myself too. I knew you wanted something from me I couldn't give. At least, I didn't want to give it. I'm still not that kind of person, although I am trying—"

"Oh Simon, I just wanted you to feel what I was feeling." She paused, corrected herself. "I wanted you to show what you felt the way I showed it. I suppose, looking back, that was unreasonable. I should have realized we grieved in different ways. It didn't mean you were grieving less." As she said the words, she realized how true they were, and how, for the first time, how genuinely she meant them.

Simon shrugged as a heavy sigh escaped him. "Grief is unreasonable. It's part of life and yet it feels wrong."

"It does." Ava's throat had thickened again, and she swallowed hard. "It always felt so wrong, Simon." Her voice broke then, and Simon moved towards her, pulling her into his arms.

"Oh, Ava. I know. I *know.* And I'm sorry, for everything. So sorry. I do miss her, you know. Our Charlotte. I miss her every day. I think about her every day, even when I don't want to."

Ava pressed her face against Simon's shoulder, breathed in the wonderful, familiar scent of him—of soap and coffee. Her shoulders shook from the force of her sobs, and she could feel Simon's grief like a living, pulsing thing, connecting them, binding them together.

After a few long moments her tears finally subsided and she stepped back, wiping her face as she took a shuddering breath.

Simon wiped at his own eyes. "Do you think," he began, and then cleared his throat, "do you think we can try again, Ava? Knowing how different we are? Knowing that I can't…"

She gazed at him, at his wire-rimmed glasses and sandy hair and crooked smile, and knew she loved him as much as she ever had. *But was that enough?* They'd managed not to sort out their differences or really even speak properly to each other for an entire year. How could they make sure that didn't happen again? That another tragedy wouldn't tear them apart, simply because of the different ways it might affect them?

Yet maybe now that they were finally being honest, things could be different. At least, they could start to be. It wouldn't be easy or natural, perhaps it never would be, but it could still happen. Perhaps they'd needed this time apart to realize just how important their marriage really was… and how much they had to work at it.

"Ava?" Simon asked softly, and she knew there was only one way to go forward. One step at a time, inching their way together.

Smiling a little, crying too, she walked towards Simon. He held out his arms.

It felt so good to be held by him, her cheek pressed against his shoulder once more. He rubbed her back the way he always did, and she closed her eyes. No, it still wasn't simple or easy. But it was right.

CHAPTER TWENTY-NINE

November 1942

Sophia curled her knees up to her chest in an effort to keep warm. She was shivering uncontrollably, both inside and out. The *andarte* had led her to one of the old goatherds' huts on the mountainside, a bare stone-walled space with holes in the roof and a door that did not latch. With no fire or even a blanket, she had spent the night trying not to freeze to death and wondering what on earth was to become of her—and what had become of her family.

And Alex. *Alex, dead.* Her mind refused to accept it; she kept silently repeating the words and then blotting them out, as if denying the fact made it untrue.

But it was true, it had to be... and if her father and sister were in danger or worse, she was completely alone in this world with nowhere to go. No life to live. She could not possibly see a way forward.

The *andarte* had told her he would return in the morning with food and provisions. For what purpose, Sophia wondered bleakly. Would she live the rest of her life in a goatherd's hut? When would this terrible, terrible war be over? Would it ever be over for her?

A nameless terror had kept Sophia awake at night for weeks, and yet now that the worst had actually happened, she could hardly believe it. As the hours slipped by, she began to feel the truth weigh inside her like a stone, heavy and impossible to bear.

How did people live like this? she wondered, her face pressed against her knees as hot tears ran down her cheeks. How did you go on when you'd lost everything?

Sophia found out soon enough: you simply did. Time passed, the sky darkened, and she fell into a restless and uncomfortable doze. She hadn't slept in over twenty-four hours, and despite the swamping sense of misery, her body craved sleep.

She woke several hours later, cold and aching, her senses snapping into alertness as she heard the crunch of boots on snow. She shrank back into a corner of the hut as the door slowly opened, half expecting the beam of a soldier's torch, the shouted order, the end of it all…

"Sophia?" It was the *andarte*, and Sophia nearly wept with relief. He stepped into the hut, blocking out the weak dawn light. "Here."

She watched as he took some dried plums and a hunk of bread out of a burlap sack and handed them to her. She had not thought of food since she'd first come to this hut, but as she took the bread, she realized she was starving.

He took other things out of the sack: boots, several men's sweaters, more food. He glanced up at her, his face serious. "You will have to go."

Sophia swallowed a lump of bread, her heart starting to thud. "Where?"

"Away from here. The Nazis are looking for you all the way from here to Karditsa. You cannot stay."

"But how—where…?" She shook her head, overwhelmed at the thought of simply walking out into the night and disappearing.

"There are clothes here, and enough food for a few days. There is a woman in Makrakomi, a widow who will look after you. She will leave a red ribbon tied to her shutter."

"Makrakomi—" Sophia had never been farther than Lamia.

"Thirty kilometers away," the *andarte* confirmed. "You can walk it in two days, but you will have to stay in the mountains and forests."

"With no shelter? I'll freeze to death!"

He pressed his lips together and gave a little shrug. "It is your best chance."

And yet it felt like no chance at all. "What will I do in Makrakomi, with this widow?" She could not imagine it.

"Stay and gain your strength. Move on, eventually. She cannot keep you for very long, for her own safety. But it is up to you, where you go." He gave her a small, grim smile. "You are mistress of your own fate."

She stared down at the pile of clothes and food. So this was her payment for a life given in service to the Resistance. For the loss of everything she'd ever had or wanted. A pair of boots and a bit of bread.

"Do you know anything of my family?" she asked after a long moment. "My father and sister Angelika? What has happened to them?"

The *andarte's* jaw bunched. "The Nazis came to the village. They took your father and Angelika out—"

Sophia's stomach churned and she doubled over, the little bread she'd eaten threatening to come up again. "No—"

"Your father will live," he said. "He was badly beaten, but he is alive."

Sophia swallowed bile. "And Angelika?"

He said nothing, and she looked up to see him staring at her grimly. He gave a little shake of his head. Sophia bit her lips to keep from crying out in anguish.

"What—what happened to her?"

"They shot her right there in the street. At least it was quick."

"Mother of God." And then the bread did come up as she retched helplessly onto the cold dirt floor, tears spilling down her cheeks. The *andarte* said nothing; he just waited until she was done before he packed up the things that he'd brought, back into the sack. Sophia wiped at her mouth and her eyes, knew that he had nothing else to give her. No advice, no salvation, no hope.

"What of the *Englezoi*?" she asked after a wretched moment, her heart an unbearable weight when she thought of her sister—so playful, so naïve. *Dead.* "Are they... are they all right?"

He shrugged, indifferent. "As far as I know. They are returning to Egypt. We have no need of them now."

His obvious indifference stung, even though she knew it shouldn't. "But what of Alex—the explosives engineer—he died on the bridge!"

The *andarte* stared at her for a long moment. "No one died on the bridge," he finally said. "Except for some damned blackshirts."

Sophia blinked, staring at him in disbelief. *No one died on the bridge...* Could Alex possibly be alive, then? And if so, why had Perseus told her otherwise? Had he lied deliberately, or had he been mistaken?

"I must go now." He rose from the floor, brushing the dirt from his knees and adjusting his rifle. He paused by the door, his back to her. "God go with you," he said gruffly, and then he was gone.

CHAPTER THIRTY

Now

Lukas Petrakides was quick-witted and spry for a man of his years, with sparse white hair and a faded scar curving down one cheek. He invited Helena and Ava into his home in Lamia with genial alacrity.

It had been two days since Simon had arrived, and Ava's mind was still reeling from his presence. He'd insisted on sleeping on the sofa, even though she ached to have him hold her at night. But she understood that he wanted to take it slowly, do things right. And they had been talking more, or trying to, about what had happened in the last year and how they'd both felt. All those conversations had been good and necessary and even healing, but Ava wasn't sure she wanted to talk about it any more. Like Simon perhaps, she'd had enough. She wanted to get on with living... whatever that looked like. However hard it felt.

The future was something they had not yet discussed. Would they go back to their little house in York and pick up where they had left off? Perhaps that was all they could do. Just keep on, and eventually things would smooth out and feel normal. Good, even. She knew she couldn't stay in Greece forever, although what would happen to her grandmother's house or the cat she'd befriended she didn't know. What about the life she'd made for herself, small as it was? Would she just say goodbye to it all?

Maybe she would have to.

Lukas led them into the living room and plied them with cups of thick Greek coffee as Helena explained the purpose of the interview. Although Helena had told her that Lukas had been in the Resistance, Ava didn't know how likely it was that he knew or remembered Sophia. After Parthenope's revelations, she longed for more information about her grandmother. What had happened to her, and how had she made it all the way to England?

"Of course, you want to know about Sophia Paranoussis," Lukas said after they had chatted briefly about the war.

Ava sat up straight and nodded. "Yes, my grandmother—"

"As it happens, I did not really know her. I grew up in a different village."

"Oh, I see." Disappointment swamped her. So he wouldn't know anything more. She'd never learn the answers she'd been looking for.

"Actually, I don't think you do, young woman," Lukas said with smiling severity. "You have the look of her, you know."

"Then—you knew her?"

"In a manner of speaking. I recruited her."

"Recruited…" Helena stopped abruptly, realization dawning. "Then you were a leader in the Resistance."

"One of them," the man once known as Perseus agreed with a gracious nod. "Sophia was working at a coffee house in Iousidous. It was run by a woman named Kristina who suggested I approach Sophia to help with our cause."

"Why?" Ava asked, eager to know more, to understand her grandmother as she never had before.

"Because she was quiet and discreet. And she didn't want to help us, which made her more desirable. Too many people wanted to help and then bragged about it in the village square, threatened everything we were working for. Sophia would never have done that." He smiled faintly. "She only knew me as Perseus."

"So what did she do for you?" Ava asked.

"She brought the SOE agents from their drop to shelter. Gave them food—and saved them from being executed by that butcher Velouchiotis." Lukas shook his head in remembrance, and Ava leaned forward.

"Saved their lives?"

"She was brave when she needed to be. I always knew she had it in her." His smile of reminiscence faded slightly. "I have sometimes regretted… but it is too late now, of course."

"What did you regret?" Helena asked softly, and Lukas shrugged.

"Perhaps only a small thing; who knows? There was a soldier, one of the *Englezoi*… Sophia was attached to him, I could see, and he felt it too. It seemed dangerous. People do all sorts of foolish things when they are in love, yes?"

"Yes," Ava agreed quietly. She knew that only too well; she'd left her home because she'd loved Simon. And even though she knew it had been necessary to gain some distance, she half wished they'd been able to work it out without her taking such drastic measures.

Lukas sighed heavily. "So I told Sophia that this soldier—Alex, his name was—died during the explosion. I thought it was for the better, for both of them. Alex went back to Egypt and Sophia… alas, I did not know what became of her until now. But I have wondered if it would have lasted, if I hadn't said such a thing."

"They were in love?" Ava's heart twisted as she took in Lukas's words. It hadn't lasted, because it hadn't been given a chance. If Sophia had known her sweetheart was still alive, would she have come back? Would she have looked for him? Would she have taken such a risk on an uncertain future?

"She's never mentioned an Alex," she told Lukas quietly. She felt a pang of inexplicable grief for the unknown Alex. "But she married another Englishman. My grandfather Edward. I never knew him, but I believe they were happy."

"I hope they were." Lukas smiled sadly. "Perhaps it was all for the best, then. I have a photograph, if you'd like to see it, of the English SOE agents."

"Oh, yes," Ava said eagerly, leaning forward in her excitement.

Lukas rose from his chair and went to rifle through a drawer in a heavy wooden sideboard. "This was taken right after the bridge blew up. All the men were celebrating." Smiling, he showed Ava a black-and-white photograph of a dozen men. Some stood, some sat; they all looked dirty, exhausted, and jubilant. "There, that one." Lukas pointed at a man in the back row; he wasn't looking at the camera, but rather off in the distance, as if searching for someone.

Ava took the worn photo and peered closely at it. "But... but that's my grandfather!" she exclaimed. "At least, I think it is."

"What?" Helena stared at the photograph as if she could find an explanation there.

"There was a picture of him in my grandmother's house, back in Leeds, from the war years. I knew he fought in the war, but not that he was in the SOE. And his name wasn't Alex."

"Perhaps a nickname? Or even an alias? Many soldiers had them then."

"Yes, that must have been it..." Ava shook her head. "It's just so strange." Her mind was spinning.

"It is good," Lukas said with a laugh. "She must have found him, after all."

"She must have," Ava said softly. She felt bizarrely near tears. How incredibly difficult it must have been for her grandmother to go all the way to England and find the man she loved. But she had. She'd tried and persevered and at last succeeded. She'd been so strong.

Stronger than you think.

Yes, Ava thought as she handed the photo back to Lukas. Yes, Sophia was strong—and so was she.

*

Ava and Helena were both quiet when they finally took their leave. Once outside, Helena ducked her head shyly and said, "I'd offer to take you out for a coffee, but I'm actually meeting Andreas."

Ava couldn't conceal her grin. "Oh, really?" she said, and Helena blushed. She laughed and pointed to Simon, who was waiting by the garden gate. "I've plans myself." She hadn't even told Helena that Simon was here yet. Clearly they were going to have a lot to catch up on.

Helena went on her way, and Ava started walking towards Simon. He quirked an eyebrow as she came towards him. "Is everything all right?"

"Yes. I just learned quite a few things about my grandmother." She stood before him and Simon smiled at her.

"Good things?"

"Mostly," Ava said. She thought of all she'd learned of her grandmother during the war, and all she'd learned of herself in Greece. So many sad things: the needless tragedy of war, Parthenope's betrayal, and her condition now. It was unlikely the old woman would recover. Ava had suggested Eleni take on her half-feral cat, a small comfort now that her mother would be staying in care.

But there were good things about her time in Greece too: Andreas's strengthened relationship with his daughter, and his fledgling one with Helena. Her friendships with Helena and Eleni, and the lessening of her own grief. She would always mourn her daughter, always remember her. But it felt less like a burden than simply part of who she was and always would be.

And, of course, Simon. *He was*, Ava thought with a smile, *a very good thing.*

"What are you smiling about?" he asked, uncertainty and laughter both audible in his voice, and she put her arms around him.

"You," she said, and kissed him. Simon kissed her back and Ava closed her eyes as he pulled her closer. She'd missed this—him—so much. "Us," she amended softly. "I'm smiling about us."

CHAPTER THIRTY-ONE

May 1946

Sophia stared at the terraced house in a busy little market town in the middle of England, a place she'd never imagined finding herself. It had been a long—an endless—journey to get here: first making her way across Greece, avoiding both Nazis and then the violence of the civil war, freezing and starving on hillsides when she could not find someone in the Resistance to help her. She'd never even been able to say goodbye to her father, although she had at least written him since she'd left.

Then she'd arrived in Brindisi and worked at a small seaside taverna to make enough money to pay for transport. She'd paid a piratical-looking sailor to stow her on his ship, and landed on the darkened shores of England in the summer of 1945.

The war was over, the world was being rebuilt, yet Greece was still gripped in the deadly claws of a terrible civil war. She'd heard no word of anyone, not her father or her aunt or any of her friends, despite her own letters back to Iousidous.

And as for Alex… she had heard nothing. She did not know whether he was alive or dead, if he was in England or some other country, or even if he would want to see her after all this time.

And yet she hoped. She clung to hope, frail thing that it was, because it was all that had sustained her through so many years of suffering and sorrow.

And now she was finally here, in front of this little house, a scrap of worn paper in her hand, her heart in her mouth.

The curtains twitched and a head peeked out from behind them. A woman, Sophia saw, and determinedly, knowing she must be just as brave as she once had been on the snowy side of Mount Oeta, she started forward.

She knocked once, twice, and then the woman answered the door, looking a little suspicious. "Can I help?"

Sophia had learned a bit more English in the last four years. "I'm looking for Alex."

The woman frowned. "No one by the name of Alex lives here."

Sophia's heart sank, her hopes blowing away like so much ash. "Did anyone by that name live here?" she asked desperately. "During the war?"

The woman shook her head. "We've lived here for over twenty years, and my husband and son both answer to Edward. I'm sorry." She eyed her up and down, not unkindly, although Sophia knew her clothes were both cheap and worn. "You're looking for someone?"

"Yes… he gave me this address." Sophia swallowed past the lump in her throat. "He must have got it wrong," she said quietly. "Thank you for your time." She turned away, and the woman watched her leave with a little frown.

Sophia's steps were heavy as she went down the little paved path. She realized how much she'd put into this moment, how much hope and love and desperation. And for what? Had Alex given her the wrong address? How could he have done, unless it had been on purpose? And yet why would he do such a thing? He hadn't had to give her anything at all. She hadn't been expecting it. Why would he have been so needlessly cruel?

The back of her neck prickled, and she stopped. Turning around, she saw a man coming down the street. He was still quite far away, yet she recognized that jaunty stride. As he came closer, she saw the streaks of gray in his dark hair, new grooves from his nose to his mouth. But he was the same.

He was Alex.

She stood there, unable to move, to think, and then Alex looked up. Sophia felt as if she were pinned in place, trapped by his gaze, praying he would be happy to see her.

A look of disbelief flashed across Alex's features and then Sophia saw it turn to wonder. "Sophia!"

He started running.

Sophia still couldn't move, even though tears were now streaking down her face. Tears of both incredulity and joy.

Alex caught her up in his arms, kissing her thoroughly before he pulled back and looked at her as if he were trying to memorize her features. "I've been looking for you for years... I've asked everyone, followed every lead I could. I was afraid I'd never find you. I was afraid..." He trailed off, but Sophia knew what he'd been going to say. *He was afraid she'd been dead.*

"I was afraid you wouldn't be here," she managed through her tears. "The woman at the door said there was only an Edward—"

"My name is Edward," Alex said, and he kissed her again. "Alex was just an alias."

Sophia shook her head. "I do not know that word—"

"Not my name," he explained. "I just used it as a cover. We all used them, just to be safe. I never even thought to tell you, how stupid of me—"

"It doesn't matter." Sophia glanced at the woman on the stoop, who was staring at them in confusion. "But you might need to explain. Is that your mother?"

"Yes," Alex said, "and I know she'll be delighted to meet you when I tell her everything." He kept his arm around her as they started towards the house. "You're never leaving me again, do you hear?" His voice wavered and he pulled her back into his arms. "I was so afraid we'd never see each other again," he murmured against her hair. "But you found me, thank God. Thank God."

Sophia buried her face against his coat, filled with gratitude. She knew she'd found more than just her wonderful Alex—she'd finally found her safe haven, her home. Her future. With Alex's arm still around her, she turned back towards the house and the life, whatever it held, that awaited her there.

A LETTER FROM KATE

Dear Reader,

I want to say a huge thank you for choosing to read *Beyond the Olive Grove*. If you enjoyed it, and want to keep up to date with all my latest releases, just sign up at the following link. Your email address will never be shared and you can unsubscribe at any time.

www.bookouture.com/kate-hewitt

There are so many fascinating stories of ordinary people's bravery during the Second World War, and when I discovered during my research how Greek villagers helped with the destruction of the Gorgopotamos Bridge in what became known as Operation Harling, I knew I had to highlight their remarkable courage in a story.

Several characters in *Beyond the Olive Grove* are real—Aris Velouchiotis and General Zervas were the leaders of the communist and republican factions of the Resistance; the destruction of the bridge was the only time they worked together. Barba Niko, who cooked for the British SOE agents, was also a real person, and he was helped by a local village woman, who inspired my Sophia. The events leading up to the explosion are based on real-life accounts, including the parachute drop being bungled and Resistance members under Velouchiotis leading the British SOE agents to Zervas. Greek citizens had a particularly hard time during the war, thanks to blockades that left them starving; it was both harrowing and fascinating to research about life during that very difficult period.

I hope you have enjoyed *Beyond the Olive Grove*, and if you have, I'd love for you to leave a review. They mean so much, and it's always wonderful to hear how my books have touched people.

Thanks for reading!
Kate

 katehewittauthor

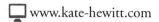 www.kate-hewitt.com

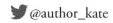 @author_kate

ACKNOWLEDGMENTS

Thanks must go as always to the wonderful Bookouture team, in particular Radhika, who worked on this book, as well as my editor Isobel, and all the other staff who work tirelessly to bring my books out into the world—Jenny, Alexandra, Alex, Kim, Sarah, Alba and Rhianna.

Thanks also to my family and friends, who are always supportive of my writing, and recognize it's a "real job"! Thanks especially to my dear mom, who is always willing to hear about my stories, and has read most of them. Love you, Mom!